ALWAYS LOOKING WEST

A Novel

Book One of: The Clausen Family Series

By Duane Kent Clatworthy

ACKNOWLEDGEMENTS

I would like to thank my wife of sixty-seven years, Leona Wood Clatworthy, for her help in the production of this novel. It was with her encouragement that I started to write the story. Thanks for her many hours of research. I appreciate the time involved with editing and compiling the data I used.

   I am also most thankful for the men who were examples to me and took a little of their time over the years to show me how to do many of the things I have mentioned in this book.

****

CHAPTER 1

My earliest memories are of a farm with chickens and pigs running around the barnyard. My mother and father laughed and played games with my younger sister and me.

I remember, ducks, geese, and guinea hens always raising a big fuss over anything new. The gander goose walked around with his neck straight out and made all kinds of hissing sounds. I learned at a young age, he acted as mean as he sounded. I was better off staying out of his way. He delighted in catching me unaware. He grabbed me and pinched and twisted his head and left a big red welt everyplace he bit.

One summer evening my father came home from town. He seemed very quiet. He and Mom went into the house. Mom was crying and saying, "It's not fair." Dad said he had no choice. He must go right away. I didn't understand what they talked about other than it seemed really scary.

Dad came out on the front porch and said, "Kenneth, I need to talk to you. Come sit here on the steps by me, please."

I sat down beside him. He put his arm around my shoulders and said, "Ken I must leave for a long time. I want you to become the man of the family and take care of Mom and Sissy."

"Dad, where are you going? Why will you be gone a long time?"

"I don't suppose you heard Mom and me talking about the war between the North and the South. The army requests that I go and lead a group of men."

"What will we do without you? Who's going to keep our men working?"

"That's going to be your job, Son. You'll need to make sure the men get the crops in this fall. You talk to Bull. I left him in charge of the farm, but he will need you to help."

Now, Bull was a huge black man who never seemed to smile. He frightened me. He seemed to be not only strong, but maybe mean. I had visions of him scowling at me and not doing what I asked, or worse yet, laughing at me when I asked him to do a job. He had huge arms and hands. The veins stood out along his arms and hands like ribbons of steel.

Dad and I talked a long time that night. I didn't imagine this would be the last time I talked to my father. He told me how proud he had become of me, and he depended on me to grow to be a fine man. He wanted me to be honest and respectful to grownups, especially my mother and sister. He would take Ben, the saddle horse, with him. He would leave the team for us. I shouldn't worry, because the men knew how to harness and work the large team of brown horses. They were not the gentle type, but spirited and would run if given the chance. They ran away with Dad the summer before. I was afraid of them. I had never seen anyone except Dad work them. I wondered if anyone else would be able to control them. If I had been older, I would have realized that Bull, with all of his strength, probably could have picked one of them up.

When I awoke the next morning, Mom stood on the front porch crying. She looked down the road. Dad left before dawn. I realized we were alone and had a lot of chores to do.

Dad left Tuesday, April 30, 1861, on a hot spring morning, with a clear, blue sky. I walked to the barn and fed the cow her hay. When I got ready to milk someone chuckled behind me. I turned and there stood Bull with the milk pail in his hand.

He asked, "Are you planning on milking the cow this morning? If you are, you forgot the bucket."

I thought, "He really doesn't seem so mean this morning."

Bull said, "Young Ken, have you ever milked Daisy?"

I threw my head back and looked him straight in the eye. "No, but I don't think it's going to be so hard."

He grinned. "We will see." He handed me the bucket and the stool.

Now, I would milk that old cow or die trying. After all, how much different is it from milking the dumb goat? I had been milking her for a while so Mom didn't have to.

I sat down on the stool; like I had seen Dad and Mom do many times. I reached out very slowly and brushed the straw from her bag. She looked back at me. I think she had a smile on her face. She stepped to one side and took aim. She sent the empty pail flying across the barn, which startled the chickens and everything else, including me. That caused an awful amount of squawking and screeching.

Bull stepped over and asked, "Are you alright? She didn't get you, did she?"

I didn't know if I dared move or if she might be taking aim again; at me this time. I got a new respect for Bull. He gently picked me up, turned, and placed me out of the way.

He turned to the cow and said, in a very deep voice, "Now listen to me cow; we won't have any more of your foolishment. The boy will milk you if he wants to. After all, he is the boss man now, and don't you forget it. Do y'all understand me cow?"

He asked, "You still want to try, or would you like me to milk for a while longer, until you think you're ready?"

I stared down at the ground and mumbled, "Maybe I'd better wait for a while."

He smiled, roughed my hair and said, "When you want to try again let me know." (So he would be there to watch the fun, I thought.)

I learned Bull was my friend. Over the next three years he helped me grow and taught me many things I would put to use in the years to come. By the time fall came, I was milking the cow.

Now, at the age of eight, going on nine, I was not very big. I might have topped the scales at forty pounds. But, I have always been strong for my weight. My body was all skin and bones and never looked strong. As the summer passed, I learned how to get a stool, stand on it, and drag the harness up and over the team's backs. I learned what straps went where and how to hook them up to the wagon. By summer's end I drove the team in the field while the men loaded the wagon with hay or grain or whatever needed to be harvested.

Bull and I became good friends. We spent many evenings down along the creek that ran close to the farm. He showed me how to catch fish and how to read tracks in the dirt along the bank. I learned what animal left which tracks and if the animal was hunting or just walking through. Bull taught me how to walk without making any noise, how to not leave tracks, and move through the deepest bramble patches; where it seemed like only a small animal could go. His knowledge surprised me. Of course to me, being just a boy, he seemed to be so smart. He showed me how to make a bow out of a hickory sapling, and to make string out of bark by braiding long strands of green bark together.

One afternoon, while I worked my way along the riverbank, I came to a small clearing with a cabin setting along one side. The cabin had been built so you had to be almost on top of it before you could see it.

A picket fence surrounded a garden. Lots of flowers grew along the fences. I stood and watched for a while. When I turned to leave, a white-haired Darky was watching me from inside of the house. It kinda spooked me to see that, as quiet as I had been, he was still aware of me. I had the feeling he knew I was coming before I got to the opening. I turned and worked my way back and went for home. At the dinner table, I told my mom about the little cabin and the old man.

She said, "Oh, you found Obadiah's cabin. Did you stop and talk to him?"

"No, I wasn't sure if I should."

"Oh, he's a nice man and would love to visit with you."

"You know him? I've never seen him around before."

"Yes, I know him. He's Bull's father. Your grandfather gave them permission to build the house where it would be hard to find. He's a runaway slave. He worked for your grandfather and raised his family. They sold his wife. The plantation owner planned to sell the children, so Obadiah took his family and ran from a big farm way down south."

"Why would they do such a thing?" I asked. "That's not fair."

"Remember the talk your father had with you about the war?"

"Yeah, but what does that have to do with Dad and slaves. We don't own slaves, do we? The men are not slaves are they?"

"Well, not really, but on the other hand, yes, they are. Someday I hope you will understand."

"Did Dad go to fight with the South or the North?"

"Eat your supper and don't worry. He did what he thought would be the right thing to do."

Sissy cut in and said the men did not think well enough to work without a boss and, after all, all of her friends had slaves and she didn't think anything was wrong with slavery.

Mom said, "Okay, eat and get ready for bed."

Two weeks later I got away from the farm and school to go down along the creek again. When I got close to the cabin, I stopped and watched for a while. I was ready to turn around and go back home when I had a feeling someone was watching me. I spun around and the white-haired man stood about fifty feet from me, leaning against a tree, smiling.

He said, "I was awonderin' when y'all would come a pokin' around again. You must be the young man from the farm Bull's been tellin' me about."

"Yeah my name is Kenneth. My mom told me about you."

"Oh, is that so? So, what has she told you about me? That I am a mean old man, or a little touched in the head for living out here in the woods by myself? Well, she's partly right. Would you like to come in and have a glass of goat's milk and a cookie or two?"

I wasted only a second, and said, "Sure."

When we got to the cabin he stopped at the door, removed his shoes and asked me to do the same. As we entered the house, I was surprised. The room was spotlessly clean with pictures on the walls and the odor of spices strong in the air. He had braided rugs on the floor and bright curtains at the windows. His house was a lot nicer than ours, and a lot cleaner, too. He had a homemade table and chairs made from small tree limbs.

He set out a pitcher of milk then went to the cupboard, got a bowl with big fat cookies, and set that on the table. They sure looked good. I had a hard time not just diving in, but my mom taught us to wait until the host passed the cookies.

When fall and winter came, I spent a lot of time exploring the area along the banks of the creek. I caught a few catfish for the table. I made a habit of dropping in at the cabin. There was always a kind and respectful attention given to me. Obadiah asked what we heard about the war and if we had any word from the master. The answer was always the same, no word from Dad. I understood nothing about the war. I guessed it was away off someplace else. The schoolteacher said the North was trying to take the lifeblood out of the South, and wanted to release all of the slaves. I wondered why the men in the south couldn't do their own work, like Dad did. But what did I know? I was just a kid. I didn't realize the men, as Mom called them, really were slaves in a way. They were tied to the farm by public opinion and considered slaves by other farm owners. If others had known my father paid the men wages, they would have been upset. On the other hand, the men were not free to go and work for anyone else, so in a way they were slaves.

CHAPTER 2

The second winter turned into spring. Mom told Bull and me we would not be planting much of a crop this year. Money was short, and the buyers hadn't come around wanting to contract the cotton crop. My thought was, "Good! Not so much work this summer." I could spend more time wandering the area and playing in the creek bottom.

A big farm down the road from our place, owned by Mr. Wagoner, had many fine riding horses. He also had some racehorses. One of his riders began riding some of the young horses down the road past our place while he trained them. I liked to walk out and watch him as he galloped them up and down the roadway. The trainer, a young, black man, always waved as he rode by.

One morning he stopped, rode over to me and said, "Hi, I'm Rick. What's your name?"

"Hi, I'm Ken," I answered.

"Do you like horses?"

"Yeah, I like them."

"Do you have a horse?"

I said, "Yes, we have a team."

He laughed, and said, "No, I mean, do you own a horse?"

"No. I never had a horse. I don't know how to ride."

"Do you want to learn?"

"Well, yeah. I would love to."

"Let me talk to Master Wagoner and ask if he will let you come to the ranch and ride."

He was riding a fine, big white horse. I could imagine me riding up and down the road on something like him. Would I like to learn to ride? Of course I would like to ride the way he rode, and on something as beautiful and big as the white horse.

"I'll ask Master today. You ask your mom and dad. I'll stop and talk in the morning."

Now, I didn't tell him my dad was gone. I felt sure Mom would let me.

At the supper table, I made the big announcement. I was going to go to the Wagoner farm and ride horses. I had forgotten one important thing; I had not cleared the plan with Mom.

When Mom heard this she said, "Now where did that come from? I haven't heard anything about it before."

By the tone of her voice, I realized my mistake. So I told her about the invite to learn to ride from the man riding the horse up and down the road.

"Ken, do you realize the young man has no authority to promise you anything? He's a slave who rides the horses for his master."

"Mom, you must be mistaken. He doesn't sound like a slave. He rides all of the horses and teaches them to do all kinds of things."

"Well, you will see. Nothing will come of it."

"But Mom!"

"You just worry about the work here on the farm."

"But Mom, the men can do that. There is not going to be as much field work this year with only half of the cotton crop in."

"I've talked with Bull. He thinks we can plant a field to potatoes and do okay. So, there will be plenty of hoeing and work to keep you busy."

"But Mom!"

"Quiet. Now go finish your evening chores."

As always, my sister found an opening to pick on me. She said, "I can picture you with a black suit and a bow tie, riding some big black horse down the road in front of a bunch of girls, and at the last minute falling off. What a sight that would be. Why don't you let him, Mom? I think watching him fall would be funny."

"Oh, you just wait. Someday I will be a great rider." I jumped up and went out. I shut the door a little too hard, which got me a scolding about losing my temper.

I didn't go to the road the next day. About a week later Rick waved and rode in and asked, "Did you talk to your folks?"

"Yeah, but Mom said no."

"Well, so did the Master."

"I guess that takes care of the riding plan."

"Maybe not, let me work on another plan. I'll be back later. Bye."

He rode off. I thought I hated my mom for being so right. I went to work doing the chores and helping Bull and a couple of the other men cut seed potatoes to plant in the empty cotton field.

One of the men plowed the big field with the team while we cut the seed, a lot of seed, it seemed to me. I remember when I thought no one could work the team but Dad. I learned things seem different to a kid of nine than they do to someone eleven with a lot more experience. Growing up and understanding a thing in a different way was hard. Dad had been gone for two years. I missed him.

One morning Rick rode into the barnyard and he asked if our cow was giving milk.

I said, "Yes, her calf came a week ago."

He got a big smile and said, "Good, I have something you'll be interested in. Will your mom let you keep a pet?"

Mom walked out and Rick turned to her. "Good mornin', Mam."

"You must be the man who works for Mr. Wagoner my son told me about."

"That's right, Mam. It's good to meet you. Mam, will you let Ken have a pet?"

"Well, that depends on what the pet is. No hound pup or anything like that. We don't need more cats. We might even send some home with you, so I don't know what else you could give him."

"I'll bring it by one of these days, okay?" He said, as he turned his horse and rode off. "I better get on down the road. I'll be back in a couple of days."

Three days later a buggy turned in the driveway and came to the barn. The driver asked one of the men if a young man lived here by the name of Ken. I came out of the barn.

He stepped down from the light wagon and asked, "Is your mother home?"

Mom came out of the house and walked toward the wagon. She said, "Yes, I'm right here. What can I do for you?"

"I'm your neighbor, Mr. Wagoner. I want to give your son a pet, if you will let him keep it." All of the time, he smiled a big smile.

"I don't know," Mom said. "It depends on what kind of pet."

"I raise very expensive horses. A mistake happened last year. One of the mares got away and went down the road. A few days ago she dropped a catch-colt. It's not something I want to keep on the place. We thought your son might be able to raise him. I understand your cow is fresh, so you have milk."

"Well, yes. And a second cow will be dropping a calf any time, but I don't ......"

Mr. Wagoner cut her off and reached in the back of the wagon. He removed a canvas covering. The biggest, ugly head appeared. The ugliest mule colt, anyone ever did see, stood up. He was all head, legs, and a very long slim body. He looked like nothing I had ever seen.

Mom put her hand to her mouth and asked, "What will we do with anything so ugly?"

Mr. Wagoner laughed and said, "That's what I wondered. What would I do with him? But I have a soft heart, and didn't want to put him down. My boy, Rick, said he had a place for it. He said I should give the colt to Ken. I decided I would come to make sure that was okay with the boy's parents. Truthfully, I think he will grow to be a great saddle mule. His mother is a runner. She has won many races and is a grand old lady. I just can't have her on the place with a mule colt. I would be the laughing stock of the racing world. So, what do you think? May I leave him with your son?"

I stood in the barnyard, hoping. If I had known what the future of that colt would be, I would have never believed it.

He stood in the back of the wagon looking around. He turned and walked to the tailgate. He made an awful face by sticking his nose in the air and rolling his eyes back. Then he let out a loud, harsh sound that was supposed to be a bray. Everything in the barnyard stopped what they were doing. He turned to me, reached out with his nose, and looked me straight in the eyes. He shook his head and tried to jump into my arms. If Bull had not been standing close, I'm sure he would have jumped the tailgate and knocked me down.

Mr. Wagoner laughed and said, "I guess the decision is made for us. What do you think, Mrs. Clausen?"

Mom shook her head and asked me, "Do you realize what this means? You will need to get up and feed that thing in the night for a while. As he grows, he will need lots of care."

"Yes, Mom, I do. And I will. I promise. Can we keep him, please?"

"Well, I guess so. But where are you going to keep him?"

"I can make a box stall out of Ben's stall in the barn, if Bull will help."

Mom hesitated. "Okay, I guess."

"Thanks, Mom."

"Bull, will you help me with the barn? Mom, I need some way to feed him. What do we have for him to suck on?"

Mr. Wagoner laughed and reached into the wagon. He handed me a whiskey bottle with a nipple on it. "Here, this bottle has raised many a colt. He'll be eating grass and hay in a month or less, and then he will only need a little milk morning and evening for a while. In a couple of months he'll be big enough to go it alone."

"Thanks, Mr. Wagoner."

"So, what are you going to name him?" asked Mr. Wagoner.

"I don't know. I think the name will wait for a day or two."

Bull and I began to prepare the barn. Mr. Wagoner stayed and visited with Mom for a while, then drove off. We had the box stall fixed with some boards to hold the colt so he couldn't run all over the barn. I started to the house to get some milk. Mom came toward the barn with the full bottle of warm milk. I took the bottle and climbed into the pen with the colt and tried to feed him. He didn't like the nipple.

Bull said, "Put your arm around his neck. Hold him and squeeze some milk into his mouth."

I did, and it only took a couple of times until he was following me around the pen.

Mom said, "He's one smart little fellow. Look how quick he learned."

I leaned back against the wall and took stock of my colt. He was not a handsome piece of horseflesh, to say the least. His head was twice as large as it should be, with the longest set of ears I ever saw. If you bent them over, they almost reached his mouth. His neck was skinny and his legs were so long they made his body seem very small. He was a yellowish brown, with a black stripe the full length of his back; which was short compared to the length of his neck. Two black markings ran from his back to his front knees, one on each side. His mane and tail were black, as were his legs from the knees down. A small white stripe started in the center of his face and ran to his nose. That was all of the white on him, except; he had white rings around his eyeballs. They made him look like he was wild.

I spent a lot of time feeding him. He was always hungry. He soon figured out that if he brayed, someone would come running to stop the awful noise.

Mr. Wagoner was right. By three months old he had almost stopped wanting milk and lived on grass and some hay. We became very close. He wanted to go every place I went, and followed along behind me. If I slipped away and hid in the barn or someplace, he put his nose to the ground and trailed me. Then he stood with one ear up and the other back and acted like he was bored with life.

As the year came to an end, Bull and the men dug the field of potatoes. Bull had been right; food was short, due to the war. The demand for potatoes was great. Our patch of ground produced twenty wagonloads. The local store bought all of them as soon as they were out of the ground. Mom was very proud of the job we had done. When Mom collected the money from the store, she called the men and Bull into the house.

She said, "Now, we will divide the profits for the year like we always do. We received $600 dollars for the potatoes and $200 for the cotton. We have $800 dollars. So, each of you gets $100 dollars and we get $400. Now, do you want me to buy anything for you at the store so you don't get in trouble for using your own money?"

They all told her what they needed for clothes and things for another year. If a black man went into the store, with a bunch of money, the storekeeper would say he had stolen it and keep the money for himself. So Mom did the buying for them.

As they were leaving I thought Mom did something funny. She said to them, "I hope you are saving most of it for a later date."

One of them said, "Yes'm, we surely are. Just like the last few years, like you asked us to."

"That's great, because if this war ends and the North wins you're going to need it."

After they left I said to Mom, "Why will they need the money then more than now?"

She said, "Sit down, both of you." Sissy and I sat at the table.

"When the war is over, slavery, which we have never had on this farm, will end. If the North wins this war, there will be hundreds of black families with no homes. A lot of the farms will go broke and can't pay for their labor. But these men, by saving some of their money, will be able to buy land or food."

Winter came and the colt grew. He filled out and became a respectable animal. He was very smart. I would show him once and he would do what I wanted him to with no trouble. I took him along when I went hunting and playing down along the creek. He really enjoyed it when I hid in the bushes and he had to find me. He would put his nose to the ground and trail me. I couldn't hide from him for long. One day

I climbed a tree, so he couldn't find me. He trailed me to the tree, but was lost. He walked around the tree three or four times. He stopped and looked in all directions, then put his head in the air and brayed as loud as he could. I couldn't keep myself from laughing. He looked up the tree, got a disgusted expression on his face, and walked off, headed for home.

I still had not given him a name. One day my sister said, "What are you going to call the colt? He needs a name, you know."

I said, "Yes, I know. Nothing seems to fit."

"Then," she said, "I think I will call him Charlie."

"Why Charlie?" I asked.

"I don't know, but don't you think that's as good a name as any?"

"I guess so. Okay, Charlie will be his name."

So that's how he became Charlie, the mule. He seemed to like it.

CHAPTER 3

Winter progressed. Charlie had a problem. The king of the barnyard decided the time had come to show the young, awkward thing, who was the boss of the farm.

The king happened to be a BIG rooster. He did not like anything getting close to his hens. He had long gray legs and a big, curled, red and green colored tail. The colors on his wings went from gold, to orange, to red, with a little green mixed in. He strutted and swaggered when he walked. He stayed between the hens and anything that came into the farmyard. He walked around with his neck stretched out and said what he was going to do to you. He walked sideways and scratched the ground. When we walked away, he thought he had scared us off, so he would make a run, fly in the air, flap us with his wings, and hit with his spurs. He acted so aggressive that Mom or Sissy wouldn't gather eggs without a stick for protection. He weighed about ten pounds.

The rooster had been threatening Charlie for about a week. One day, when Charlie stood in his way, he flew into the air and flapped him and pecked Charlie's back. He scared the colt pretty good. Charlie ran for the protection of the barn. Mister Rooster thought he had won the battle. He walked around, crowing and strutting his stuff.

A couple days later, when I walked to the barn, he came at me. I stepped beside Charlie. The rooster knew the colt was afraid of him. He walked around both of us and let us know we were in his territory and we had better leave, right now.

I watched him and so did Charlie. Mister Rooster got too close to the left foot. The next thing I saw was Mister Rooster sailing through the air. He slammed against the barn, about six feet up the wall and let out a squawk as he sailed. The slam into the side of the barn did something to him. He slid down the wall. All he could do was squeak, no squawk. He lay quivering on the ground. I thought we would have rooster for supper. It took him about two minutes before he could stand up. He walked in circles with one wing dragging. He didn't see things in any type of proper order. He got inside of the barn door and lay still, making funny sounds, like he had no breath left. That went on for a few seconds, and then he jumped to his feet. With a loud squawk, he made a dash for the chicken coop. He didn't come outside for about a week. When he decided to come out into the world he acted like a very nice, peaceful chicken. He respected everyone and was careful not to get too close to Charlie.

The war came closer to our area. We heard the canon fire in the distance, but we never saw any troop movement or soldiers of either army.

One morning Bull came to the house and asked to talk to the lady. When Mom stepped out on the porch she asked what he needed.

Bull said, "The men left in the night and left no word about where they've gone."

Mom had a shocked expression on her face and then she asked, "Are you going, too, Bull?"

Bull shook his head and said, "No, Mam. I got people here and I can't go running off and leaving them. My father is old and he can't travel like he used to, and then I done promised The Man I would stay and help with the farm and watch over youns."

"That's good of you, Bull, but you better go to Obadiah's place and stay out of sight in case some of the army comes along. I'm sure we will be safe enough," Mom said.

Bull said, "But, who will do the work?"

I said, "Bull, you have taught me how to do everything. I'll try to do what needs done for a while."

Bull walked off. We watched him going through the field with his head bent and his shoulders slumped, like an old man.

I turned to Mom and asked, "Why is Bull so worried?"

She said, "The other three men are his brothers. I think he's afraid he will never see them again."

A few days later, after I finished chores, Mom called to me and said, "Do you suppose, if you go down along the creek, you can find a young pig? We're out of meat."

A lot of wild pigs lived in the brush along the creek. I killed three or four of them in the last year for meat. We had not had the cow bred. Dad always took her to the neighbor's bull. Now we didn't have a calf to eat. I went in the house, got the rifle down, and found some shot. I made sure I had everything I needed to butcher a pig. I went out to the barn and found a piece of rope to tie the hog on Charlie's back. I had done this a couple of times. The first time he didn't like the idea, but I talked him into carrying it, anyway. He walked along and huffed and puffed, but by the time we got home he decided the hog wouldn't hurt him. The hogs liked to go and root under some big, old acorn trees. A bunch bedded down close by. I followed the creek down a ways. I came close to Obadiah's cabin, so I went over to visit with him and Bull. His home gave me a good feeling and was always so peaceful. He was at peace with the world. When I got there, he and Bull were working in the garden, laughing and kidding each other.

I walked up to the fence. Obadiah said, "Well, would you look who is here. I'll bet that stranger wants a handout. What do you think, Bull, shall we invite him in or run him off?"

Bull smiled and said, "Oh, I think the Bum smelled them molasses cookies you just took out of the oven. I told you to hide them someplace, but no, you had to put them out for all of the bums in the country to smell. It didn't take long for this half-starved one to come a beggin'."

I said, "I didn't come for no handout. I wondered if you wanted me to shoot you a big, fat boar pig that's been rolling in the mud." (Now, you know, a big boar pig is not good to eat. The meat is strong flavored and they stink something awful. Cooking only makes the smell worse.)

They both laughed. When I opened the gate to go into the yard, Bull stood up and said, "What is that? Sounds like shots!"

He turned and ran for the farm. I started to follow him and he turned and said, "Master, y'all stay and let me check into this."

I heard a lot more shots and some screams. I had to go back up the creek. I couldn't take Charlie up through the brush the way Bull went. It took me about fifteen minutes longer to get back to the house. Meanwhile Obadiah went up the trail. He got there before me. I couldn't hear any noise from the farm so I didn't really hurry.

When I came into the farmyard, everything was still, no sound at all. Nothing moved in the yard or around the barn. Bull was lying out by the barn's double door. Obadiah sat on the ground, swaying back and forth. He held Bull's head in his lap. I went running up to him.

He was crying and saying over and over, "Why, why, why would they do this?"

I got really scared and ran toward the house. Mom was lying on the porch, all covered in blood. I started to cry and say, "Mom, Mom, answer me please."

I knew Mom would never answer. I looked through the door and Sissy was lying on the floor in the kitchen, covered in blood. I knew she was also dead. I fell to the ground and cried and cried. When the sun went down, I staggered into the house. Then it hit me! I was the only living person left on the farm.

I went outside to the barn. Whoever had been there, and did all of the killing, had taken every living thing except the goat. There were tracks from twenty horses or more. I had forgotten Obadiah until I heard him crying. I walked over to him.

He said, "We must get to my house for the night. We need to be back here early in the morning. We have a lot to do. These people must be put in the ground soon."

I didn't want to leave, but he took my arm and steered me to the path. I started down the path when I remembered Charlie and stopped and turned back.

Obadiah said, "Leave the mule. He'll be alright tonight."

"No. I want to take the blanket and stuff off of him."

So I went back. I took the blanket and ropes off of Charlie, put my arms around his neck and hung on for dear life. I cried until there were no feelings left in me. I just felt hollow and numb.

While holding onto Charlie the thought hit me. What am I going to do? Then the rage came. I wanted to follow the killers and kill every one of them. I didn't know who they were, and there were a lot of them. I could track them, but I only had a small rifle and ten shots of powder and ball.

I walked back to the barn. Obadiah had gone to his house, so I walked into the barn, fell down in some hay, and cried myself to sleep. I dreamed terrible dreams all night. When I awoke the sun was just coming up. I tried to get up, but couldn't move. Something was lying next to me. I rolled away from it and stood up. Charlie stood up at the same time. He had lain down beside me and kept me warm throughout the night.

I walked out of the barn and came face to face with the terrible picture of yesterday. Bull's body lay in front of the doorway, where he died defending our home, as he had promised the man. He had a pitchfork lying beside him. He must have challenged the raiders because he had been shot many times. The shock of yesterday hit me again, but as I stood looking around, I realized many things needed done.

I went to the tool shed and got a shovel. I decided the best place to dig the graves was in the garden. At least the top part of the ground was soft. I got about a foot of easy digging. I had one grave about deep enough when Obadiah came. I was shocked. He had aged many years over night. He walked with his shoulders stooped and his face was thin. The bright light was gone from his eyes. He said nothing, but got another shovel from the tool shed. He walked out in the field and began to dig.

I went to him and said, "Let's put them all over in the garden."

He answered, "No. That's where the lady of the house and family is to be put."

I said, "Obadiah, Bull gave his life for them. He has been part of our lives ever since I can remember. He will be buried with the family."

It took most of the day to dig the three graves and lay the bodies in them. When we finished, I realized we had not eaten all day. I went in the house to find something to eat. When I went through the cupboards, I soon realized the raiders had taken everything eatable, and what wasn't taken was dumped on the floor and destroyed.

From the doorway Obadiah said, "Come on, Son. We'll go to my place and find something to eat and get some rest."

I held out my hands and asked, "Why did they do this? Are they animals or what? I can't believe anyone would be so cruel and so destructive."

He answered, "People have been like that forever. I know. They have abused my family all of my life. Come on, let's go eat and then you can decide what you're going to do."

CHAPTER 4

The next few days were busy ones. I tried to clean up the house and find my way over the loss I experienced. I went through the house trying to find the money Mom got from the sale of the crops last fall. She had a special hiding place somewhere in the house. While going through the cupboards for at least the tenth time, I slammed the door in anger and heard a funny little sound, like something falling or dropping. I opened the door. A board had fallen down, leaving an opening in the wall in the back of the cupboard. A leather pouch hung out of the hole. I reached in and took out Mom's operating money. I dumped the pouch out on the table and counted a hundred and ten dollars. All week I had been making plans in my head about what to do and the money would help.

That afternoon I rode Charlie down the road to the horse farm. I wanted to find out if anyone still lived there. The place was a shambles. All of the people and animals were gone, the same as our place.

I went in the horse barn hunting for anything I might be able to use. A saddle and blanket hung on the wall. I guess the raiders didn't need saddles to go with the horses they had stolen. I also found a set of hobbles and a leather halter. I put the halter and saddle on Charlie. Nothing much else would be of use to me. The house had burned with all of the food supplies.

I returned home to pack the things to take: a couple of blankets, some clean pants, and two shirts. I put a coffee pot and a small kettle in my roll with a knife, fork, and spoon. I took the butcher knife we used to cut up the meat. I went to Obadiah's cabin, where we had been eating one meal a day.

I said, "Obadiah, I'm packed and I'll be riding in the morning. I don't know where I'm going, but I can't stay here with the bad memories. If Dad ever comes home, tell him I've gone west, some place beyond the big river. Every time I go in the house I see Mom and Sissy lying on the floor. I'll stay with you tonight, if that's all right. I'll leave at daylight."

Obadiah nodded his head and looked very sad. "I hate for you to go, but I understand. I also had to leave my home, and it's hard. So, be a good, honest man your father would be proud of. I love you as a son. Now get some sleep so you can leave early."

I sure didn't realize what the next morning would bring. I woke up before daylight. Obadiah was still sleeping. I fixed some breakfast and got ready to leave. Obadiah had not stirred. I went to his bed and touched him but got no response. He also had started on his last journey. He died in his sleep. I couldn't leave without taking care of him. I went out and got a shovel and dug a couple of hours to make a grave for him. I went into the house and wrapped him in a blanket, as we had done with the other three. I picked him up and was so surprised at how light he was.

After I buried Obadiah, I went in the cabin and searched for some food to take with me. I found small sacks of things, like flour, beans, salt and other things I could use on the trail. I also found a leather sack with twenty dollars. That gave me a good-sized traveling fund. Before I went out, I picked up the lamp and poured oil on the bed and set it afire. Then I made my way to our farmhouse and did the same thing.

I rode away, trying not to turn back, but had to take one last look. The smoke billowed from Obadiah's house down in the brush. Our house burned big. The clapboards were so dry they went fast. One more look, then I went forward with great fear, not knowing what would happen to me in the future. I could not hold back the tears because I was afraid. I had never been more than ten miles from home in any direction. What would I do? Oh, sure, I had camped out overnight down on the creek, but not more than one night at a time. And always close by the farm to run home if I got in trouble.

I was going on thirteen and still not very big, about five feet five, and not over eighty pounds. A strong, muscular eighty pounds because I had been working on the farm for four years lifting sacks of grain, potatoes, cotton, and loose hay. The past year I had been doing half of the work alongside of Bull. Now I had to take care of myself.

I wasn't much to look at as I started this new adventure. As I said, I was about five and a half feet tall. My boney shoulders had not started to muscle out, even though I had worked hard. I lifted a hundred pounds easily and worked all day. I was slender and not very muscular by appearance. My face was thin. My hair grew to the bottom of my ears as black as coal. I took after Dad. My eyes were a watery blue. When I got mad, they had a way of getting almost green. I had long and slender hands, with a good grip from milking the cow twice a day for the last three years. I dressed in an old pair of bib overalls and a pair of knee-high boots, I had nearly outgrown. The plain gray shirt and plaid jacket were about two sizes too big, but they kept me warm. The jacket was one Dad left hanging in the house and wore to do chores. The sleeves had some worn, ragged spots. I picked up the old felt hat from one of the men a couple of years ago. The hat was worn and dirty from fieldwork, and the brim had a way of falling down. I wore the hat so that part hung in the back. It didn't make much difference. There really wasn't any shape to it, anyway.

I rode Charlie with an old beat up saddle from the Wagoner's farm. Charlie and I were not the most handsome couple ever starting out to see the world. I carried the squirrel rifle in my lap. I suppose I most resembled a tramp or a runaway kid.

I had a few days of food, the rifle, and a hundred and thirty dollars. At the last minute I picked up the old cap-lock pistol Dad left behind. I didn't know if it would fire or not. I had never shot the gun. I don't know why I picked it up.

I didn't know where to find a camping spot, but had an idea what I should be looking for. The first night I camped along a stream in, a small opening, and set out some snares, the way Bull taught me. The next morning I caught a nice rabbit, which I took time to cook. I hadn't eaten for two days, so the rabbit tasted good. I ate half and took the other half with me for the night meal.

The first week of travel went pretty much the same. I got up before dawn and ate some rabbit or squirrel I snared during the night. Charlie had a good long walk but I don't know how far we traveled each day. As the days went by, he got so he could walk a lot faster. The first week or two we met very few people on the road. When we did, I pulled off to the side and let them go by.

One day, about a week later, along the middle of the morning, I came to a store beside the road. I stopped a ways back and watched to see if anyone was trading. No one went in, so I rode up to the front and went inside. A heavyset woman was working in the store. When I went in, she turned and walked behind the counter and, with a big smile, asked what she could do for me.

Now, I had never been in a store before nor had I ever bought anything. I stood there and she got a funny expression on her face.

She said, very kindly, "Young man, do you want to buy something or just look around?"

I had the biggest urge to run out the door. Finally I got control of myself and in a stammering manner told her what I needed.

She asked, "How far have you come?"

I told her, "I don't know, but I came from Wagoner's Corner." Anyway that's what I thought Mom call the store close to home.

She said something to a person behind a curtain covering a doorway. Then she turned to me. "And where in the world is Wagoner's Corner? How many days have you traveled?"

I shrugged my shoulders, "About two weeks, I think."

She asked, "And how long since you had a good meal, young man?"

I really didn't remember, but it was before Mom died. I answered, "Maybe three weeks or longer, I think."

"Are you from the area where the raiders went through a while ago?" She asked.

I nodded my head. Now, I was uncomfortable. I had not planned on spending much time in the store before moving on.

She turned her head and said, in a loud voice, "James, you get in here!"

A black man came from behind the curtain. He said, "Yes, Mam, what do you want?"

"Would you take this young man out back, help him put his mule away for the night, and introduce him to the water trough so he can get cleaned up to eat?"

I stepped back. I guess I acted scared, "I just came in to buy some things for the trail, not to beg for food or a meal. I really can pay."

"Oh, hush. You go on out back and get yourself cleaned up. We'll talk about what you need after you get some good food in your belly."

James motioned for me to follow him. When we got outside he looked me up and down and said, "There's no use arguing with that woman. You can't win, so be thankful for people like her. Come on, let's feed your mule and get some soap and water so you can clean up."

We went in the barn and I took care of Charlie. James had a big pan of water setting on the feed box with a washcloth and towel ready for me to use.

He said, "Just wash and change clothes in here. When you get ready, come to the house."

I washed and put on the clean set of pants and a clean shirt out of my bedroll. I decided I would wash the dirty clothes in the next stream I come to.

They were waiting for me. She asked, "What do they call you, young man?"

I told her my name was Ken.

"Ken what?" She asked.

"Ken Clausen," I replied.

She smiled, "How old are you, Ken?"

Now, I was getting a little nervous with all of the questions. I guess she realized that, so she set a big bowl of stew on the table and she and James took a smaller bowl. I sat down and began to eat.

She said, "In this house we give thanks to the Lord for our daily bread, young man."

I had never seen that done, so I sat blushing, not knowing what to do. They bowed their heads and said a prayer to the Lord.

I don't think I ever tasted a stew as good as the stew we ate. It might have been because I was so hungry or because I'd been living on rabbit and squirrel with not much else for a couple of weeks. Now, don't get me wrong, I had plenty to eat. Sometimes I ate two squirrels and sometimes a rabbit for breakfast and a squirrel for supper. I always found wild onions, or things from an abandoned garden. I learned to be a good scrounge and took advantage of opportunities as they came my way.

When we finished eating the lady said, "I guess we better go in the store and get the things you'll need."

She turned to James and said, "You'll take care of the dishes for me, won't you?"

"Yes, Mam," answered James.

We went into the store. I told her I would like to buy some flour, salt, a few dry beans, and something to make the flour rise when you make biscuits.

She laughed and said, "I'll tell you how to use this later," and gave me a can of stuff. When I thought I had everything, she said, "I have some dried meat and a few cans of fruit, if you want them."

I thought and said, "No, I think I better not. I need a pair of shoes that won't hurt my feet when I walk. How much do I owe you for all of this stuff?"

"Better try some shoes first, and then we'll add it up." She replied.

I must have tried on four or five pairs of shoes before I found some big enough, but not so big they were loose on my feet. I had small feet for a boy.

"Okay, let me add all this up." She took a pencil and paper and wrote down everything on the counter. With serious expression on her face, she asked, "Do you have five dollars?"

I pulled the money pouch from around my neck, counted out five dollars and handed the money to her.

She pointed at me and said, "Now you listen to me! The next time you go into a store to buy something, you take some money from the pouch and put it in your pocket so you don't show your pouch to anyone. Do you understand me?"

"Yes, Mam. I never thought about anyone wanting to take my money."

When I collected my stuff, she asked how I planned to carry everything on the mule. I shrugged my shoulders. I had no idea. I looked at the things and realized they would not work in my bedroll.

"Why don't you go out in the barn and get a couple of grain sacks? We'll make you two packs to hang off of the saddle. While you're doing that, I'll fix a few things to help you cook."

I returned from the barn with two sacks. Cans, spoons, a jar, and some other things were lying out on the counter top. She explained what each was for.

"This jar is for you to soak your beans while you travel. Just put a few beans in and cover them with water and screw the top on. They'll soak as you ride. This pail will serve as a water pail to collect water from a steam. You can wrap this rag across the top and strain water into the bucket. You already have a coffee pot to boil water and a pan to cook in. However, this is a small, heavy pan to make pancakes or fry meat. This small can is for you to drain fat into when you fry meat so you will have grease to fry with. I think that will get you to wherever you're going. Do you have a canteen to carry drinking water on your saddle?"

I shook my head no. She went to the other side of the room and got a round metal thing, wrapped in many layers of cloth and with a web strap to hang it from.

"Now," the lady said, "I think you're all fixed. Take this stuff to the barn and get ready for traveling. Come back in and we'll all eat a nice meal and have a chat this evening. I suppose you'll want to get an early start in the morning."

I packed all of my treasures out to the barn. I was looking at them in awe, and trying to figure out where to put what, when I realized I had not asked what I owed her for all of these things. Before I returned to the house I opened my pouch and put some money in my front pocket, as she had instructed me. I balanced the saddle over the feed manger, as if it were on Charlie, and tried hanging the two, small connected sacks in different places. They were finally hanging where I thought they would fit best. I found, if I put the sacks there, I could tie them in place with some rope from the throw-away can by the feed box.

I couldn't believe the meal she fixed for us, just like Christmas dinner. There was a big roast of meat with sweet potatoes, onions, carrots, cabbage, and a pie. Everything sat on the cupboard, waiting to be eaten.

We ate for about an hour. We talked and really enjoyed each other. Finally, I stood and said I needed to get to bed so I could ride out at sunrise. I turned to the lady of the house and said, "Thank you for all you've done for me. I think I owe you more for the things you gave me and, most of all for your friendship. I'm sure I'll be able to use the things you've taught me."

She smiled, walked over and gave me a big hug and said, "You can stay awhile, you know. I have work for you if you want it. I'm sure James will be moving on soon. It's too dangerous for him to stay in one spot much longer."

She didn't know how temped I was. Something drove me now, other than just looking for a place to live. I still had a lot of summer to travel.

"Thank you, but I'd best ride on in the morning. I'll think of you and be ever so grateful for your help. Now, can I pay you for the other things you gave me in the packs?"

She shook her head and said, "No, just go and be safe. A lot of men are deserting from the armies and they're roving the country, like the group that went through your home area. They rob, kill, and take anything within sight. I don't know if you have heard, but President Lincoln was murdered the fourteenth of April. So, watch carefully and trust no one while you are on the road."

James and I walked out to the barn. He went into an empty horse stall and I laid my bedroll on a pile of hay the other side of the alleyway. After we lay down, we talked for a while about our plans.

I asked him where he was going. He said, "I don't know. Some place where it's free and I won't have a master with a whip. I got sold from a big farm down in Georgia and that there man planned to take me way across the big river to some place called Texas."

"Why did you run away if he was taking you way out to another farm?"

"Have you ever been whipped with a buggy whip for not moving fast enough or for trying to learn how to read and write?" He asked.

"No. Dad used to threaten to whip me if I didn't pay attention to the teacher instead of teasing Lucy Pool," I answered.

We talked for a while longer. I was sleepy, so I rolled over and shut my eyes. I had a funny, lonely feeling so I got up, took my knife from the pack, and put it along side of the bed. I went to sleep, feeling a lot safer for some reason.

I have no idea what time it was, but I woke up with a scary feeling that things were not right. Then I heard Charlie making the funny little puffing sound, like he did when something is wrong. I lay still and listened. The hair on the back of my neck was all tingly. A shadow crossed in front of a crack in the siding.

Someone said, in a whisper, "He has to be in here someplace. You look on that side and I'll check out this side."

I picked up the knife and lay very still. I didn't know if they were after me, or what, but I was very scared. I was sure of that!

They poked around in the hay and, all of a sudden the one on my side said, "Here he is!" And he jumped on me.

I put my arms up trying to keep him from landing on me. I forgot about the knife in my hand. The next thing I knew, he landed full length, knocking the wind out of me. He laid there, for what seemed like a long time, but I think it was just a few seconds. Then he jumped to his feet and went running out of the barn.

He started to cuss and swear and in a loud voice said, "Let's get out of here! He has a knife and he stabbed me. I'm bleeding something awful. Let's get for home so Maw can stop this bleeding."

I jumped out of bed and crawled to the door. Two men were running down the road. One ran kind of lopsided. I turned back and called James' name. There was no response, so I walked over where his bedroll had been. It was gone, along with James. He must have left before the two came in the barn or during the fracas. I know he was long gone when I tried to find him.

I decided, since I was up, I might as well follow James' example and leave as soon as I could saddle up and go. Sunrise found me about five or six miles down the road, watching to make sure no one followed. I hoped that big, long butcher knife didn't do too much damage to whoever it went in, but, on the other hand, he may be a little more careful what he jumps on in the dark.

When I opened my pack to fix a small meal, I found a lot of dried meat in a package, along with a smaller package. I opened the small package and saw my five dollars. She must have put it in when I went to the barn. For supper I put some of the meat in my small pan to boil and made some soup.

CHAPTER 5

I had been traveling for at least two months. I didn't know for sure, because one day ran into the next. I couldn't say if today was Monday or Saturday. Camping spots away from the road became a lot harder to find. The country flattened out with more farms farther apart. A few times I had to ride until dark and sleep along the road next to a fence. I traveled, what I thought was a westerly direction, but seemed to be going more north. I came to a small river and followed it downstream. I found a bridge and crossed over to the other side, and worked my way down the river. The country seemed more like home, with small rolling hills and valleys with some timber in them. Most of the valleys had water and a shack with gardens, chicken coops, goats, or a milk cow. I found plenty of places to make a camp with feed for Charlie, and lots of squirrels and some small rabbits to catch. One small creek seemed promising, so I took out my fishing line and, low and behold, I caught catfish and had a real feast.

The sky showed signs of rain, so I stopped at one of the shacks to ask if I could sleep in their lean-to barn. A girl about my age and her little brother, a couple years younger, came out the door. She seemed very afraid and stayed away from me. Her brother hauled out a double-barreled gun bigger than he was. He said, "Better move along, mister, as this here thing is loaded and I don't want to hurt you."

I looked straight at him. He seemed so serious and so small with the big gun he was trying to hold up. I pictured him pointing the gun at me and pulling the triggers and when it went off, going air bound from the kick of the monster. I began to laugh.

He glared at me and said. "Oh, crap!" His face got red. "The gun ain't loaded anyway." And we all laughed.

"Hi, I'm Ken. Is your Mom or Dad home?"

"I'm Elisabeth." She waited for a long time, and then said, "No. My Daddy left and went to war and we haven't seen him since. Momma left this spring and hasn't come back."

I noticed a well kept garden. Their clothes were clean, so I thought they were doing okay. "I think it's going to rain. Do you suppose I can sleep in your lean-to shed tonight? I've been riding a long time and it's hard to find some place to camp around here."

The brother asked, "Did your Pa go to the war, too? Ours went two years ago to fight them Damn Yankees. When I get old enough I'm going, too." He spat on the ground.

His sister spun on him and with a voice as sharp as a knife said, "Bob, you are not! You're going to stay here and help take care of this place, like Pa told you to. You hear me?"

The brother acted like his sister was not even there he asked, "Is the mule yours or did you steal him someplace? Pretty nice mule for some kid."

As I listened to the tone of his voice, I decided I really might not want to sleep around here. I'd better move on and find someplace else to camp." I told them.

I turned Charlie around and asked the girl "Is there a store close by?"

She said, "About three miles down the road."

I decided since I was getting low on food maybe I better move along. I rode off, not wanting to stay any longer. On top of that, the answer the boy gave me about his pa going to fight the Yankees made me think, who did my Dad go to fight? Did he fight for the Yankees or the South? He did not like slavery, however all of the neighbors had slaves, and hadn't he kept the men working for him? Sure, he paid them, but did he pay them enough or was that just Mom's way? I hadn't thought about any of these things before. While I rode along, I worried. What is my dad fighting for, slavery or freedom for the blacks?

There was not just a store but a small town with many buildings. I stopped at the top of the street trying to make up my mind if I wanted to go on in. I'd never been in a town this big, with so many different stores. People were walking between the stores. I guess the posts are to tie the animals to. I decided I should get a haircut. My hair reached to my shoulders by now and was hard to wash. I had run out of soap and most of my food. I rode down the street and people turned and looked at me.

CHAPTER 6

I was getting mighty uncomfortable, when a man stepped out of the blacksmith shop. Anyway, that's what his sign said. He smiled, motioned me over to him and said, "Welcome to Farmington. I can tell by the looks of your mule you've been traveling for a while. Where are y'all from, anyway?"

I answered, "Oh, over east a ways. Can you tell me what all of these stores have in them? I need some food to replace mine and I need a feed for Charlie and a day or two of rest for both of us."

"Well, sure. The building next to us is a livery barn for the mule. The one across the street is a grocery. That's where you get food for yourself. The next with the open door, is a barbershop, which you might need. You can also get a bath. He has a room in the back and even has hot water. What else do you need?"

"Well, I need some place to sleep."

"I might let you sleep in the hayloft of the barn. I own the livery and this shop."

I decided I better stay for one night anyway, since the day was nearly gone. I asked, "How much is this going to cost for the bed and a feed for the mule?"

He answered, "Oh, about ten cents a day for the mule. That includes a feed of grain. For the haircut and bath, Harry charges twenty five cents, if you get both the haircut and the bath."

"Do I pay you now or when I leave?"

He shook his head. "You wouldn't be a thinkin' about running out in the middle of the night would you?"

"No sir. I'm not sure how many days I want to stay. Charlie needs a couple days rest. If I don't get out of this saddle for a while, I don't think I'll ever be able to walk right again."

"Well, if you promise not to run out on me, I can wait until you decide to go. If you're short of money maybe we can figure out some way for you to work out the expenses for the feed and grain. If you're going to get a haircut and a bath you better go. Harry will be going home for supper in about an hour."

I checked my pocket and made sure I had enough for the haircut and bath. I would come back and get more for supper later. I put my saddle, with the packs, in the stall in front of Charlie and the pack with my money down in the manger, under the hay.

The bath, with the tub full of hot water, sure was great. I soaked as long as I could.

Harry opened the door and said, "You've got to get out now. I need to close."

I dressed in my clean clothes and went back to the livery to get more money. When I got to Charlie's stall, my saddle was not in the stall or hanging on the side. The packs were both gone. I thought I would get sick. "What am I going to do now? All of Mom's hundred dollars and the other money had been in the packs."

I started to panic when the owner walked in and said, "If you lost something I put everything in the saddle shop and locked the door. Some people will steal anything of value and I didn't want you to lose your camping supplies. Oh, by the way, I'm John," and he held out his hand.

I was so relieved. I put out my hand and said, "I'm Ken, and thank you! I thought I'd been robbed. Everything I own is in those two grain sacks. How is the eating place down the street, and how much do they get for a meal?"

"The food is good. I eat there every night. They charge fifty cents for all you can eat. The pie is really good."

"Pie! I guess I better go before it's all gone. I haven't had but one piece of pie since I left home. What kind do they make? Apple, I hope. That's my favorite, with a big glob of cow's cream on top."

"Well, I don't know about the glob of cream, but the pie is always good. From the sound of you, I guess I better go now, or there might not be anything left for me."

He laughed as we walked down the street. Suddenly it dawned on me; he treated me like a man and not some little boy. This man was treating me like I was grown up and not thirteen, although I was almost fourteen. That made me feel good, I'm sure I grew a couple of inches in those few seconds. I know I grew about a foot in confidence. He had a friend for the rest of his life.

I lay in the haymow watching the stars through the big double doors in the end of the barn. I thought, maybe I should stay and work for a few days and learn something about blacksmithing. I'm comfortable with John. He's easy to talk to. He seems like he's also alone and needs someone to be friendly with. I made up my mind I would talk to John in the morning about working for him a while.

I got up early and fed Charlie. As the sun came up I turned him out into the corral with the rest of the horses. I stood by the gate petting Charlie and brushing him when a brown mule walked up and stopped a little distance from us. She stood, watching us. I talked to her while I worked with the brush on Charlie's back. I turned and slowly put out my hand. She backed up and laid one ear back but kept the other one forward, looking at me. I ignored her and went on about my work. She walked up, almost to me, like she wanted some attention. I got a sugar cube from my pocket and handed it to her. She, very dainty like, took the sugar from my hand.

"I don't believe what just happened." John said, almost scaring me out of my wits and causing me to jump. "I've had the mule for two months and you're the first person to get close enough to her even to take a hold of the halter, if you wanted to. We've tried everything but roping her. She likes you or Charlie. I believe, if you work with her a little, she'll let you pet her."

I smiled at him. "Well, if I was to do that I would need a job of some sort to pay my way. Living in town and eating in the café costs a lot of money."

John nodded his head as he spoke. "Have you ever worked with a forge at home? Did your daddy use one?"

"No, I never was close to one until I watched you make plowshares yesterday."

"I guess you could learn to pump the bellows for a starter. That would make my work a lot easier. I could work with both hands. How much do you think you will need for wages?"

"I don't know. We'll see how things go today."

He smiled and said, "Okay, but pumping the bellows and keeping the fire stoked is a lot of hard work."

I had watched him the day before and it didn't look too hard. He pumped the handle up and down with one hand, as the piece of iron heated. Once in awhile he put a small shovel of coal on the fire. He took the iron bar, or whatever was in the fire, out and pounded the metal into the shape he wanted.

We went into the shop. He took off his shirt. He got out a leather apron and tied it around his waist. He put coal on the fire and showed me how to work the handle on the bellows. It wasn't all that hard, so I started to work the bellows.

He looked up and said, "No, not too fast! Pump slowly enough for the fire to get going. I need a good bed of coals. If you pump too hard the fire will blow out."

"Okay, this is going to be easier than I thought."

When the fire was just right, he put four pieces of flat bar in the pot, as he called it. I kept up a steady, slow pump on the handle and, while I watched, the bars turned red, then almost white. That's when he took the first one out and shaped it on the anvil with a couple of hits with a big hammer. He worked all four of them really fast. In about thirty minutes he had made four horseshoes. I was fascinated with his speed and how quick he turned the rods into shoes.

We worked, to what I thought was almost lunchtime, when a customer came in. John said, "I'm ready for your team. If you want to leave them we will do them right now, so you can get on your way."

Wait a minute! I thought, what about lunch? Now, he had me jumping. I took him a shoe from the forge with a set of tongs, as he called them. He walked out and held them close to the horse's hoof as he held the foot in the air. Then he put the metal on the anvil and worked the shoe to fit the foot. I took his shoeing kit out to him with a bunch of other tools. When the team was shod, he straightened up, looked at me and laughed.

He said, "You worked up a sweat on that little job. Wait until we get a big job, then you'll earn your keep."

When the day ended I was ready to drop. As soon as we finished supper I went to bed and right to sleep.

The days ran into a week and that week turned into week two. The work got a lot easier. I began to understand what he needed for different jobs without being told.

Every morning and evening I talked to and worked with Molly, as the mule was called. She got so she trusted me. I brushed her all over. She even tried to push Charlie out of the way so she could be first. I asked John where he got her.

He said, he was working in the shop one day and this young girl came leading the mule down the road. She said she needed to sell the mule because they didn't have any money for food.

"I asked about her folks. She told me her dad had gone off to war and had not returned. Her mother disappeared one day and they have not seen her again."

Now, the story seemed like one I had heard before from the girl out of town a few miles. "John," I asked, "Was the girl about thirteen with brown hair and wearing a dress put together from feed sacks?"

He looked at me kind of funny and said, "Yeah that pretty much describes her. How do you know about her?"

"When I was coming in the other day I stopped at her house and her little brother ran me off with a shotgun." So I told him about the meeting.

He got a funny expression on his face and said, "Those two kids are all by themselves with no one to help." He walked away while shaking his head. He was very quiet the rest of the afternoon and seemed preoccupied about something.

Later, in the afternoon, he asked, "How far out to the kid's place did you say?"

"Oh, about five miles maybe, or a little farther, I guess. I rode maybe one hour on into town. Why? Are you going out there for something?"

He took off his apron, cleaned up the shop some, and banked the fire, like he did every night. He turned to me saying, "Let's call it a day. We're almost caught up with everything here. Why don't you go rest or work with the Molly mule?"

I got the message. He was going to go out and check on the kids. In the afternoon I thought about my situation and decided now was time for me to move on. Charlie was rested and I had a restless feeling again. I had gained some weight and, even with working hard, felt rested. Charlie was ready to go. He did a lot of walking around the corral while looking down the road.

John left and came back about dark. When he came in the barn he seemed very sad. "Did you find them?" I asked.

He said, "Yes," and went on putting his horse away.

He finished, and walked down the alley to the front door. "That's a sad thing with the kids. They have no food and no oil for their lantern. They have eaten all of the chickens and killed the milk goat today before I got there. They are going to starve if someone doesn't help them. The young boy is a feisty guy. He tried to run me off with the same shotgun until I told him I knew he had no shells. I think I'll give him a job here, working with us."

While I lay in bed, I made up my mind to move along. The next morning, when John came to work, I was in the corral feeding the stock. He walked up to me as I glanced at him. "I think it's time for me to move along. I've been here for a month and have the feeling now's the time. What are you going to do with the Molly mule after I leave? No one else can touch her, and I don't think she will take to many people."

John stood for a while looking at the stock in the corral. He said, "You haven't learned to make things yet. Why don't you give me another week and I'll show you how to make some tools? You can take them with you when you go."

That day was the most fun I had since starting to work. John had me get the fire ready. He put a piece of thin metal in the pot. While the metal got hot he explained how I was going to make a hoof knife, to clean the hooves out and trim around the frog of the horse's feet. He showed me how it would work on Charlie. I worked on the knife and learned how to handle the hammer right. I made the knife in the morning and made a set of nippers in the afternoon. Working the forge was fun and I liked finally making things. Over the next couple of days I made the knife, nippers, a different type of nippers you use to remove the old worn out shoes from the horse's hooves, a clinching block, and some nails.

After three days of working in the shop he said, "Now, let's put a set of shoes on Charlie and get you ready for the rest of the summers travel."

I had watched him shoe horses and mules and it looked pretty easy. But, when I picked up Charlie's front foot, I found out I was wrong. Charlie stood still and was okay with me holding his foot up, but when I tried to smooth the bottom with the rasp, that was a different thing. He gave his foot a jerk and put it down. Now, I was determined to do the work myself. He was just as determine that his feet did not need shoes. John stood back and gave me advice on how to hold the foot and not let him take it away. Oh, sure, I'm an hundred and thirty pound kid and Charlie must weigh in at a thousand pounds, and I'm supposed to master his feet. I ended up on the ground looking up a couple of times.

John said, "Here, let me make him understand how he's supposed to stand."

He lifted the front foot. When Charlie tried to take it away, John held on and Charlie couldn't get away. I saw the difference between why John could hold the foot and I couldn't. When Charlie strained against him, John's arms got twice the size and the muscles stood out like ribbons. I hadn't noticed how huge his arms were. I made up my mind; I didn't want this guy mad at me. I told him to go ahead and shoe the mule. I was wasting his time. He showed me how to tie up the feet when I needed to if Charlie was not co-operating. Charlie ended up lying on his side and I did the shoeing job. While we worked, I asked him again about the Molly mule.

"Why do you want her?" He asked.

I answered, "Well, I think she and Charlie have a thing going and I need a pack animal. No one else can handle her without abusing her. How much do you want for her?"

I wondered if he was going to ignore my question, but soon he said, "You'll need a packsaddle, blanket, ropes, a set of panniers, and some canvas for a cover sheet. Then we'll find out if she is broke to the saddle."

I thought about all he said. I knew I didn't have enough money for all of those things, on top of the price of the mule.

He said, "You've worked for me for a month, give or take a day or two, and we never did set a wage. I suppose we can make a packsaddle. The store has the rest of what we need. Jim, down at the harness shop, has leather for the breeching and breast collar. The first thing in the morning you go find out what the cost will be for all of the leather, rope and canvas we need. I've made trees for pack saddles for Jim before, so that's no problem."

Early the next morning I headed out to search for all of the parts we would need for the saddle and fittings. I was sure I couldn't afford to buy everything I needed at the store. I figured that was out of the question. I might as well forget Molly and get going in the morning. They wanted thirty dollars for everything. I asked Jim, at the saddle shop, what kind of a price he wanted for what I had on my list.

He said, "New or used?"

Well, now, I hadn't thought about anything used. "Used would be good but I don't want anything rotten or broken."

He walked over to a rack, took down the things on my list, and laid them on the counter. "I think I could give you the whole thing for fifteen dollars, cash."

I couldn't believe what he was saying. Now, all I had to do was find out what John wanted for the mule. As I walked out of the store, I said, "Just leave everything out. I'll be right back as soon as I buy the mule."

I hurried down to the shop and told John what I found. He smiled and went back to his work.

"Well," I asked, "What do you want for Molly?"

He turned back to me and, after a few seconds, said, "I'll tell you what, you've worked for me for the month and never quit when you were so tired you wanted to drop. So you take the mule and we'll be even."

I had eaten a hot meal twice a day, had a place to sleep at night, and now he was giving me the mule. I could hardly believe my ears. I reached into my pack, got out twenty dollars and went back down the street and got my stuff.

The next problem was getting the saddle on the mule without getting killed. I went back to the corral and snapped a lead rope to Molly's halter and led her out the gate. She acted fine until I tried to lead her away from the corral. She noticed Charlie was not coming and planted her front feet and stopped. No amount of pleading, or pulling moved her.

I was getting upset when John said, "Go get Charlie and walk him down to the shop. I think Molly will follow."

I did, and she walked along without even pulling on the lead rope. Now, John and I looked at each other and knew what was going to happen next. We were going to put a set of shoes on her and we would have a fight. We finally had her lying on her side.

John asked, "Do you want to shoe her or do you want me to?"

I said, "I'll shoe her. You tell me what to do. That way she's going to know I'm the boss later on."

He nodded his head. "That's probably a good idea."

I proceeded to work on her and, after an hour, I finally had shod my first animal, all by myself. I was very proud of the job, but knew that was not something I wanted to do any more than I had to. When I let her up, she stood in one spot and kicked and kicked trying to dislodge the shoes from her feet. After a while she settled down, so I led her back to the corral and tied her up to the center post. I got the saddle and tried to put it on her. She was having nothing to do with that. This was not going to happen, as far as she was concerned. An old man, sitting on a bench in front of the livery barn, stood up and walked over to the corral.

After I tried a bunch of times to get the saddle on her, he said. "You're going at it the wrong way. She's afraid of that thing, so cover her eyes with your coat and she'll settle down."

I walked in the barn, got my old coat, and went outside to talk to her. I gave her a sugar cube, petted her, and then slipped the coat over her head. She fought for a little bit, and then I petted her. She let me put the saddle on and tighten the cinches.

He said, "Now, go ahead, put your panniers on and put some weight in them. Not a lot, but enough so she will get use to the weight. Untie her and tie the halter rope to the saddle. Take the coat off and get out of the way."

I did what he told me. When she saw daylight, she stood for a moment, and then started to move. She felt the saddle and the loaded panniers. She let out a bawl and went into all kinds of fits. I got on the outside of the corral. We watched her buck, bawl, roll on the ground, reach back and try to bite the load.

After about ten minutes she stopped and, with sides heaving, walked over to the fence on the other side of the corral and stood pouting.

"Now, you go have something to eat. When you come back walk around the corral and talk to her. Give her some of the sugar you've got in your pocket. Leave the saddle on her all night. In the morning catch her and take it off. She'll be so glad to see you she will walk up asking for you to take the stuff off."

I said, "I don't know about that, but if she tries to kick me I'll leave it on all day."

He shook his head and said, "No, then she would start to hate you, so just leave it on until morning."

I did what he said. I took the load and saddle off the next morning. Molly walked away and lay down and rolled in the dust of the corral. Then she got up and walked right to me. I petted her, gave her a treat, and brushed her back. She liked that.

Later in the afternoon I got out some money and went to the store and got the food things I needed and more clean clothes. Now, I had some room to carry extra things. I bought a small axe and some powder and balls for the squirrel rifle. I had only used the rifle a couple of times because I had just a few balls and not much powder. I didn't like to use it anyway, because the noise might let someone know where I was camping. I asked John if he knew how to load the pistol I picked up at home.

He looked at the pistol and said, "Yes, I know how but if I was you, I would throw it away. This pistol will only shoot one shot and then you have to reload. If you miss anyone can be on you before you can get a new load. This was built for pirates on ships and is mostly bang, not much power. I don't think you could hit anything over ten feet away. I doubt if you can hit anything, even at that distance. You might do more damage to yourself than to them."

CHAPTER 7

While packing the panniers I put the pistol on top. A big bang might be all I needed. I finished packing before going to bed and planned on an early start in the morning. Packing the panniers, and putting saddles on two mules, takes a lot longer than just getting up, saddling Charlie and leaving. In about an hour I had everything ready to go down the road. Molly had to learn what to do. I needed to practice packing in a more orderly manner.

I made good time, though. Molly wouldn't let Charlie get ahead of her, so she kept up really well. They seemed to enjoy traveling together. I passed up several good campsites. Along towards evening, I was in a farming area with a lot of fenced fields but not much for small streams.

As darkness settled in, I turned into a lane leading towards a farm about a half-mile off the road. When I got close to the farmyard, I slowed down, watching for someone to talk to. I needed a place to spend the night. I rode up to the front door and hollered to find out if anyone was home. No chickens or life of any type showed up. I got off, walked to the door and knocked. Still no one answered. I walked around the house. The back door stood open. The room was empty, no furniture or sign of anyone living in the house. I took the mules to the barn, unsaddled and found some hay. I ate a cold supper of dried meat. The well pump worked great, so we had lots of good, cold water.

I slept hard. The next morning I left before the sun came up. I traveled for some time before meeting a rider coming my way. He was a big man on a big horse. He had a star on his chest.

He pulled up and greeted me with, "Hold up young man, where are you going?"

I didn't like what I saw. He appeared to be a tough type of a person. "I'm headed to the big river and beyond." I replied cautiously.

He swelled out his chest and tried to seem important while he looked over my outfit. He wanted to know where I had stolen the mules and all of the equipment.

I said, "I didn't steal anything. I raised the mule I'm riding, and I bought Molly, the pack animal."

"Yeah, I'll bet that's what you did, all right. That saddle mule is out of some fancy riding mare. Where would a rag-tag pup like you get that kind of animal? I think we better go to town and talk to the judge about some things. We'll find out what you have to say then. What else do you have in them packs?"

He turned and motioned for me to ride on and he came up behind Molly. I waited to see what he would do. I was scared, since I had never seen a police officer. I had the feeling that if he checked the pack and found the pistol and my hundred dollars he would find some excuse to take it. Never fear, as Molly went by him, he took a swipe at her rear end with his bridle reins.

The next thing I knew, Molly stopped, planted her front feet, and let fly with both hind feet. I heard a loud crack as one newly shod hoof hit a shinbone and a dull thud as the other took Mr. Sheriff full in the stomach, knocking him from his horse. When he hit the ground he had an awful sick look on his face. I figured it would be a while before he got his breath back.

I kicked Charlie into a fast pace and rode on down the road, hoping the man would finally get some air into his lungs, and his leg wasn't too badly broken. I rode all night and all the next day before hunting for a campsite. I found one off of the road about a mile and hoped no one tried to find me. I bet if, or when, the man with the star gets to where he can walk again, he doesn't swat a mule on the rump when he's sitting right behind, and in the firing range. I gave Molly an extra sugar cube that night. I came to the conclusion he was one of those carpetbaggers I'd been told about. He must have been from up north where they don't work with mules, or he would have known enough to stay away from the dangerous end.

I stayed in the campsite a couple of days and rested the mules and myself before venturing out on the road again. The campsite was along a fair sized stream of water. I got out my fishing supplies and caught two catfish for supper the second day. They sure tasted good, but would have been better with some fried potatoes.

Some time, in the middle of the night, the rain came. In just a little while I realized what I forgot to put in my packs. I had no waterproof clothes. By the time the sun came up I was wet, cold, and a lot wiser. I needed to get something or some way to stay dry during the rain. I vowed, right then, not to ride around the next town I came to, but go in and buy a warm, waterproof coat. The rain lasted all day.

Toward evening I searched for a place to camp. I was very wet and cold. I turned off into a draw and found a lean-to someone had made out of branches and covered the roof with dirt. Not a house, but it was dry. I made a fire to dry out my clothes and get warm. It rained for three more days. I stayed there and kept partially dry.

When the weather cleared, I noticed the mornings were a little colder, and the days didn't seem really warm. I decided fall would soon be here, and winter was not too far away. I still wanted to get to the big river, but had no idea how far away the river was or what I would do when I found it. I knew I had to get there as soon as possible and plan for winter. John told me not to go on after I crossed the river because he heard the weather got really cold, with lots of wind and snow out west.

After riding for the better part of a month, I came to a beautiful area. The grass was green and the trees hadn't shed their leaves. I didn't find any camping places and the people were not very friendly. In the last three weeks I had been run off, told they didn't allow bums to camp on their land, and all of the excuses you could think of.

One man thought he could take advantage of me and said he would give me feed for the stock and a hot meal if I worked for him the next day. Since I needed a break in traveling, I thought that sounded okay. I slept in the hayloft and worked for him all day, hauling hay into the barn. He said we had done a good job.

The next morning, when I was packing to move on, he walked up and asked, "What are you doing?"

"I'm getting ready to move on down the road, but I want to thank you for the dry place to sleep and the food for the mules."

He watched me for a little bit and reached out and took the lead rope of Charlie's from where I had tied it to the ring on the side of the barn. In a very gruff voice he said, "You're not going anywhere until you pay up on the board and room for you and your mules."

"What do you mean? I worked for you and that was supposed to pay for everything."

He smiled, "Well that paid for the first night but what about last night?"

I did some thinking and figured things out. There was no way I could ever get paid up. He would always have me owing him money.

"Well, I guess you'll have to figure we're even. With the plan you have worked out I will never be paid up, right?"

He smiled, a mean looking smile, and nodded his head as he said, "That's the way I have it figured. So unload the mule and let's get to the hayfield."

No way was I going to work for him the rest of my life, or even the rest of the day. I continued to saddle Molly. I put the load on her while trying to think of a way I could leave. Then I remembered the pistol in the top of Molly's pannier. When I lifted the pannier up and strapped it in place, I put my hand down inside of the pack. Sure enough, the pistol was close to the top. I closed my hand on it easily. I pulled the gun out, walked around and took Charlie's lead rope from where he had tied it to the barn again.

He turned back. "What do you think you're doing? Tie the mule up and let's get to work."

I held the pistol up. He got a shocked look on his face. I told him I was leaving. He did a lot of sputtering and fuming but when I swung into the saddle and sat looking down at him, with the pistol pointed somewhere in his general direction, he backed up and let me ride away.

I traveled a couple of days. The weather was warm in the daytime, but at night it was plenty cool. I thought about what to do for the winter. I wanted to find some place to work for my room and board and make enough wages for feed for the mules.

CHAPTER 8

One afternoon, as I rode along the main road, a man working in his garden caught my eye by the way he dressed. I had never seen anyone dressed in animal skins. I started to pass.

He straightened up and smiled, "Hey Sonny, where are you headed with those nice mules? From the looks of you you've traveled a fair piece. Must be time for a rest?"

Now, I was leery because of what I got into a few days earlier. After all, this guy seemed a little strange. The big man, dressed in well-worn leather, appeared to be greasy and dirty. I don't think he had an ounce of fat on his body. His dark beard, streaked with grey, hung almost to his belt. He was completely bald on top. The little bit of hair growing around the sides of his head had a greasy, yellow color. He had some kind of shoes that must be soft and comfortable. When he put the hoe down and walked over to the fence to talk with me, I had the impression he walked so light on his feet he wouldn't leave any tracks. He had long legs with no sign of age in his stride

"Now, where would y'all be headed this time of year? Not over the river, I hope."

"That's what I had in mind, unless I can find some place to winter. You wouldn't know where I can find a job for the winter would you?"

"Well, get down, and let's put the mules away for tonight."

I worried some about going into the house because of the way he dressed. I thought the house might be full of, who knows what.

"Come on in. Let's get a bite to eat for supper. A kettle of stew has been cooking all day. Should be done by now."

The house was made of large logs, with a shingled roof covered with leaves and some grass growing on top. When I went inside, I couldn't believe my eyes. The house was very clean and tidy and the inside walls shone. The table had a checkered cloth covering. Two beds stood along the walls with bright colored covers on them. All kinds of things hung on the walls: bows, arrows, and funny shaped axes, I later learned were tomahawks. Bright bead work of all different shapes hung along with the other things. The wood floor shined from many scrubbings. A fireplace, at one end of the room was built of colored rocks. A big black rug lay about midway on the floor. When I asked about the rug he laughed. "The rug is a black bear I killed two years ago."

I was amazed, taking everything in. Something smelled awful good. After setting the table, he walked over to the fireplace and removed a large, black pot from a hook. When he set the pot on the table, I noticed he moved very fast, but didn't seem like he was hurrying.

He turned, put out his hand and said, "I guess we need to get acquainted. I'm sorry for not introducing myself. I'm called Bart, and you be......"

I shook his hand and was surprised at the strength, kind of like getting caught in John's vice. "I'm Ken, and I'm happy to meet you."

I wanted to say, "Now let's eat." I was so hungry I thought I could eat the whole pot of stew. I had eaten nothing but some dried meat and drank water for the last two days. Not too filling on a growing boy. I hadn't found a good place to build a fire and cook or to pasture the mules, so I started early and rode late.

We sat down and he filled a bowl and handed me the stew. He had potatoes, carrots, beans, turnips, cabbage, and some other things in the stew. I didn't stop to try and figure out what everything was.

When I was getting full Bart leaned forward and asked, "How do you like the muskrat stew? Sure makes for some mighty fine eating, don't you think?"

I didn't know for sure what a muskrat was, but I thought it did make fine stew. "Yeah, do you mind if I take a little more, please?"

"Well, you can eat all you want, but I baked a fresh pie this morning, if you would like some." Bart replied.

Now, I never turn down pie. I held out my plate and said, "I'll take the pie if you don't mind. Thank you."

I don't know why I slept so hard. Maybe because I felt safe for the first time since the raiders destroyed the farm and my life, months before. I completely relaxed. I didn't wake up at daylight, but slept until the sun shone high in the sky. I sat up with a start, jumped up into my clothes and headed out the door before I realized how late it was. I couldn't find Bart, so I went where the mules were grazing and got ready to saddle up to move on.

From the garden Bart asked, "What are you doing? Where are you going to take off to this morning? We need to talk a bit before you go and get yourself into more trouble than even you can handle."

I turned as he came from the other side of the garden. He was carrying a bird. He hung the big bird on the fence and walked over where I was standing by Charlie. "Did you sleep well?"

"Yes, sir, I did. I don't know why I slept so hard, but I need to move on if I'm ever going to get to the big river this fall."

"The big river, you say. Is that what you're trying to find?" Bart asked.

"Yes sir. I hope I can get a job someplace until spring, and then I'm headed on west."

"To where?" He asked. "Do you know what's across the river?"

"No, I only know I need to get across the river and out into a new country. Lots of opportunities are out west." I replied without much confidence.

"That's for sure, but, opportunities to do what, and go where? Do you realize how big the country is? Sometimes you can ride for a year and never meet another person. Are you prepared to live off the land completely, make all of your clothes, and go for months without talking to anyone other than those two mules?"

Now, I didn't realize I wouldn't find people or farms along the way. I guess I thought the county wouldn't be much different than where I had been.

"What are you telling me? Aren't there people and farms across the river? How can that be? People have been going west for years. Where are they?"

He laughed, "Yes'r. That sure is true. But you could move all of the people this side of the river out west and you wouldn't even cover half of the ground between the river and the great divide. The Stake Plains, as they call them, go on forever."

I walked over and tied Charlie to the nearest fence post. "So, what do I need to do to get ready to go on west? How far is it to the big river?"

"Well, the river is just over the hill to the west of us. Come on, we'll walk up the hill and you can see for yourself."

I turned Charlie loose and we walked for about an hour to get to the top of the hill. When we topped out and looked to the west, there was the biggest river I had ever seen. I could hardly believe the size. Some small boats were tied up along the other bank. They seemed like toys. The river must be a couple of miles across.

"I don't believe it! Where does all of the water come from?"

Bart gazed at the river and answered, "It's called the Mississippi River, and comes from about a thousand miles away. The headwaters are at a place where the snowmelt runs east to here. Water, on the other side of the divide, runs west to a great ocean."

"Have you been to the ocean?" I asked.

"Oh, yes. I've been across the divide and on to the Pacific Ocean, not once, but four times. The country is so vast you can't even explain the size to someone. Okay, now you've seen your big river. Will you let me get you ready to travel on across so you can travel to the ocean next spring?"

I was still shocked at the size of the river. Now I had one more thing to worry about. How in the world was I going to get across so much water? I knew the mules and I were not going to swim that far.

While we walked back to the farm he explained the things I needed. The first thing we had to do was kill two buck deer and tan the hides. He would make a couple pair of pants, shirts, and moccasins, a warm coat, and a cap to keep me from "freezing my ears off," as he put it. We needed to dry the meat.

The next morning, when I got up, Bart was still in bed. As I walked out of the cabin, he rolled over and complained about the cold weather. I did the chores, and he fixed breakfast. We sat at the table, eating our meal.

"I think the first thing we need to do is get a bunch of dry wood. A good place to start is the big dead tree in the field."

I walked to the door and looked at the tall, dead tree out in the pasture. I thought we would work all of the next three months to cut that thing down. The trunk is at least ten feet around. Some of the limbs are as big as a good-sized tree. I said to myself, "Another impossible job. We are going to cut the tree down with an axe? Not in a million years."

I turned and shook my head. "How in the world can we cut that old tree down? We'll work all winter to get it off of the stump."

He chuckled and said, "You might be right. That's why I haven't tried before. I needed someone to help on the other end of the crosscut saw. Have you ever pulled a saw?"

"No. I have never cut down a tree with an axe or saw. I guess there's always a first time for everything. Besides, we do have all winter, don't we? By the way, I've lost all track of time. What month is this, anyway?"

He walked over to a cupboard and took out a calendar. He said, "I think it's about the middle of October. We haven't had a freeze yet. We never go past Thanksgiving time without a freeze that kills the garden."

In the afternoon he went to one of the outside sheds. He took out the longest saw I have ever seen. He laid it on the outside table and got a file from the house. We sat down. I held the saw in an upright position while he filed the teeth until they were sharp. As he sharpened the saw, he explained to me that you had to have the cutters sharp and sloped just the right way, so the saw left a grove wide enough for the base of the teeth to slide easily through the wood. Also, the long teeth in the middle were straight. They cleaned the grove and dragged the shavings out as you pulled the saw back and forth. He worked most of the afternoon to get the saw sharpened to suit him.

"Okay, we're ready to start in the morning. Now, let's go in and see if the turkey is done."

Then I remembered the big bird he killed this morning. I forgot about it while we worked around the place. He cooked the turkey in the open fireplace. The bird was all brown and juicy, with a thick crust, and sure was good. We cut pieces off and ate them with some salt. I ate until I was way too full.

Bart leaned back and asked, "Do you want some of the pie we had last night? We still have half."

I was so full of turkey I couldn't eat any more. I wanted to roll over on the bed and sleep. "No, I think I'll wait awhile."

He smiled and went over to his bed and lay down with a sigh. "I'm not as young as I used to be. It seems like I get tired awful easy. I guess the trip up the hill was a bit too much. The walk felt good, though. I haven't walked that far for a while. Maybe I'm just too old." In about three minutes he was asleep.

I walked around outside for a while and talked to the mules. Then I went in, got undressed, and went to bed. I didn't sleep very well. A million things went through my mind. I thought about what Bart had said. Sometime in the early morning I woke with a start. I could hear Bart outside, coughing and coughing. After a while he came in. He was as white as a sheet, with a trickle of blood on his chin.

"What's the matter?" I asked.

He shook his head and said, "Oh, it's nothing, really. The last two or three months, every once in a while I start to cough and can't seem to stop. The last couple of times I've coughed up a small amount of blood. I don't think there's anything to worry about."

I lay in bed awhile longer, then got up and dressed. Bart had gone outside. I could hear him chopping wood. The day was wet and rainy, so we decided to wait for another day before starting on the tree. Along about mid-morning Bart turned to me and asked, "How good of a shot are you with your squirrel gun?"

"Oh, I miss the squirrel's head once in a while if he's running along a branch, but not too often," I answered.

He looked at me like I was joking. I thought he was not happy that I would miss. Finally he smiled and said, "Think you're pretty good, don't you? If you're so good, why don't you go over by the hill? When you get there you'll find a trail where the deer travel to a salt lick to your left. Now, if you'll climb up in the big gum tree, and sit a while, one is sure to come by. We need a big buck to start with. Do you have a knife to clean it? You do know how to clean one, don't you?"

"Yes. I've shot a lot of pigs and cleaned them." I answered.

"Let me see your knife."

I went to my pack and got out the butcher knife to show him. He said, "Well, that's some knife all right. But, let me get you a good hunting knife."

He went to the cupboard and got a knife in a leather scabbard from the top self. He handed it to me and said, "Try to keep from cutting your hand off with this. It's really sharp. I'll be waiting to hear you shoot. I'll come help drag the buck home."

I got everything ready. He told me again where to go, as if I couldn't remember his first instructions. I went out into the rain and walked to the bottom of the hill. I searched for a trail, but couldn't find one. I climbed up the hill a ways and still no trail. I backtracked and finally found a very faint sign of a trail, winding through the timber. Then I hunted for a big gum tree. There was a sound off to my right, so I very carefully backed up against a nearby tree.

A doe deer came wondering along the trail. She was feeding on mushrooms growing up through the leaves. I didn't want to spook her, so I stood really still, hoping she didn't see me or smell my scent. I guess the rain was keeping her from getting my scent, because she walked within a hundred feet of me and continued on down the trail.

I needed to find the big gum tree to hide in so I wouldn't be caught in the open again. I caught a movement to my right. There was my buck. He caught me on the ground with very little cover. I didn't want to move, so I froze. I eared the hammer back on the rifle. The buck stood still. It seemed like forever before he took a step forward and put his head behind a small tree. I used the time to change my position and raise the rifle. I took a lean against a small tree, to help support the rifle, so when he stepped out from behind his tree, I had a good shot.

Again he stood, and the rifle was getting heavier by the minute. Then he whirled, and in one leap, disappeared into the brush. I was so surprised I just stood watching. I had never hunted deer before. The pigs I shot always walked out in the open and gave me a good shot. Not that deer. He was gone in a flash.

I looked around a little more and found a big tree to climb. I got up in the tree and sat down to wait. I waited and waited and nothing came along. When the sun reached about noon position I gave up, climbed down, and started home. Whoa! What was that? I whirled around. There stood the buck. Before I could raise the rifle, he was gone. I walked on toward the house. When I got there, Bart stepped out and said, "I didn't hear any shots."

I proceed to tell him about my morning. He laughed, then said, "Welcome to the club. That old buck has made fools out of half the hunters on the river; so don't feel like you're a failure. I'll tell you what; you keep hunting him for the next month or so. When you get smart enough to bag him, you'll be ready to start into Indian country."

CHAPTER 9

The next morning Bart went to the toolshed and came back with an axe with two sharp heads.

"I've never seen that kind of an axe. Why the two heads? How are you going to drive wedges?"

He explained, "This is called a double-bitted axe. I got this the last time I was on the west coast. They use them as falling axes. The blades are a lot thinner so when you cut the undercut in the tree, the axe will take a deeper bite into the wood and make a bigger chip and you can cut faster. Cutting is easier with a thin sharp blade."

Then he went to the grinding wheel. He sat down astraddle the framework, pumped on the pedals and made the wheel turn. He laid the blade of the axe against the wheel and pointed to a can on the ground at his side. "Pour some of the water on, will you?"

I picked up the can and began to pour the water out.

He said, "Slower. Just a thin line so the stone can hone the blade."

He did the same to the other side of the blade. When he thought the blades were sharp enough, he rolled up his sleeve, spit on his arm, and shaved the hair with a downward stroke. The blade shaved like a razor and left a clean area. "I think its sharp enough for now, so let's get to work on the big tree."

I had no idea what he was talking about. I had never seen a tree chopped down. I think he knew I didn't understand anything he told me.

"You'll understand when we get started. Come on. Let's try to get the tree down this morning."

Now, that big, round tree had been dead for a long time and was hard. Bart took one end of the saw and told me to take the other. He showed me what he wanted me to do, so we got a little cut on the base of the tree. He took the axe and chopped the bark away above the cut we made. We went to work again. I was supposed to pull the saw toward me every time he pulled it away. Sounds easy, but when I pulled the saw my way. I didn't get much for shavings, and when he pulled, I tried to help by pushing down on the handle.

He soon said, "Stop. You're working too hard. We'll get too tired too soon. You just let the saw do the work. When I pull my way you let it ride on the bottom of the cut. When you pull your way, pull down on the handle and I'll let it ride on the wood."

In about an hour we were working together. We got a rhythm and our work went a whole lot easier. After the third or fourth rest stop, Bart looked at me and nodded his head. "I think we're starting to get it a little. At this rate we will only take a week to put this tree down. Now it's your turn to chop on the face."

I paid attention while he chopped on the face of the cut. I picked up the axe and swung at the face of the tree. Man, I hit the trunk of the tree with all of the force I could muster. The blade sunk in about a sixteenth of an inch. I took another swing and hit a long ways away from my first cut. I looked at Bart and he was smiling.

"Oh, lordy. At this rate we will surely be working on falling this thing yet next year. Here, let me show you how to swing an axe. There is a system and you better learn how now, because if you are going to build a house or even a lean-to to keep warm in, you must know how to use an axe."

He worked with the axe a while longer. He kept getting paler all of the time. Finally he said, "You work for a while. I need to sit down and catch my breath."

He was puffing and sweating hard. He walked over to the bench in front of the house and sat down. I noticed how old he seemed. He sat while I whaled away at the tree. When I started to get tired, he walked back where I was chopping and not getting anywhere.

He took the axe and said, "You're tired enough now to stop and listen to what I have to say. Take the axe this way." He showed me how to hold it. "Now, don't try to sink the axe to the hilt, but try and place your cuts in each other and every third cut you come up from the bottom." He handed me the axe and walked off towards the house. "I'm going to rest and get some lunch for us."

I worked like he showed me. After about an hour I began to understand what he had been trying to teach me. I went to the house when he shouted and waved. We ate and I rested. I went back to the tree and finished cutting the wedge out of the face, then went to get him to come help me.

I found him asleep, so I was as quiet as could be. I got the rifle and powder horn and went after the buck again, determined today would be the day. I came back to the house about dark, still empty handed. I had been made a fool of again.

We worked on the tree for a couple more days. The fourth afternoon the top started to tip. The back cut began to open up. Down the tree came with a loud crash, and broke about half-way up. Limbs flew all over the place. I walked around it wondering what in the world we would do with all of the wood. Some of the limbs were a foot thick and twenty feet long.

Down the length of the tree stood a mama raccoon and her four half-grown kits. She acted like, "What happened?" I suppose she had lived in the hollow of the tree for many years. Bart had no idea she was there. I walked towards her and she reared up on her hind legs and gave out a snarl. The hair down the length of her back stood up. She turned and casually walked to the top and jumped off of the tree. She continued on across the pasture. About every twenty feet she turned around and bared her teeth before moving on. When she got to the timber she turned for the last time and, rearing up on her hind legs, gave us a mean look before going into the trees.

After the tree hit the ground, Bart brought out a small saw that one person could use. He called it a buck saw, and told me we could cut the limbs into lengths a lot easier than with the ax.

About a month later we had the tree all cut into stove wood. Bart thought we had enough wood to last for many years. The wood was dry and hard and burned really hot. I had learned how to chop with the axe and saw with a saw. My hands had grown calluses and my arms and shoulders were filled out. By the time the tree was all cut, split, racked, and ready for the stove, my muscles had hardened up. I no longer had kid-size arms. My hands had thickened. I was becoming a man.

But, the old buck still walked through the trees. However, I had killed a smaller buck and two does. We dried the meat. Bart started the hides to cure and I learned to scrape them as they cured. I worked to get all the meat, fat, and inner layer of membrane off. Bart showed me how to stretch the hides over a log to scrape them, and how to work them to start the softening process.

While the hides were still fresh, he put wood ash and water in a large tub and soaked the hides until the hair slipped off easily. Then he made a mixture of brains and some saltpeter and rubbed that into the hides to cure them. They became stiff and hard. He had me work them on the log until they were soft and pliable.

The first of the year came and the buck was still around. I spotted him a few times. One day I got up early, way before daylight. I stepped out of the door and Mr. Buck was grazing by the light of the moon, right in the front yard. I quietly stepped back in the house, picked up the rifle, and went outside. He was still eating. I got all excited. I took a lean on the end of the cabin logs and put the sights on him. The thought went through my head, "Ah! I've got you now." I sighted very carefully and eared the hammer back on the gun, and sighted in on him. As I watched I thought, "Not him, he has won the battle. Go get a couple more young bucks for your clothes and let him be." I lowered the rifle and stood it against the cabin. I watched as he fed over to the timber and then with a switch of his tail, glanced over his shoulder and walked into the trees. I leaned against the cabin and looked at the stars. I had a good feeling about what I had done.

After Bart got up, he said, "I saw you go out this morning. Was something wrong? I noticed you got the rifle."

I shook my head no. He began to cough again. I worried because the coughing spells were more often and harder. Sometimes he coughed up a bunch of blood. He was coughing hard almost every morning, and sometimes in the afternoon. He wasn't eating as much as he had been when I came three months ago.

One morning I asked him if we had enough hides for a set of buckskins. He nodded his head, yes, and went over to my bunk. He pulled the hides out from under the bed and told me to lay them out on the table. He measured me with a piece of string. He drew a pattern on the hides and handed me a knife and said, "Cut on the outside of the lines. Get the cuts as smooth as you can."

I worked slow and careful. When I finished, he took the pieces and held them up to me. He made a few small cuts, to make them fit better, he explained. He had me cut a lot of the scrap pieces into strings to hold the big pieces together. Before he sewed the pieces, he rolled the edges and sewed them with a big needle and thread he had made out of sinews. I don't know when he made the sinew thread, but he had a lot.

"Why don't you go get us a squirrel for supper while I work on these skins? Maybe you'll spot the buck again."

I went to get the rifle and, I don't know why, but I felt like I should tell him about the buck being out in the pasture and me letting him go. "I don't think I'll bother the buck any more. We've made a truce. He will live to have more kin and I'll admire his cunning from a distance."

Bart stopped working on the skins and smiled. "Yeah, I know. I saw you the other morning, when you got up early and had him in your sights. I was afraid you were going to pull the trigger. I am very proud of you for letting him walk off. You're nearly ready to go west now. A few more lessons on cooking and you won't starve, so now go get a squirrel."

I grew another foot that morning and walked with a lot more confidence. I had passed a test. I came back with the squirrel and Bart was still working on the clothes. He had the pants, or leggings, as he called them, done. As the day wore on he finished the shirt. I tried them on and they were a bit big. I commented on this and he said, "Oh, you'll grow a bunch from now until the time these are worn out, so you need them a little big."

The weeks flew by. Bart taught me how to take care of the cast iron skillets by always wiping them with a greasy rag; I would carry along for that purpose, before putting them in the panniers. He told me to put beans to soak at night in a jar with a tight snap ring. I learned how to cook in a Dutch oven, and how to carry sourdough starter so it would be ready to make pancakes or biscuits.

He had a tin pail with a lid that clipped down tight. When he made pancakes or biscuits for breakfast, he put his starter in the pail along with a healthy amount of flour so it was stiff enough not to leak out. When he made camp for the night, he mixed the water into the pail and made his starter for the next morning. If he planned to stay in camp for a few days, he made biscuits and baked them on a reflector oven, either in the sun or by the coals from a small fire. If Indians were around and he didn't want to start a fire, he used the reflector oven, setting with the opening toward the sun. The oven made no smoke and he didn't worry about anyone finding him.

The mornings had been foggy and cool for most of the winter. The last two mornings a thin coating of ice formed on the water trough. Bart stood in the cabin door while I fed the mules. When I came in from doing chores he went to the table and sat down.

He said, "We've had our last frost. The air will begin to warm up in a couple of weeks. Are you about ready to leave?"

I stood there wondering, am I ready? Do I want to leave here? I've grown to love his old man like a father. I have been here about six months and he's taught me so much. He is getting thinner and thinner.

His color is almost yellow. His coughing is harder and more often. He has a coughing spell at least four to five times a day, and every time he raises a bunch of blood. Will I ride off and leave him here to try and feed his mule and the chickens by himself? He had a hard time walking to the outside privy, let alone to the shed to feed the stock. He couldn't pack water to the mule or chickens.

I answered, with a shrug of my shoulders, "Oh, not for a few more days. I'll wait until the grass is green on the prairie so there's plenty for the mules to eat."

He was very quiet the rest of the day and went to bed early. The next morning, after we had eaten breakfast, he said, "Would you go saddle Jenny for me and you're Charlie? I want to take you to town and show you where to get on the boat to cross the river, so when you decide to go you'll know the way."

I went out and saddled the two mules. I tied Molly up so she couldn't follow us.

When we reached town he said, "I'm going to the bank for a few minutes. Stay with the mules and I'll hurry back."

He was gone for a short while. He came back and said, "Now, we need to go over to the barbershop."

The barbershop? I thought he hadn't had a haircut for a long time, maybe for years. He still didn't need one since he had no hair on his head except a few strands right at the back. The barber could trim his beard that nearly reached his belt. That really needed done.

"Come on. You need a haircut as bad as I do. When you go out on the plains it will be a long time before you can get one."

I hadn't even stopped to think about my hair. I suppose it had grown a little long. I hadn't done anything other than wash it for the better part of a year. We went into the barbershop and the barber glanced at us.

He said to Bart, with a very serious look on his face, "It's by the pound this time, Mr. Brown. You got me the last time you came back from out there. It took me a week to catch all of the critters that dropped out of your beard."

Bart acted like he couldn't believe what the barber said, and answered, "You must be slowing down considerable as you get older, Alf. You used to get the job done in a couple of days. I guess the boy better go first so he doesn't pack anything out with him."

They both laughed and shook hands and said how glad they were to see each other.

The barber asked me, "How much do you want off?"

I sat in the chair and said, "You better take it pretty short. I might not have another haircut for a long time."

While Alf cut my hair, Bart said to him, "I have a favor to ask of you."

"Sure, anytime. You know that." Alf replied.

Bart took a paper out of his shirt pocket and handed it to Alf. He said, "I had this dawn up a few minutes ago. I wonder if you will act as a witness to what is on the paper, and sign your name."

Alf read the paper and looked at Bart. He said, "You're sure about this?"

Bart nodded his head and said, "Yes, it's time."

Alf walked over to the counter, signed the paper, and handed it back to Bart. He shook his head and said, "Give this to the boy to read."

I took the paper and read it through, not understanding what was going on. The second time I read, I understood what he had done.

"Ken," he said, "fill your name in on the line with the X in front."

The paper said, "I Bartholomew Brown, do hereby leave all of my possession to," and I wrote Kenneth Clausen in the blank space.

"Now, I guess everything is legal. I'll take this back to the bank. Thank you, Alf. You just go ahead and finish the boy up right fancy while I go take care of this. Then you can do some fancy cutting on this darn beard. It's getting so heavy I can hardly chew. I should have come in when I got back last fall, but one thing or another kept getting in the way."

While Bart was gone, I asked Alf how long he had known him. He smiled and said, "At least forty years and maybe more. I made a couple of trips across with him when we were young. We both got married and settled down on a few acres. The second year after they were married, Bart's wife died during childbirth. He left soon after and came home about every two or three years. I think it's been five years this time. You've been living with him this winter?"

"Yeah, I been there since October, I guess."

He stopped cutting and asked, "How is his health?"

I wondered what to say and told him about the coughing and the blood this last couple of months.

"That's no big surprise, I guess. He was shot though one lung about ten years ago and barely made it home. We patched him up so he could travel again. We tried to get him to stay for a while, but in six months he left."

Bart stepped through the door and said, "If you didn't talk so much you'd have the kid done by now."

"Okay! Okay. I'm about through, unless he wants a shave." Alf said as he stepped back and looked. "Nope there's not enough to waste the soap on. You're done." He removed the cloth from around my neck.

I asked, "How much for the cut?"

He waved me off and shook his head no as he answered, "Nothing, the first one is free."

Bart stepped to the chair and sat down. He merely said, "All five year's worth since it will probably be my last one."

I was surprised. I thought he had the beard all of his life.

CHAPTER 10

I walked out to the mules and watched the people walking by. A man rode up and said, "A fine looking mule you got, boy. Who does he belong to?"

I answered, "Me, why do you want to know?"

He was sitting on a big, three colored stallion. The man's scared face was disfigured on one side and his ear was missing. The scars made him look like he had a lopsided grin. His eyes were cold and generated nothing but hate. He had no other expression on his face.

"What do you want for the mule? I need some mules and will pay you a good price," he said.

I shook my head and answered. "Charlie isn't for sale at any price."

He turned his horse and started to ride off, and said, "We'll see about that, Sonny."

I was sure I would meet Mr. Scarface again. Bart came from the barbershop, looked down the street, and asked, "What did that fellow want?"

"He wanted to buy Charlie. I told him Charlie was not for sale. When he rode off he said, we'll see about that, Sonny. That man scares me. He has the deadest eyes I ever saw. They're black, and filled with hate."

Bart said, "Don't worry. He's some drifter who wants to scare you into selling him the mule."

We mounted up and left for home. As we rode down the street, I showed Bart the three-colored horse standing at a hitch rail. He nodded his head and said, "Let's stop at the store and get a few things."

We no more than tied up when a man walked up to Bart and said, "A man in my office claims the mule the boy is riding was stolen from him over in Kentucky, Mr. Brown."

"Well, now Joe, you know I've never been over in Kentucky in my life. That man tried to buy the mule from the boy just a few minutes ago. Now, if he was stolen from him, why would he try to buy him back?"

Joe had a star pinned to his shirt. He turned to me and asked, "What's your name?"

I studied him for a spell and then said, "Kenneth Clausen, and I did come across a small part of Kentucky, I guess, on the way out here, but I didn't steal Charlie from anyone. I raised him from a three-day old colt."

"Do you have a bill-of-sale?"

"No, I said I raised him from a colt. He was given to me by a horse raiser who didn't want a mule colt out of one of his racing mares."

Bart said, "You know, Joe, the guy's a drifter trying to cause trouble for anyone he can, to get anything he wants. Does he talk with a southern or northern accent?"

"Come to think of it, he sure doesn't talk like a southern horse raiser to me," answered Joe."

"I will vouch for the boy. You tell the would-be bad-boy to go back where he belongs." Bart said with force.

Joe turned and, over his shoulder, said quietly, "You watch out for him, Bart. He's dangerous. You're not as young as you used to be. You aren't even carrying a gun these days. So be careful, will you?"

I had not paid any attention to Bart when he came from the barbershop, but as I turned to mount Charlie, I got a good look at the man I'd been living with for six months. He didn't look like the some old man, but more like a very strong man of maybe sixty. His face was tanned a deep brown, except where the beard had covered it up. His jaw was square and he had an air about him that said, "Don't mess with me." I was surprised. He really was a handsome man. He stepped up on his mule like a younger person. Wow, what a shave had done for him.

We started out of town. We hadn't gone far when he began to cough and nearly fell from the mule. She stopped and waited for him to quit coughing. When he was sitting straight, Jenny went on as if he had spoken to her. She walked like she was walking on air, so as not to cause Bart any discomfort.

When we got home, I told Bart to go in and lay down for a while. I would take care of the mules and come in and cook supper. He didn't disagree with me. I could tell that the coughing had drained him completely. The only one upset about our trip to town was Molly. She let her displeasure be known. When I led her to water, she tried to bite me. Then she walked so close, I had to jump aside to keep her from stepping on my heels. She was not happy about getting tied up and left.

The next day Bart asked me if I had any idea where I was going when I crossed the river.

"Not really," I answered. "Just west, I guess, searching for work or something to do."

He frowned and said, "If you don't make a plan of some sort you'll wander the west, like so many others, and end up with nothing. The west is a land of opportunities, but you must be smart enough to do something for yourself. A lot of opportunities will come your way if you're clever enough to take advantage of them. Now, I don't mean a guy must steal, take advantage of people, and be deceitful; but be honest, work hard, and win the respect of the people you deal with. Do you know which direction you want to go after you get across the river?"

"No, I don't. I would like to have a farm or some land of my own, but I don't want to be a sharecropper, like so many of the farmers back home." I explained.

He nodded, "You won't find sharecroppers in the west. The men are too independent. The men all want the same things you do. They're willing to fight and work hard to get it. However, some men will do anything to get what other men have. They also will fight, steal, or murder to get what you've got, because they think they're entitled to everything free."

I said, "Some men are like that on this side of the river, too. That's what happened to my mom and sister. They were murdered for maybe fifty dollar's worth of things."

"You said you would like to get land, so you will want to go way on beyond where most of the settlers are going. Do you want land to farm or to raise cattle?"

After thinking for a while I said, "I'd like land to raise cows and horses."

"Okay. I'll tell you about a place that would make an ideal cattle ranch, if no one has filed a claim. If worked right, you would make a ranch to run thousands of cattle, with the best graze in the west. When you leave here, take the boat across the river. On the other side you'll find a road running north and south along the river bank. Take the road north and go about a two-day ride. When you come to the first big canyon coming from the left, turn in and follow the canyon until you reach a large plateau. This will take at least two or three weeks to ride to the top. You will find water and game in the canyon. Other travelers also use the trail, so travel carefully. Look behind you often. Ride up on one side of the canyon or the other so you can check your back trail. Always travel a good distance up on the side of the hill before returning to the bottom. I've used this trail many times and it's the least used of most of the trails west. Always camp so you will be hard to find, and always stop before dark, cook your supper, then leave a clean camp. Do you know what I mean by a clean camp?"

"Yeah, I leave no sign. I cover my fire so nothing shows and leave nothing that is not natural, like papers, flour, or anything out of place."

He nodded and said, "You can't completely hide a camp from an experienced tracker, but you can make it hard for him to find. Now, as you get to the top of the canyon, you will come out onto a large plateau. This runs for a few hundred miles, west by southwest. Stay on the left side until you reach the wagon trail coming from the southeast. As you travel the rim, many small draws drop off to the left. Always drop down into one of those before you camp at night. I've marked the ones I use with two stones along the trail on the right, about five feet apart, then one on the left side of the trail. If you turn at the last stone, you'll find a small game trail leading to the top of the draw. You will find water in most of these, and where you find water, game will not be far away. Sometimes you need to go into the draw a ways to find a small campsite with enough grass for a couple of horses for a day or two. Never stop on top of the draw. Always stop just out of sight and walk back and watch your back trail for at least ten or fifteen minutes before you go in and bed down."

"Why watch so long? If the country is open, won't I be able to see someone following me before I turned off?" I asked.

"No. Sometimes the person following you might be three or four miles behind. And again, go down a ways and stop, cook, eat, and move on away from camp to bed down."

"Anyway, when you come to the wagon trail, from the south, follow the trail until you climb a long, gentle slope. As you climb, the grass will turn slowly to sagebrush and the ground will become rockier. Sagebrush is a small, gray bush about three feet tall and gives off a sharp odor. The climb will be about a hundred miles or so before you reach the top. That is the continental divide. A small creek begins not far down on the other side. You'll know you're in the right place if you look west and, way off in the distance are two tall mountains that appear to be about three feet apart. They tower above anything around them. They are the pass into California."

"That's where you leave the trail and stay on the right side of the creek. The creek gets bigger quite fast, and really marshy, so stay up on the hillside away from the water. You'll find a meadow and a campsite close to the top of the divide. The timber will be along your side and gets thick in some places. I mean real thick. The trees are called lodge pole pine. They are straight and tall and mostly not more than three or four feet apart. Sometimes you have a hard time finding your way through them. Now, work your way away from the creek about a mile. Go down until you come out on a huge rolling plain. The land is too rolling to farm, but would be the most wonderful cattle graze in the west. The open country runs for at least a hundred miles west and maybe as far north. In the center of this is a great, deep valley. It's the shape of a large bowl. A river runs to meet the one you were following, coming from this bowl-like area. Go down onto the floor of the bowl. If you follow this river to the north, and stay along the east side of the bowl, you'll find a canyon coming from the east. A creek runs from it and the water is warm. Follow the creek back into the canyon about two miles or so and you will find a large cave."

"The cave stays dry and doesn't take much work to keep it warm. I spent one winter in it. The water comes from under the wall about fifty feet to one side of the cave. You can take a hot bath any time. The nice part of this is a larger spring, about a hundred feet on the other side of the cave, is cold, clear and sweet. Water from the two springs work their way down the meadow and swing father apart. They enter the creek about a half-mile apart. Plan to take about two months of steady riding to get to the cave after you leave the Mississippi River."

I lay awake for a long time and listened to the outside noises. I suddenly sat up. It had become silent outside. No noise. Why not? I heard the snuffing of Charlie. I jumped up and went to the door. Sure enough, someone was trying to get a rope on Charlie. I saw another figure, off to the side, by the gate. I eased the rifle out of the door and yelled. "Get away from my mules!"

The man, who was after Charlie, turned and fired at the house with his pistol. I heard the bullet hit the wall. I shot at him without even thinking. He let out a yell and went limping out the gate. He mounted his horse and said something to his companion. Then they rode my way and fired their pistols as fast as they could. I was surprised. I had never seen a pistol with more than a single shot. They turned to leave.

This time, when I shot, one of the men slumped over the saddle horn and started to cuss. They both took down the road at a gallop.

By now Bart was up and had a pistol in his hand. He jerked the door open and went running outside, but they were gone. All you could hear was their horses galloping down the road. He asked, "Are you okay?"

I smiled, "Yeah, I'm alright, but those guys aren't. I think I hit both of them."

Bart went back in the house and asked, "How did you know they were out there? I never heard a thing."

"Neither did I. All noise stopped. I guess that's what woke me up. Charlie has this puffing sound he makes when he doesn't like something or if he thinks things are not right."

We went back to bed. Well, anyway, Bart lay down and started to cough. I could tell this was going to be a bad one. He coughed for about five minutes. He got a lot of blood up, and was completely spent. He lay still, white as a sheet. He finally went to sleep and was restless until morning. I got up, did the chores, and the fire going when he spoke.

"You know, I'm not doing very well. I thought I would come home and get well, but that's not going to happen. I want you to listen. I put my place and all of my things in your name. Will you be sure I'm buried beside my wife and baby? The graves are unmarked, but I'll show you where, as soon as I get a little strength this morning."

"I don't think we need to hurry about that. Here are some eggs and toast," I replied.

He sat up and said, "Yes, there is a need to hurry. I'm not doing very well. I was shot in the lungs a few years ago. The Doc told me scar tissue would build because he couldn't get the bullet out. He said one day I would cough and start to bleed and then it would just be a matter of time. I think the time is near, because I'm bleeding inside more all of the time, and it's going to get worse. Soon I will drown in my own blood, like the Doc said."

After breakfast we walked out to a spot under a big tree. He pointed to two small indents in the ground. He said, "I want to be laid beside them. Forty-six years ago I put them there. I have missed them terribly all of those years. I wonder how the little one looks and, oh, how I've missed my wife. I never drank or caroused around because I promised her I wouldn't. She was very religious and did not believe a person should drink or use tobacco in any form. To this day I've lived up to the promise I made. Now, I feel really weak. I'm going to go lie down and rest. Hope you didn't hurt those fellows too bad this morning, but remember what the sheriff said about the man with the scarred face. Say, how many were there? They fired a lot of shots in a hurry."

I walked over to the front of the house to count the places where the bullets hit. I counted ten holes. I wondered what type of a gun would shoot so fast. I went inside and told Bart the number of shots fired.

He shook his head and said, "I guess they must have one of the new six-guns. The Henry repeating rifle has been around for a while. I've seen a few of them, but that didn't sound like a rifle. The sound, was different, a sharper crack like a pistol. A rifle sounds like more of a boom. Kind of a dull, deep sound, but this was sharp and loud. Real loud in here when they hit the old, dry logs. I think it was loud enough to wake up the dead."

He closed his eyes. I went outside to let him rest. I made myself busy for an hour or so. Then I went back into the cabin. Bart was lying in his bunk looking out of the door.

I asked, "Feeling better yet?"

He nodded his head and, with tears in his eyes, answered, "Not much, I think my time is really short now, so listen to me. I've learned to love you as my own son. I wish I could go west with you, but remember what I've tried to teach you. You're a smart young man, so be careful and listen to others and learn as you go. Now listen to me on this one thing, you will meet the man with the scars again, and when you do, be ready to shoot or fight. He's a mean man with a lot of hate. He'll use every mean trick he has learned to take the mules away from you, if for no other reason than plain spite. Better leave the old pistol you brought, and take mine. It's not the best, but it's better than yours. Better yet, go to the store and buy a newer six-shot one before you leave."

"I'll think about that, but they probably cost a lot of money and I don't have much."

"Just go to the bank and get what you need. There's money in an account of mine. I told the banker he was to change the account to your name after I'm gone."

"I'll get what's needed when the time comes, okay?"

I worked around the place for the rest of the afternoon. I had a sense of pride, thinking I was working on my own land. I didn't know if I wanted to leave here. I was truly torn between the feelings I had of ownership of this land and the urgent need to keep going across the river. I had driven myself across a couple thousand miles to get to this point in my life. I was drawn by the need to keep going on, but why? What was out there pulling me?

I was now fifteen. I had chopped wood, hoed gardens, pitched hay, worked in a blacksmith shop, been ran off by a shotgun, and called a bum. I had been made fun of by other kids, who, with the backup of a couple companions, had dared me to fight. I had helped housewives, who needed dishes washed. I fended off sheriffs who wanted to take advantage of this boy. Why would I want to go on and make myself subject to more abuse when I had a home here? What did Bart find out there? I didn't know, but when he talked about the vast open spaces, the look on his face that was indescribable. A kind of fire would light up his eyes and he stood a little straighter. When he walked, he was a little more alert.

CHAPTER 11

Bart died in the night. I heard him up, coughing really hard. When he didn't come back in, I went out to find him. I found him by his family's graves, sitting with his back against the tree. He had a peaceful expression on his face.

Even though it was still dark, I went to the toolshed and got a shovel and an axe and began to dig a grave. I worked most of the day to get the job done. I cut through a lot of tree roots, as well as moving many rocks. When I finished digging, I went into the house and took his blanket from the bed to roll him in. Then I put him in the grave.

I sat by the grave for a long time and thanked him for all the things he had done for a homeless youngster. I told him all of the things I had been thinking about the last while and asked him to help me make up my mind. I thought I should say some words over the grave, but I had no idea what to say. I turned my face to the sky and said, "He was a good man, Lord, please help him and me. Thank you."

I filled up the grave. Only then did the mules let me know I had not given them anything to eat or water for the day. I turned the chickens out and took some water to the mules. They were really thirsty and showed they were not happy with me. The chickens ran around clucking and scratching.

I had a hard time the rest of the week. I missed Bart, a lot. I decided to go to town and tell his friend Alf about Bart's passing. I saddled Charlie, went in the house and got the paper Bart had given me. It deeded everything to me and he had left an account in the bank. I wondered how much money was in the account.

When I got to town, I went to the barbershop first. Alf had a costumer, so I stayed out on the street and watched the things going on. I was surprised to see so many wagons. Some were big wagons with a smaller one hooked behind. These had five teams hooked to them. Some were smaller with three teams and some with only two teams. They all seemed to be waiting for something. The drivers stood beside their wagons. Many of them visited in small groups.

I turned to see if the customer in the barbershop was through. He came out of the door clean shaven and hair cut. He asked me, "Are you next?"

I shook my head, no. When he walked by I asked, "What are all of the wagons about? Is there a celebration of some kind happening today?"

He laughed and said, "In a way, yes. This wagon train is forming, heading for California. Have you been to California?"

"No, but I'm going to head out that way as soon as I can. Maybe we'll meet each other on the trail." I answered. I walked into the barbershop.

Alf turned to me and said, "I thought I just did you the other day."

"Yeah, you did, but I needed to come in and tell you, Bart died a couple of days ago. I buried him next to his wife and baby like he wanted. So if you go out that way you might stop and pay your respects."

Alf lowered his head and was real quiet for a little bit, then he looked up with tears in his eyes. "He was a good friend, a good man and also my brother. We were very close."

"I didn't know, or I would have come and got you to be with me when I put him in the ground. I'm sorry. If that's the case, I need to give you the deed for the land and anything else you want."

"No, I have all I need. We raised each other. Our folks died when we were about twelve and fourteen. I have a lifetime full of memories and the love of a good brother He wanted to leave everything to you, so it's yours. I have my own land and a good family."

I visited a few minutes and then walked across the street to the bank. I had never been in a bank before, so when I walked through the door I stopped and stared. The building was big and beautiful. All of the wood was polished and the floor was so clean it shone so you could see yourself. One of the men, behind a counter of some type, asked if he could help me.

I didn't know what to say, so I asked, "Can I talk to the banker?"

He turned to a man sitting behind a desk and said, with a big smile, "There is a boy, I mean a man, here who would like to talk to the banker."

A big, tall man stood up and walked toward me. He told me to come on in. When I walked in behind the counter, he put out his hand an asked, "Do I know you? I'm Mr. Sullivan, the president of the bank. What I can do for you?"

"I'm Kenneth Clausen."

"Oh, yes. You're the young man I helped draw the papers for last week. How is Bart doing?"

I looked at the floor and said quietly, "He passed away the other day. I thought I should come and tell you. I buried him out at his place beside his wife and baby, like he asked me to. I stopped over at the barbershop and told Alf. I wasn't aware they were brothers. I should have come in and told him."

"No. That's what Bart wanted. Now what are you going to do? Are you going to stay, or are you going to go on west?" The banker questioned.

"I'll be going west for awhile, but I don't know what to do with the place. I don't want to sell. I might want to come back and use it as a home, like Bart did. Will you tell me how much money is in the account he had here? I might need some things to go west with. Bart said to come and get what I needed.

He frowned, and said to the man behind the counter, "Would you please bring me Bart's file?"

"Yes sir, the file is right here." He turned and picked up a folder from a number of files on the top of his counter.

"Thank you. Now let me see what we have here." He studied the papers and looked at me. He said, "The amount is almost a thousand dollars. As a matter of fact, the balance is nine hundred, forty-two dollars and fifty cents. What do you want to do with it? Do you want to take some west with you?"

I was still stunned. I sat thinking for a minute or so and then said, "No, I will need some for supplies, but that's all. Oh, by the way, do you know someone who would farm the place for me on a share-crop agreement? If you will put the money in my account and I need some later, I will write to you."

"Let me think on it. How soon are you planning to leave?" He asked.

"I want to leave next week. A lot of people going now, so I better be on my way. Oh, Bart never said how many acres are in the farm. Is the deed here?"

Mr. Sullivan answered, "Yes, the deed is here in a strong box. The farm is a good one and big enough. If you want to stay and farm, you can make a good living. It still needs some clearing, but there are a hundred and sixty acres of good, rich bottom land."

I asked him about taking some money from the account. He asked how much I wanted. After thinking and adding it to the hundred dollars I still had, I decided to take forty-two dollars and leave the rest.

He smiled and said, "I can understand why Bart thought so highly of you. You're like him. He never spent freely. He was very wise.

We talked a little longer. When I left the bank he had agreed to take over the management of the farm and I would get one-third of the money from the crop deposited into the bank account. I could leave now. Everything was going to be taken care of. On the way home, later in the afternoon, I had a feeling of freedom I had never felt before. I had enough money to go west, a home to come back to, and I had made a major decision about the rest of my life.

CHAPTER 12

I spent the rest of the week getting everything ready to leave. I shod Charlie and Molly and used up the better part of a day. The mules had forgotten the lessons about the shoeing they had last fall. Molly was the worst. We had a major battle, which she almost won. I outsmarted her and she ended up lying on her side while I attached her new shoes. The packsaddle came next. She also had to be refreshed about that. All in all, she had to be broke again after the six months lay off. After the fight, she walked up to me and hung her head, as if to say, "Okay, now I remember."

Monday, the 15th day of April 1866, I left the Cabin a short while before sunrise and headed to town and the boat to cross the river. I didn't know what to do with Jenny so I tied her on behind Molly and took her along. She followed along with her ears up acting like she was pleased with the chance to go again. When I got to town the boat docked and prepared to take on wood for the trip up the river.

I tied the mules up and went on board to talk to the captain about booking a crossing. He greeted me and said the boat went about two hours up river to a dock on the other side. I gave him a dollar for me and a dollar and fifty cents for the three mules.

I returned to the mules. A group of men stood talking. Most of them had packs, rifles, and other gear. I stood aside and listened to their conversation. I got the impression the group wanted to meet a wagon train the other side of the river.

Two men stood apart from the rest. They had horses with new looking saddles and their camping gear tied on behind each saddle. I watched while they talked. They also had new pistols and rifles. The pistols were the six shot type and the rifles, the new repeater type.

One from the group walked over to them and asked about the guns. One of the two took his out and showed the pistol to the rest. They talked about how many shots the rifle held and looked at the bullets. You didn't have to pour powder down the barrel. You pushed the cartridges in a side gate and went back to shooting. I was kicking myself for not going to the store and buying one of each for the trip.

Later I found out the two men had been watching me. I had all of my camping gear and food on Molly and nothing on Jenny. The deck hand told us to load our livestock on board. I led Charlie up, to what they called the gangplank. Charlie took one look and decided against it. I talked, pleaded, and threatened, but no way would Charlie go up the plank. Finally a Darky walked down and stood, wondering what to do.

He said, "Is that Bart's Jenny behind?"

"Yeah, Bart died. Did you know him?"

"I did. Lead Jenny up here. She'll bring the rest onboard with no more trouble. If you want to lead them, I'll follow and they will load just fine."

I walked back to Jenny, talked to her a minute and led her up the gangplank. She walked right up onto the deck. Charlie and Molly followed like they had done that all of their lives. I thanked him as he walked down to help load the other horses and the waiting teams.

Later, he came back to where I had the mules in stalls. The boat was loaded with a lot of horses and mules. A wagon train crossing would take all day, going back and forth, to get all of them across the river.

He told me Bart had come and gone across the river a lot. He would cross over to hunt and just to ride out on the open land, sometimes staying two or three days and sometimes for years.

As I unloaded from the boat the two men watched to see which way I went. I had a funny feeling about the two of them. I went north on the road, like Bart told me to. I rode all day and the road never got very far from the river. The landscape seemed almost the same on this side as on the other.

Along towards dark I hunted for a campsite. I found a small draw with some trees, so I figured there would be water and wood for a fire. I turned off the trail without looking back, and saw a nice place for a camp. It had been used by others. There was a small stream and enough wood for a supper fire. I remembered what Bart told me to do at night. I walked back to check down the trail. Sure enough, the two men were walking their horses along. They got where I turned off and stopped and talked in low tones for a few minutes. They rode on up the road, out of sight. I went back, took care of the mules, and cooked supper. After eating, I loaded the mules, went back out to the road and crossed over to the other side then rode on. In the afternoon I found the draw Bart told me to turn into. I turned west, up the draw. The mules and I were tired, so at the first seep of water I built a fire, ate supper and then moved on. I traveled about a mile, pulled off of the trail, made a camp with no fire and went to sleep.

As daylight began to creep into the sky, I got up and cooked some breakfast. I continued up the canyon in this manner for about a week. One evening, when I pulled off the trail and went back to check, I spotted the men about a mile behind me. I did the same as before, but this time I set out some snares around my camp, with the small ropes I bought early on.

I woke up with a start and lay listening. I heard something walking and Charlie doing his snuff, snuff thing. All of a sudden I heard a scream and then a rifle shot. I jumped up and heard something running through the brush and a horse running back down the trail. I went to investigate and suddenly bumped into something soft. I jumped back and nearly yelled, but caught myself before I did. I went back to camp.

In the morning, when I went to find out what had happened, I found one of the men hanging from a tree. He tripped one of the snares and hung by his feet. It must have spooked his partner, because he had also been shot in the chest. I wondered what to do now. I decided to move on.

While loading the mules, I thought about the things he had, like the new guns and personal things. Those things are not going to do him any good now. I wondered about his horse, so I went to look for the animal and found him tied about a hundred yards down the trail, and led him back to the mules. He had a nice new saddle with a new rifle strapped in a scabbard. I put the new saddle on Charlie and fixed it with the breeching and breast collar to fit him.

I decided I'd better bury the man instead of leaving him hanging in the tree. By the time I buried him I had spent all day. I went through his stuff and laid out what would be of use. His clothes were way too big for me, so I just threw away the things in his pack, but I put some of his things in the panniers to use at a later date. One thing I had not bought was a razor and he had a new one.

I moved on up the trail for a couple of hours and camped in a small draw. The next day, as I went up the trail, Jenny was slow to start. I took her halter off and tied the horse to Molly and let Jenny just follow along behind.

We traveled this way for about a week. One night Jenny didn't eat. She walked off, up the hill, like she was looking for something. She lay down. The next morning she was still lying in the same spot. I walked over to check on her. She died in the night. She had come out to the open spaces she loved. Now she was with Bart, I thought, and they were looking over a whole new territory together. They are meeting the new challenges ahead of them, following the trails to the high country.

For the next few weeks, I worked my way along the rim of the plateau. Spring came quickly on the plains. The flowers buds began to open and the brown grass had new green shoots. When I looked far off, the ground had a brownish green tinge. The Black-eyed Susans were opening up. They are orange flowers with black centers. The blue bells, in their clumps, sometimes were so numerous that the plains appeared to have a blue haze. Along on the side of the hill were fields of rooster heads. They turned the hillside pink. When I dropped off, into the head of the draws, I found lady slippers, called mountain orchids. They are lavender with reddish stripes. They were growing out of the decayed wood, in moist areas or under trees, in the shade. It was a beautiful sight. I understood why Bart loved the west so much.

I spotted a group of small animals traveling in large herds. They were reddish brown with white markings. Sometimes I would ride over a ridge and spook them and they would light out on a dead run. Oh, boy, how they ran, just like a streak. After scaring a herd of them, I noticed they always ran in a single file.

I also saw bigger deer than I had seen or killed east of the big river. They didn't run, but they bounced when they went away from me. They didn't have a big white tail to wave. Sometimes, when I approached them, they just stood and watched me. If I got too close they stamped their front feet and snorted loudly and bounced off.

There was so much to see. From time to time I got off and let the horses feed on the new grass, and lay on a ridge in the sun, watching the world around me.

One day, when I came to a small, flat basin, a little animal ran across the ground. One, no two, no, the whole basin appeared to be moving in different directions. I stopped and watched, and then I heard, in the distance, a faint whistle. It was repeated many times. I saw many little animals standing upright. They looked like big squirrels. I rode down and found myself in a whole basin of holes, so many holes that the mules had a hard time walking without caving in some of them. I quickly worked to the side of the flat before the mules got a leg caught in a hole. There must to have been a thousand holes and twice that many animals on the flat. They weren't afraid of me. I could ride within a few feet of them before they ducked down.

I slowed down my travel speed to about half to see everything. I didn't always make the distance between the draws. One night I had to camp in the open, with no water or fire, because I had wasted so much time watching a mother wild dog bring a rabbit to her pups and tear it up for them to eat.

As I worked along, I found myself completely at home out here. After all, I had Charlie and Molly to talk to and they listened to me. When I asked one of them a question they would turn their heads toward what I had been looking at and flop one ear, or raise their head and look sharply in that direction.

The horse was as tame now as the mules. He found out I wasn't going to hurt him. Someone had mistreated him. He was afraid of me when I tried to catch him. Now when I woke up all three of them would be standing in a circle around me.

I stopped in a draw one afternoon and, as I traveled down into the timber, found a small deserted cabin. The roof seemed to be solid, so I camped for the night. My dried meat was getting low. I took the axe and cut down a dry tree. I cut some green limbs and made a drying rack.

The next morning I walked down into the canyon a little way and found a nice young buck deer. I had the new rifle, so I took a bead on the buck's head and pulled the trigger. There was a loud pop and the deer dropped. I was used to reloading after each shot, but with this gun all you did was jack the lever. How nice, and I hit right where I aimed. Boy, this thing is all right, I thought to myself.

I dressed the deer and tried to drag him back to camp. That's when I found out the real difference between this deer and ones in the east. I couldn't move him up the hill. I went to camp, put the saddle on the horse and rode down to the deer. I thought, well the rifle works fine, we'll find out about the horse. I put the rope around the buck's head and wrapped the other end around the saddle horn. Now, needless to say, that didn't work out as well as the rifle.

The horse took one look at the deer dragging behind and started to kick, buck, and bawl. The further up the hill he went, the harder he tried to get away. I was hanging on with both hands by now. I realized that, if he threw me off and got away, I may never find him, saddle, or rifle again. He might go all the way back to the river.

As we went by the camp, I managed to get the rope off of the saddle horn and drop the deer. We went on up the draw and out on the open ground before he started to settle down a little. Finally I talked him into stopping and letting me off. As soon as my feet hit the ground I began to tremble. I had never ridden a bucking horse before. I led him and walked back to camp. I made up my mind he was not going to act that way again. I would break him to pull.

I cut up the deer and got the meat drying on the rack. I saved some fresh steaks off of the back to eat. I ate until I felt stuffed. I woke up the next morning, made some pancakes and fried some more steak. I ended up eating a hind-quarter of the deer while I waited for the rest to dry. I spent five days there before starting out. I had misjudged the deer. He was larger, by far, than the eastern deer. I guess that's why I couldn't drag him up the hill without help from the horse. I had enough meat in one deer to feed me for a long time. I hadn't realized I wouldn't find any trading posts or stores along the way. While the deer was drying, I went through my supplies and found I was low on flour, salt and pepper. I needed to change some of my cooking habits and use corn meal in place of flour, I guess.

I rode Charlie again. I tied a rope around the horse's neck and let it drag. He got tired of trying to kick and make a fuss over it. I found a small piece of wood and tied that on the end of the rope. He fussed for a while more. By this time he had worked up a mighty sweat and was getting tired. When I found a camp for the night he just stood while I untied the rope and dropped it over his back, swung it under his belly, and over his feet. He was one tired horse. He never made a fuss about a rope again.

I rode on west for a couple of weeks. The river bottom on my left was getting closer to the rim. I figured the trail from the south, Bart told me about, was nearby.

CHAPTER 13

One afternoon, while I rested for a noon break, I thought I heard a rifle shot off in the distance. I had not heard any shots since I left the river, except for the one fired in the night by my camp. That made me nervous. I caught the animals and moved on west, but now I rode with a watchful eye. I searched for whoever might be following the river below me. I had not seen any human beings for so long; I guess I was scared to meet them.

I worried about Indians. Bart warned me to watch out for them. He said some of them would be peaceful and want to trade for tobacco, or whiskey. Since I had neither, I hoped they would believe me when I told them I didn't have any. On the other hand, some resented the white man coming into their territory and would try to kill me and take the horses and my supplies.

After I camped for the night, there were more shots, a bunch of them this time. It sounded like a fight going on. I didn't want to get involved with an attack of some kind. I lay and worried about the situation all night. In the morning I decided to drop down into the draw. The draw seamed to be fairly open and I could ride to the bottom without much trouble.

Most of the morning I worked my way down through the timber. I reached the bottom and dismounted to check the wagon trail for sign. I found a lot of wagon and horse tracks. They must be a day or two old. I mounted up and followed along the trail. I turned a bend and through the trees I saw the back of a wagon setting off to the side of the trail.

I rode to the other side of the trail, into the brush, and tied the stock to a bush so they were somewhat hidden. I stayed out of sight in the brush and walked along the trail for about two hundred yards. I found where the wagons turned aside into an opening. Two wagons, like the kind people use to travel west, stood in the opening. I crept slowly along and watched for anything out of order. I walked carefully around the wagons. Two more wagons, bigger than the first two, sat in front. Each had an extra short wagon attached to them. I saw no sign of life. I got down on my stomach and crawled ahead. The teams were still hooked to the wagons. Now, that was strange, since I heard most of the shooting the afternoon before, with some scattered shots today.

The teams looked like they had been standing a long time. There were piles of droppings behind each horse. I stood up and walked very slowly along the line of wagons. Tied to trees, in front of the lead team, were 20 mules with pack-saddles, and five saddled horses.

I recognized one horse, the big, three colored stallion the man with the scarred face rode. Between the lead team, the horses, and mules, lay a lot of dead men. I walked through the dead bodies and turned to go back to the first two wagons and found three men and two women. They had been shot in the back of the head. I went back to the dead men and looked for Scarface. He had crawled off to one side, propping himself up against a tree. He had his rifle lying beside him and had two pistols, one in each hand. He went down fighting to the end.

Who did all of the murders? There was no sign of anything being removed from the wagons. The ropes and everything were left in place. The big wagons, that I noticed when I came over on the boat, were loaded. These double-hookups had five teams hooked in front of them. I walked back to my horses and brought them up to the campsite.

Now what am I going to do? I went over to an old fire ring, tied my stock to a wagon wheel, and began to gather some dry wood to build a small fire. I needed to sit down and think about this. I guess the first thing is to get the teams unhitched and watered. That will be a big job all in itself.

There are eighteen teams in all and they don't know me. I had no idea how they would act with a stranger. I started with the ones on the smaller wagons. They were big draft horses so I figured they would be the most gentle. I walked up to the leaders of the first team and spoke to them in a soft voice. Those two put their heads down, smelled me, snuffed a little, and accepted me. I had never unhooked a line of horses like that, so it took me a little while to figure out what chains went to what horse. As I worked, I discovered a pattern to the hook up. I undid those four teams, walked them to the creek, let them drink, and returned to the wagon.

I tied them in pairs to the wagon wheels. I did those two wagons and by then I was ready to start on the big, tandem wagons. The only difference would be one more team per wagon. Evening came by the time I got to the pack mules. They were getting nervous because the other horses had been able to drink and they were really thirsty.

I hesitated to just walk up to them and drop their packs. I knew mules would kick wickedly if they didn't know you. I walked around them while talking quietly. They started to snuff and wanted to smell me. As soon as one stuck its nose out to me I would untie and walk it out and let it stand while I unloaded the panniers. Those packs were really heavy, so I knew the mules wanted them off. I removed the saddles at the same time and let the mules loose to graze with their halters on and the lead rope dragging. Only one tried to buck and keep me away from him.

I worked by firelight now, so I didn't have any patients with him and swatted him on the rump with the lead rope. He stopped and raised his head, with his ears up, watching me. I walked up to him, like I was not afraid, and told him to behave. He never moved a foot the rest of the time. I removed his load, the lightest one of the bunch. However, when it came time to turn him loose, I took the halter off and let him go. I figured I didn't want to get kicked and hurt, and I really didn't want to put up with him. He could stay behind for all I cared. Now, five saddled horses, and five with no saddles, needed water. I built the fire up to cook some food.

I went to my pack, got out some dried meat and wild onions I found a few days ago. I put my pot on the fire to boil. I was too tired to make anything else. I thought I would fix pancakes in the morning. While sitting, looking into the fire, and wondering what to do with everything, I caught movement out of the corner of my eye. I rolled under the wagon and drew my pistol.

"Okay, now step out into the firelight before I shoot."

Nothing moved, and then a very scared, child's voice said, "Don't shoot mister, please. I'm coming."

Out stepped a young girl, maybe two or three years younger than me. However, to my surprise, she had a rifle pointed at me and looked like she meant to use it. She was about my height, with shoulder length, bright red hair. When she spoke the next time, she had no fright in her voice.

She said, "You lay still and toss the gun out from under the wagon or I'll blast you."

That's when I saw she had a double-barrel shotgun, and I'll be darned if she didn't have both hammers eared back and a determine look on her face.

I said, "Okay, a truce. I have the pistol pointed on you, so let's just let the hammers down easy on both guns and we can talk about this. I promise to be good if you put away the shotgun. Please."

I crawled out from under the wagon. She was all muddy and her dress was torn in a number of places." Are you all right?" I asked. "What in the devil went on here, anyway? It looks like a war zone."

"That's exactly what happened. We planned to camp here and had just pulled in. That's why I'm still alive. I went across the trail, over on the hillside, to get some dry wood and heard the men and mules coming, so I hid behind a down tree. They were talking, when all of a sudden someone yelled, "Confederates," and everything blew up. There was a lot of shooting, yelling, and cussing something awful. About dark, they did more shooting. I was afraid to go see what had happened. I felt sure Mom and Papa were hurt."

"I was afraid to come in after dark last night, so this morning I snuck over to the wagon and saw all of the dead people. The two men lying over by the tree argued some and then they both up and shot each other. It was awful. I sat here wondering what to do, way out here, with no one around. I knew the teams needed to get to water. Then I heard you coming down the hillside. I ran into the brush and fell into a marsh and got all wet. Do you mind if I come up to the fire and get warm? I thought more of those men were coming into camp. I watched you take care of the teams and how you worked with the animals, and decided I had to see if you were one of them. Are you with them? If you are, be sure I will use this shotgun before you can get to me."

I could tell she really meant what she said and was scared enough to shoot. "Can I make a suggestion? If you help me get something to eat, I'll go get some fresh water. Then we'll decide what we're going to do with your Mom and Dad and all of the other dead bodies."

She was in shock. I knew she was not acting right. Her eyes were big and she trembled like she was cold. "Why don't you go put on some clean, dry clothes while I finish with the soup?" I suggested.

She stood like she was in a daze. Finally, she seemed to be aware of what I said, and turned and went to the back of the wagon. She picked up a lantern from the side of the wagon bed. She lit the lantern and climbed into the wagon. I heard her moving around in the bed. In a few minutes she climbed out with a clean dress on. I went into the other wagon and got some blankets and covered her parents and the rest of the bodies so she wouldn't have to see them any longer.

We ate the soup. She got some bread from a tin box on the wagon. When we finished, she stood up and said she was going to bed and climbed into the wagon. I got my bedroll and spread it under her wagon. In the middle of the night I heard her start to sob, big heart wrenching sobs. It brought back the scene of my mother and Sissy, lying on the kitchen floor at home. Tears came to my eyes again, not only for me, but for her as well. I still felt the hurt deep in my being. I lay still most of the night remembering the hurt I felt those days after their murders. I had gone from hate to longing, and back to hate, again. It was awful. She had one thing I didn't. She knew who had done the killing. I went to sleep listening to her dry, racking sobs.

I got up before the sun-rays penetrated the area through the trees. I walked around and petted some of the horses and removed the harness as I went. I unharnessed each team and led them out to a small meadow and put a set of hobbles on one of the horses. This took a long time. As I finished with the saddle horses, I became aware the fire was going and smelled bacon cooking. Now, I had not had bacon for a long time and it sure smelled good. I turned all of the horses out to pasture except the big stallion. I picketed him with a long rope. He wasn't happy about that, but I didn't want him to start beating up on the geldings.

While I took care of the horses, I searched for a place to dig graves for the dead men. I decided to bury the men around the campsite so the graves would be hidden as we walked the horses around. I would bury the girl's parents and the other couple out in the meadow away from the trail where they wouldn't be disturbed. We can put some type of a marker with them. I walked back to the fire. She greeted me with a smile and a good morning. It felt good to have someone to talk to and a smile on top of that.

CHAPTER 14

I said to the girl, "I think we should meet each other. My name is Kenneth, Ken for short. What do I call you?"

She answered. "Just call me Fannie. My full name is Frances Magee."

"Where did you come from? You talk funny," I said.

"Well, no funnier than you." She answered with a throw of her head.

She had on a clean dress and I asked, "All you wear is dresses, no pants?"

"What do you mean by pants?"

I took a hold of my pant leg and shook it.

"I should say not! Decent ladies don't wear a man's britches where I come from." She replied sharply.

I thought a little and said, "I think, if you're going to work and help me do what has to be done today, a pair of pants might be better."

"Oh, I understand what you mean. I suppose I can cut a pair of my dad's to fit me. Let's eat this before we do the unpleasant job, shall we?" She said, as she turned to dish up the biscuits and bacon.

After we ate and I helped clean the dishes, I looked in the wagons for a shovel. One was on the Magee wagon and a couple more on one of the big wagons. I turned to Fannie, "Let's walk and decide where you want your parents buried. I think along the side of the meadow would be a good place. Digging will be easier, and I can go deeper. We want to go down a little deeper for them, so the graves won't be disturbed by animals or Indians. This other couple will need to be put by them. As for the rest, we will just get them in the ground, maybe two or three in a grave."

She had a shocked expression. "What do you mean two or three? Aren't you going to dig a grave for each of them?"

"Not unless I have to. Burying ten men will take four or five days digging. I don't think we should leave these bodies out of the ground that long. They are already beginning to smell. In another three days they'll be bringing in animals, plus be a big flock of those." I pointed to the large black birds circling overhead.

"What are those birds?" Fannie asked, "I haven't seen them before."

I explained, "Those are vultures, and unless we get the bodies moved soon, hundreds of them will be here. Anyone traveling will realize something dead is drawing the birds here."

I walked over where she was standing and asked, "Is this the place for your folks?"

She nodded her head, went to the wagon, and climbed inside.

I started to dig and was thankful we picked the gravesite here because the black, soft dirt was easy digging. I worked for hours to dig two graves, so we could lay her folks out proper.

While I dug, Fannie came and asked what she should do. I asked if she would get the bodies ready to put in the ground.

She frowned and said, "What do you mean?"

"Take blankets from their beds and wrap each in one. We'll put them in the grave that way."

She stood for a short while and asked, "Won't we be able to have a box for them?"

I spread my hands out. "With what? I don't see any lumber, do you?"

"Oh, I guess not." She replied with disappointment on her face. She broke out crying and ran for the wagon.

When the graves were dug, I went to the wagon. Fannie had thrown a couple of blankets out of the back. They lay on the ground, where they landed. I picked them up and went to the two bodies, glad she wasn't there. I needed to go through her father's pockets to find out if he had anything to keep. I found some small change and a pocket-knife, but that was all. I set those aside to give to her later. Her father wasn't a big man, so I picked him up and carried him to the grave, rolled him in the blanket, and then into the grave, like I had my mom and sister.

I walked back to the wagon and asked, "Do you want to see if your mom had on anything you want to keep?"

She didn't answer. I went to the back of the wagon and looked in. Fannie lay, curled up in ball. I jumped into the wagon and shook her.

She opened her eyes and started to cry again. "Just do it. I can't watch."

"Are you sure?" I asked.

She nodded her head, yes.

I went to her mother's body and picked her up. I was surprised at how light she was. I took her to the grave to roll her in. I noticed a nice ring on her finger. I wondered if I should take the ring as a keepsake for Fannie or leave it on her mother's hand. On her neck was a gold chain. I pulled on the chain and a small, heart-shaped object came out from under her dress. I finally figured out how to open the lock. I took the necklace and the ring and set them aside for later. After the graves were filled, I went to the wagon and laid her mother's things on the seat. I dug two more graves beside Fannie's parents. I worked until nearly dark before the job was done.

I built a fire to cook some food. Fannie came out of the wagon and said, "I'm so sorry. I couldn't watch you lay them in the ground. That makes it so final. I'll cook supper. I'm sure you must be tired and hungry."

She had no idea how tired and hungry. I had worked since daylight. She cooked, and I went out and moved the rest of the bodies into the timber. As I did this, I went through their pockets. First, I took the guns and holsters and put them in one wagon. Then I picked up what rifles were laying on the ground, and put those in the wagon. I had about half of the bodies moved when Fannie said, "Supper is ready." We ate and she got up to go get water to wash the dishes.

I said, "Who was the young boy with? One of those bodies is not any older than I am. Was he with the outlaws?"

"Oh, my goodness, I forgot all about Alvin. He's with the Clements family. He's their grandson. His father got killed in the war and his mother died on the trail here. She was really sick when they joined up with us in New Orleans."

"Then I need to dig another grave over by them. That's okay, it's easy digging. I might take most of the others out in the meadow and dig the graves. It will be a lot easier than digging them here, near the hillside. I was going to put them close to the wagons and walk the stock over them so the graves would be hidden from anyone. I can do the same thing out in the meadow. The grass will grow back over the graves next spring."

After three more days digging, all of the bodies were in the ground. I went through all of their pockets and took anything I thought might be of use. They all had some small amounts of money, all except Scarface. He had a good-sized roll of bills tied with a string. I didn't stop to count, but put it with the rest of the stuff. I managed to find a couple of places where digging was easier, so I dug bigger holes. In two of them I put four bodies. I didn't bother to roll them in blankets, just got them in the ground.

I saddled the stallion, rode out in the pasture and herded the horses back and forth over the graves. After going over them three or four times, the ground became really torn up, with no sign of my digging.

Now, what are we going to do with all of the wagons and their loads? We talked after supper. We needed to know what the big freight wagons carried. Also, what the mules had been loaded with. I walked over where I dropped the panniers the first night and unbuckled the top of one. Many pieces of something were wrapped in cloth and tied with small, thin ropes, two packages in each pannier. I lifted one of the packages. The package was hard and heavy, and probably weighed thirty pounds or more. I took my knife and cut the rope binding. To my amazement, a bar of some kind of yellow metal was shining. I had never seen anything like that. Then I realized that they were gold bars.

I took a bar over to the wagon to show Fannie and asked, "Do you have any idea what this is?"

She shook her head no. I went over to the pile of money and picked up a five-dollar gold piece to show her. She still didn't understand, so I said, "Its solid gold. If all the rest of those sacks are as full of gold as the one I opened, we are awful rich. Awful rich, I mean like thousands of dollars rich."

I had no idea how much gold, but there was a lot. Then I got scared. If anyone knew what we had, they would kill us in a minute. Surely someone was searching for the gold. Now I had another worry, not just what to do with the wagons loaded with who knows what, but a whole lot of gold laying out in the open for the taking.

I lay awake most of that night, worrying. I finally came up with a plan. We would load the bars in one of the wagons, if we could find a way to make room for them. The next morning I told Fannie what I had been thinking about all night.

She asked, "What about the things in the two family wagons?"

I had not thought about those things. I shrugged my shoulders and said, "I guess we need to repack the big wagons and decide."

The next day we searched through the big wagons, one at a time. We found a lot of shells and gun-powder in wooden kegs, plus some new rifles in one of them. The others had a lot of food things and boxes of clothes. I found a hammer and pried the lids off of the boxes.

We took the clothes out and went through them to decide if anything would be useful to us. In the other wagon we found boxes of dishes, pots, and pans. I measured the boxes. Some were the right size to fit the gold bars. The ones I opened fit perfectly. We needed five of the boxes, so I moved some of the rest and made room to put the boxes of gold in the center.

While doing this, I asked Fannie what was in her wagon that she wanted to take.

She said, "A lot of clothes and things of my mother's." She thought and said, "Nothing, I guess."

I was sure that was not right, but I dropped the subject. "I'm hungry. How about you? It must be time for supper."

"I guess so," she answered and sat down on the tailgate.

I looked down at her and asked, "Fannie, how old are you?"

She said, "I will be fourteen soon."

"You're only thirteen?" I guess I sounded shocked.

"Yes. So, what! I'm big enough to do my share of the work."

Sparks were coming out of her deep, blue eyes. She was ready to take issue with anything I said, so I decided to not push my luck.

"My dad was sick. We came west for his health. I've been doing most of the heavy work since we left the boat back at the river. I've driven the teams most of the way. Dad drove for a while, but he was getting weaker the farther this way we came. One of the guys asked Mom if she would drop off at the next trading post."

My ears picked up quickly. "He said a trading post was close."

"No, he didn't. He wanted to know if, when we got to a trading post, we would stop and rest until another train came by."

I asked her to cook while I unloaded the small, trailing wagon. That wagon was nearly all food things, flour, beans, oat and corn meal, and ten sacks of sugar. I thought I'd better start over and put this stuff all together so we know what really is here. So, I unloaded the one big wagon and its little, trailer. I had a large pile by dark.

Fannie called and when I went to eat she had made biscuits, gravy, mashed potatoes, and a can of tomatoes.

I said, "Wow. You've been busy this last hour. You might be useful after all. Maybe we will get along if you keep cooking like this."

"Well, don't count on it. Our food won't last that long."

"Oh, yes it will. I unloaded the first big wagon and the smaller one. They are almost all dried food things. I even found one package that says dried apples. We'll have an apple dumpling dish one day, huh?"

"Are you going to unload all of the wagons and reload them?" She asked while she dished up a plate for me.

I began to eat and Fannie looked shyly at me and asked, "Do you suppose we could start our meals with a prayer of thanks from now on?"

I felt embarrassed because I never thought about it. My folks never asked prayers on the food. The only other time, was one meal I had eaten, way back at the heavyset woman's table. I said, "Yeah, I suppose so, if you want to. I've never asked a prayer on the food or anything else, but if it will help, go ahead."

She bowed her head and asked for help from the Lord for many things. I sat amazed, that she knew how to talk to her Lord so calmly. I was finding out many strange things about this red-headed, turned-up-nose, blue-eyed, girl who had a splatter of freckles across the ridge of her nose.

After supper, we washed the dishes. Then I asked her if she had ever shot a gun.

She looked at me and said, "Good Lord no. Why would I want to?"

"What were you going to do with the shotgun the other day? Beat me over the head with it until I was dead?"

She frowned and asked, "What are you talking about?"

I laughed and said, "The other morning, when I came into the camp and you caught me under the wagon. Don't you remember?"

"No. I must have been so scared I was doing anything to keep everyone away.

"Well, you acted to me like you meant business. The holes in the front of that big gun looked like two flour barrels would fit, one on each side. Where is the gun, anyway? I think I should check and make sure you're not going to blow a hole in something. You did lower the hammers, didn't you?"

"It's laying just inside of the tailgate of the wagon. Anyway, I think it is." She replied.

I got up and walked to the back of the wagon. I started to climb in and there was the shotgun, pointed out at me. I very gently lifted the barrels up so they were pointing up in the air. WHOA! That thing was still cocked. She had been crawling in and out over the gun. I drew it out to where I could get to the hammers and let them off cock. Then I climbed down and walked to the front of the wagon so I could see better by firelight. I pointed the barrel at the ground and broke the magazine open. Guess what, two shiny brass caps stared at me from the end of the barrels. Yes, the gun was loaded and ready to go. A pull on the trigger and it would have blown a hole, the size of a water bucket. She had been crawling in and out of the wagon for a week without tripping the hammers.

In the morning, after breakfast, I unloaded the other wagon and the short companion. I worked most of the day to unload the two. Fannie was setting things where they belonged, or showing me where to put things that were too heavy for her to lift. When we got through, only the boxes with the gold bars were left on the wagon. I noticed the bed of one wagon had screws in the floorboards instead of bolts.

I said, "Fannie, come here. What do you suppose is in there?"

She looked, and I pointed to the screws holding the floorboards in place. I asked, "Should we remove the screws or just load everything back up and check after we get where we're going?"

She asked, "Where are we going? You've never said, and I don't have a choice right now. I have to go where you go, I guess."

"I really don't know, but a friend of mine told me of a place that sounds like heaven. I guess we'd better leave the floor and get loaded as soon as we can. We've wasted a lot of time here. We need a couple more days before we will be ready, anyway. I've been thinking, in the morning, why don't you go through the other wagons and see if you can find clothes from the Clements boy you can wear. I think it will be better and safer for both of us if you dress like a boy. I can cut your hair shorter and no one would be able to tell."

"You are not going to cut my hair, now or ever!"

I laughed and said, "I'll make you a deal. You can cut my hair if you'll let me cut yours, but you better really think about it."

We worked for three days to reload the wagons and get the things she wanted from the other two wagons. By rearranging the loads and taking the tops off of the empty wagons and fixing them on the two smaller wagons, we were finally ready to go.

The next morning we started catching the teams. Some of them really didn't want to go back to work. They had two weeks of rest and had fattened up.

I told Fannie, "Now it's your turn to tell me what to do. In the first place, I don't know what horses go where."

"I know about our teams and the Clements span. Do you think eight head will be enough on the loaded wagons? They had one more team on each wagon." Fannie answered.

"For starters, let's put the two teams where they go. We can put one other team on the wheel, where there really isn't much they can do wrong. We'll harness the other teams and tie them on behind. If we need to we can change in the middle of the day. If they walk for a day or two maybe they won't be so spooky.

"Now, what are we going to do with the loose stock?" she asked, "Their saddle horses and all of the mules plus your three."

"I'll tie the stallion on one side of my wagon and Charlie on the other. I've loaded all of the saddles except one for me and one for you. We can put yours on Charlie and I'll put one on the stallion. That way, if we need to ride ahead, we will have saddled horses ready to use. They may be a little frisky to start, but I hope they will all follow. If we need to, we can catch the loose horses and tie them on behind the teams. It will make a long string, but should work."

"Let's put that big black team on your wagon. They seem to be really quiet. I think that's where they've been. I'll put the white and brown team on my wagon. I know they were a team."

It took us almost half a day to get everything hooked up and ready to go. I turned to Fannie and said, "Show me how to hold the lines. I've never driven more than two horses at a time."

She laughed and said, "I think this is going to be fun. If you can, get them out on the trail, let the leaders take the track. You have to keep the lines a little tight so they understand you're in control, but not too tight so they think you want them to slow down. You need to talk to them and let them hear your confidence in them. After a while they'll get to know your voice, and you can talk them through tight places without using the lines a whole lot. Just practice as you go along. When there is a bend in the trail, you drive them like you would a regular team. The lead team is the one you want to control, so keep that set of lines so they are doing the leading."

CHAPTER 15

I led off and went right out to the main trail. When the team made the corner they lined out up the trail as if we had been going forever. I kept looking back to check on Fannie. The extra teams walking made a lot of space between the wagons. About midday we came to the first problem. We had to ford the creek we had been following. I stopped and studied, and decided to try, so I asked the leaders to go ahead. They walked into the creek and followed up stream a little ways and went right on out. I drove on up a ways and stopped and got down. I walked back to check on Fannie.

Her teams went right through, the same as mine, but one horse, of the trailing teams, decided he wasn't going to cross. He hung back and got drug though the steam on his side. I ran back to where he lay and kicked him in the ribs and made him get up. He got up, shook himself, and stood as if nothing had happened. I walked up to him and talked a while, rubbing his nose and quieting him down. I looked back down the road and here came a whole bunch of the loose stock. I thought they might wander off and eat and not follow. The horses came up to us and stopped in the creek to drink.

I walked back up to Fannie and asked her, "How are you doing?"

She smiled, and said, "The wheel team is doing great, but my arms are getting tired. I will get broken in again."

We had been camped for almost two weeks and it felt good to be on the move. That's the way things went for nearly a month. We put in long days. I had the stock caught and harnessed before daylight and we didn't stop until nearly dark. We followed the creek drainage and then dropped over and went down another draw. I watched for the two big peaks in the distance, but the rolling grassland didn't seem to change.

We still had all of the horses but two. One night the mule, with no halter, and one of the saddle horses, didn't come into camp. I think they took off some place. We had traveled all of this distance and not seen a soul. I stopped one afternoon to give the team a break when two riders came our way. I walked back to Fannie and told her to lay the shotgun on the seat where she could pick it up if she needed to.

"Be sure, if you do, at least one of the hammers is pulled back and ready to go." We started on. Later the two riders rode up to the side of my wagon. I stopped as they came up. I had the rifle where it would be easy to get in a hurry, if need be.

We exchanged greetings and then one asked, "Where are you headed? You've got a lot of extra stock. What happened? Did you lose some wagons, on the way across?"

"We did, and we also lost some men, so we have some extra stock." I answered.

"That's quite a long string with all of the extra horses," He commented.

"Yes, and we have some loose ones coming up behind us. They catch us before bedtime every night. Are you going all of the way east, or are you just out wandering?"

"We're headed back east. We've come all of the way from California and are going to New Orleans and taking a boat to Pennsylvania. We both have family we haven't seen for three years. We're going to stay home. This country is not what we expected."

"How far ahead is a trading post?" I wanted to know.

The second guy smiled and said, "At least a hundred miles to a little town by the name of Strawberry. We didn't find any strawberries. We stayed for a week, eating our fill. The only thing we had worth eating was a dried apple pie and that cost a quarter a slice. I ate the last piece, so we decided to leave before we got snowed in. There are a few homesteaders, a blacksmith shop, a general store; with not much for sale, and that's about all."

I picked up the reins and said, "Well, we're not going to get anyplace sitting here talking. Have a good trip, and a safe one, I hope."

I said, "Ho boys, let's go," and the teams all started at once, like they were also in a hurry to get to camp."

I watched as they rode wide, around Fannie's wagon, to see if they tried to pick up some of the loose horses or mules. I wasn't sure, but I thought they rode on. We camped that night in the open with no trees for shelter and a small spring for water. When the horses came into camp, none were missing; even the mules all came in. I was surprised. I thought they would surely catch a couple of spare mounts.

After dark, I told Fannie to go to bed. I would sit a spell and make sure no one came back. We had a spot in each wagon, down inside, next to the seat, for the beds. When we climbed in we were hidden, but we were able to see through the springs of the seat. I watched for a few hours and tied Charlie to the side of the wagon. I knew if anyone came around he would wake me with his soft puffing sound. I lay down and went to sleep. I awoke before sunup, as usual. I counted the loose stock while I started the fire. They had all come in.

Travel became very tiresome. We traveled all day and ate morning and evening. While we ate, we told each other about out lives. In the morning we hurried to get on the trail. However, most mornings, we only took about an hour to get ready. We had a system, and the teams were gentle and eager to move out. They seemed to be looking forward to the new country.

Fannie looked tired. Hanging onto those reins for ten or more hours a day was hard work. We both had lost some weight and were brown as could be. Fannie finally understood the reason for me to cut her hair. Before we left camp, she found a pair of scissors in the Clements wagon. I cut her hair, and she had cut mine. We needed to do it again and to rest up for a day or two.

The trail dropped into a small valley with a stream. We found a nice, grassy campsite with a lot of feed for the stock and plenty of water.

After supper, I asked, "What do you think? Should we take a few days break and let the stock and ourselves rest before we move on? I have no idea the distance to the valley Bart talked about. I think we need a rest, don't you?"

Fannie nodded, "Yes. There's a place, up the creek a little ways, where we can take a bath and get cleaned up. Do you realize how long since I took a bath? I have not done anything like soak in a pool since before the shooting. You can get only so much off with a washcloth and a couple cups of water. It's a good thing we found the creek. Our water barrels are getting low. Some of those springs haven't been hardly big enough for the horses to drink."

She smiled, went to the wagon and climbed up inside. She got a towel, some soap, and her washcloth. When she came by me she said, with a twinkle in her eye, "What are you going to fix for supper tonight? I've cooked everything for the last month. If you don't start doing some cooking you'll forget how."

"Hey, what about my bath? I thought about it first, you know."

"Too bad, I'm the first to do something about it. And, for your information, I deserve to be first. My birthday is tomorrow. Now, you wouldn't want me to be dirty for an important event like that, would you?"

"Tomorrow is your birthday? Man, I had forgotten. You said you were almost fourteen, right?"

"That's right, but don't tell everyone. They'll think I'm an old maid." And she went trotting up the creek.

While I fixed supper I heard her singing. She was really enjoying herself. She came back dressed in a bright, flowery dress and a scarf wrapped around her head. Smiling, she walked over and sat down and waited for me to dish up a plate of food and hand it to her. I dished up my food, and after the blessing, we ate in silence.

She said, "Your turn to bathe. Then we'll trim our hair again. I'm getting used to mine being short. It's a lot easier to keep clean. The hat you took off of the dead cowboy helps. I'm glad you made me do those things. I was uncomfortable for a while, but now I don't even think about wearing some dead person's pants and clothes. But, wearing a dress feels good, even if just for tonight. Now you better go take your bath before dark."

I climbed into my wagon and found a clean pair of pants that I had taken from a dead man's blanket roll. I still had my buckskin clothes Bart made for me. They were a little smelly. However, I had been wearing what they called riding boots I had taken from one of the men. I saved three pair of those and a bunch of cloth pants, the kind you wear with a belt around the waist. I also wore a gun belt and a pistol at all times. I had not had any need to do much shooting with the pistol, but every once in a while, when I searched for the horses, or went away from the wagon, I would practice drawing and dry firing. At first the gun seemed very heavy and I had a hard time drawing and holding it. But, after weeks of holding the reins of the ten-horse team, I had developed enough strength in my wrists that I had no trouble drawing and pointing the pistol. I pretended to draw and point my finger where I wanted to hit.

When I got to the pool I stripped and started to wade out into the water. I got the shock of my life. That water was so cold I thought I was going to freeze. How could Fannie say she soaked in the pool with a straight face? That's okay. I will get even with her some way. I took a short bath and dried off, and yes, I felt better even if I was half frozen. I made a beeline for the fire as fast as I could. As I came running up to the fire I finished putting on my shirt and bent over the fire to get warm.

Fannie smiled at me and asked with a straight face, "Now, wasn't that nice and refreshing?"

I frowned at her and shook my head. "How anyone would be so mean and not tell me the water was so cold it would freeze a person to death?"

"Aw, it wasn't too cold. But was a wee bit chilly, maybe. I thought you were getting to be a tough man. Now I wonder about you."

"I will get even one day, you just wait."

We leaned back and basked in the warmth of the fire. The night seemed so peaceful and quiet.

I heard the horses snorting and walking around, like they were getting nervous. I walked over to the stallion and mounted him and rode out where they had been feeding. I rode around through them and talked quietly. I didn't see anything that should have spooked them. Some of the mules had worked their way closer to camp. One of the horses and a couple of the mules were watching something out on the valley floor.

I pulled the rifle from its scabbard, jacked a shell in the chamber and rode in the direction they were looking. I had gone a couple hundred yards on beyond the stock when I saw, in the moonlight, a dark object standing by a small bush. As I got closer, I realized it was an animal of some kind. It looked like a deer, but a lot bigger. I sat very quietly and watched. A bunch more moved across in front of me. I rode towards them and they moved out of the way. They stayed about the same distance from me. The stallion didn't seem to mind them, so I decided they were not a threat and turned and went back to camp.

"What's spooking the horses?" Fannie asked.

"I'm not sure. I think a big bunch of deer, but when I rode close they moved away from me. They are the biggest deer I ever saw, if they are deer. In the dark you can't see them clearly. If they are deer, they looked about the size of a cow. That would be a big deer. Anyway, the stallion was not really worried about them, so I figured not to worry and came on in."

In the morning, before the sun came up, I dressed, took the rifle, and walked out to where I had seen the animals last night. They left a lot of tracks, like cow tracks, but I didn't spot anything on the valley floor. Now I was curious about this, so I followed the tracks. They had worked their way around the horses and went to the water to drink. I found some droppings. They looked like deer droppings, except they were twice the size. I followed them out on the flat, the other side of the water. They went over towards a small stand of timber. When I got close, one of them stood up and looked at me.

Wow, that was some big deer. She stood taller than any cow, and was a light tawny color. She had a long neck and big fuzzy ears, which were brown. She turned and walked away from me. The rump had a yellowish patch of color with a short tail. I walked a little closer and about twenty or more jumped up, trotted out into the open, stopped, and looked my way. They turned and trotted off, toward the hillside above the valley.

I turned to go back to camp, but decided to walk up the creek and try to find a deer. We had not had fresh meat for a long time. I had not walked very far when a doe stepped out and turned her head to watch me. I raised the gun, took aim, and shot. She dropped and I dressed her out. I tried to pick her up. I soon realized she was like the other one I shot on the trail earlier. She was really heavy. I drug her back to camp. Fannie came and helped me drag the deer across the creek. We hung her in a tree so I could skin her.

For supper we had fresh fried steak, fried potatoes with wild onions, mushrooms, hot biscuits, canned tomatoes with canned peaches for dessert. We sang happy birthday to Fannie and laughed a lot.

The moon was high in the sky and shining bright. It was a beautiful night. I turned to Fannie and said, "I suppose, when we get some place where there's a stagecoach, you'll be wanting to go back to your grandparent's farm."

She sat quietly for a few minutes before she answered. "I don't know why. They're old, and if I go back what would I do? I don't think I would be content after being in the west. On top of that, it would be awful quiet, sitting around talking to two old people."

I told her, "We have a lot of money. You know, you can go to school and never have to work again. You would have an education in anything that pleased you."

There was a soft laugh and she answered, "You think learning to drive a ten-horse team hooked to two wagon loads of goods over rough roads is not good enough? Then, there is the suspense of looking forward to what new will come tomorrow. I'm afraid that would get awful dull."

We stayed in camp for a couple more days before we moved on. The last night I asked Fannie if she thought the days were getting a lot shorter.

"Yes, it may not be long before we will have to find someplace to stay for the winter."

"I would like to get to the valley Bart told me about, if we can find it. He said there's a big cave where we can stay all winter. A hot springs comes out of the rock close to the cave. It's supposed to be well sheltered and not too cold during the winter."

"I guess we better start pushing hard then, with no more two or three day stops. If we hurry to get to the valley, the horses will have all winter to rest." Fannie replied.

We left before dawn the next morning. We traveled until after dark every day. Some nights we didn't even take the harnesses off of the teams, just watered them and staked them out for a few hours, and then were on the trail again. A couple of days we didn't find water and made a dry camp. We were climbing slowly uphill, and the grass began to be replaced with a gray, stubby bush along the trail. It gave off a strong odor. As we climbed, the nights got colder, with dew on the grass every morning.

The graze for the stock became harder to find. We both wore coats in the morning, and timber for firewood became scarce. I chopped up the bushes. They burned hot but didn't hold a fire all night.

In the middle of the third week, we reached the top of the long grade we had been climbing. We topped out and I stopped to let the horses blow. The other side of the hill was a gently sloping meadow to the west. A spring was running out of the hillside about two or three hundred feet down the hill. I looked on down the grade and tried to figure out where the trail went. I glanced up at the horizon and there were two big peaks, way off in the distance. Then it hit me. Those two peaks are the ones Bart had been speaking about.

I started the team and drove down to a flat area and stopped. From here we would start down into the valley. We would have to make our own trail. I jumped off of the wagon and had Fannie bring hers up alongside of mine.

Chapter 16

"This is where we leave the trail and swing down into the valley I told you about. We'll make camp here and ride down and try to find a trail to the bottom."

We unhitched the teams and set up camp. I took one of the teams and dragged a dead tree over, close to camp. What a great campsite, with lots of grass for stock feed and a lot of wood for our fire.

I took the harnesses off of the teams and turned them out to feed. The loose stock came grazing into camp. We had a while before dark, so I chopped up a supply of wood, enough for a couple of days.

The middle of the afternoon a cold breeze blew gently from the west, cold enough to make us put on our coats. The night was the coldest night I had seen since we left the river.

The next morning I awoke before daylight, as usual. I lay in the bed, wondering if I really wanted to get up. My nose was cold and the air felt frigid. After about half an hour, I got up and dressed. Boy, those pants were cold, and the boots were even worse. I quickly split some kindling wood and started a fire.

Fannie said, "Call me when the fire warms up the air."

She made me laugh. No fire would warm up the air this morning. I took the water pail and walked to the spring. When I dipped the bucket into the water, I saw ice on the grass. I turned back to camp and reached down and picked up a small piece of ice. I walked up to Fannie's wagon, stepped up on the tongue and looked down under the seat. All I saw was a tuned up nose sticking out of the covers. I leaned over and laid the piece of ice on her nose.

There was no reaction for about two seconds. Then a screech and one red head came out of the covers, fighting mad. She let me know what kind an ungentlemanly man I was and what she would do to me. Some of those things sounded pretty bad.

I learned a lesson that morning. I would never go to bed again until I had dry fire starter laid aside. I didn't like getting into those damp, cold clothes. It took an hour or more for my feet to warm up.

By the time the fire heated up, Fannie came out of the wagon. She still threatened me for the ice chip. I saddled the stallion and Charlie and put some dried meat and cold biscuits in the saddlebags. I got one of the rifles and some shells out of the wagon to put in both saddlebags. I tied the rifle scabbard to the saddle on Charlie. I had Fannie get on him and fixed the stirrup lengths for her. She wasn't sure about riding the mule. He stood really tall and she knew no one had ever ridden him but me. I assured her that once she rode him she would never want to ride a horse again.

After we ate we left camp and rode down the hillside. We rode for about an hour when we hit the thick timber. The trees grew so close together we couldn't get those big wagons through. I remembered, Bart had said we would have to swing out about a mile from the water. We side-hilled to the right. After a couple of hours the timber started to thin out. We found an open space with no trees. We followed down a long ways before we hit more timber, but not too thick.

I said, "I think we can cut some trees and get through this way. Let's keep going and see what we find on below."

Fannie and Charlie were becoming fast friends. Charlie liked her because she didn't weigh as much as I did. She liked him because he had a nice soft gate, not rough or choppy like a horse. When we got toward the bottom of the downgrade the land leveled out. We discussed our options and decided what we needed to do was leave camp where it was and bring a team of horses down here. We would fall some trees, cut them up and pull them out of the way. With not too much work we will be able to get the wagons down into the valley. We rested for a while and started to work our way back up the slope. As we climbed the hill seemed steeper than when we were going down. I stopped, turned the stallion sideways and looked back down where we had been. The slope was a lot steeper than I had thought. I started up again and passed Fannie. She had turned Charlie sideways on the hill.

She asked, "How are we going to keep the wagons from running away on this hill. I don't think we can hold them with the braking blocks. If the wagons push too hard the horses can't hold them."

I stopped and looked again and she was right. We had a lot of horsepower when going forward, but when the wagons began to roll on their own, only two horses to hold them back. The other teams had only chains between them and the wagon tongue. We had to figure some other way. Even if we both held on to the brake we wouldn't have enough power to hold that much weight.

"I think you're right. We can't go down that steep of a hill. I guess we do some more looking. Let's ride towards the stream and check things out."

We rode a couple more hours to get over to the stream. We worked back up towards camp and the timber got thicker all of the way to the top. We unsaddled and took care of the horses.

While we cooked our supper Fannie asked, "So, what do you think? Should we follow the trail down or do we search farther along the north ridge?"

"I don't know. Bart said we would not be able to ford the stream down in the flat country. It's too deep and the bottom is muddy. If he couldn't cross with his mule, we can't get these big wagons across."

"Which way do we ride in the morning?" Fannie asked. "If we go south we don't know what we'll find. If we go north we also don't know what we will get into."

"We have to do something. I don't want to leave the stuff parked out here in the open, free for the taking by someone coming on up the trail."

Fannie assured me, "Well, I'm not going to stay here by myself while you ride all over the country for days trying to find a trail into your basin. I say we ride north in the morning, take a mule with some camping stuff and see what we can find. Surely no one is within a couple of days behind us on the trail or we'd have seen their campfires at night, don't you think?"

"I guess so, but all that gold is in those wagons. I sure would hate to lose the load, wouldn't you?" I asked.

"Of course I would. But, stop and think where the gold is. Do you know how long someone would have to search to find anything buried in the middle of the load?" Fannie said with force.

"I guess you're right. I'll go out and try to catch a mule out of the loose ones. I might be able to coax Molly to me. They've been following free for weeks. They may be a little spooky. I know we saved four of those packsaddles. Fannie, do you want to get one out of the top of the short wagon on your string while I go try to catch any one of the mules?"

I walked where they grazed and talked to them. To my surprise, most of them came to me, and some of them walked right up to get petted and wanted to be caught. Molly hung back. I didn't want to start them moving around and getting stirred up, so I put a rope around a big black mule's neck, lead him to the wagon and tied him next to Charlie. He seemed happy to get the attention. He even nuzzled me while I was brushing him off. He wanted a friend, I guess.

Fannie called from the wagon and asked me to help her get the packsaddle out from under some boxes. They had shifted over on top of the breeching and she couldn't pull one out.

After we ate and made our packs for the next day, I put the saddle on the stallion and rode up to the top of the pass. I could see for miles down the back trail. No fires burned anywhere. I rode a short distance along the ridge and, as I went through a small clearing, some old wagon tracks followed along the top of the ridge. I rode north about a mile and picked up the tracks in a couple of different places, mostly in small clearings. The ground was covered with small rock and made tracking difficult.

We got up early and moved out shortly after sunup. We rode north along the ridge. I pointed out what I found the night before. If we followed those tracks, we would need to cut a trail through the trees that had grown up after the wagon went through. We rode the ridge and found the trail every once in awhile. The trail came to a saddle and, instead of going up the other side; someone had cut a trail off to the left, and came out on an open ridge and went down toward the valley.

We could see forever to the west. The trail followed the open ridge a long way down. Today we studied the trail a whole lot different than yesterday. Every once in a while, one or the other would say something like, "That big rock will be a problem," or "May have a little trouble down that loose rock." But, when we got down a mile or so, the ridge flattened out and we found ourselves on an almost level bench. We stopped by a spring and ate our lunch. Now we wondered if we would find someone in the valley and all of this would be for nothing. I turned back toward the river to the south. I couldn't find any trail in the tall grass. We rode the rest of the day, going southwest.

Somewhere down below, a small river ran through a sunken valley. We crossed the head of some small draws. I decided to ride out on one of the ridges. I rode for about half an hour when, suddenly below me, the great expanse of the valley came into view through some trees tops. We had been riding along the top of the bowl for a long time.

Fannie excitedly asked, "Well, what do you think? Can we get down to the valley floor?"

"Yes. I think so. I've been riding along thinking how we can slow the wagons down on the steeper grades. No trees grow on the steepest part of the hill. I think, since we have lots of horses, we can cut some trees and drag them over to the top and chain them on behind the wagons. That will slow the wagons down. All we have to do is get enough of them digging into the dirt so the lead teams can keep the tugs tight. It might take more than one good-sized tree, but there is a whole hillside full of them between the camp and the top up there. If we can get down on this flat, then surely we can make it down to the valley floor. Does that sound like it will work to you?"

"Maybe, but we have some food and camping stuff. Let's stay the night and try to find a way down to the next level and make sure another wagon isn't already there waiting for us." Fannie suggested.

"Hey, what's the black mule staring at? He sees something out in the valley. His ears are picked up and he is standing stiff as can be. Do you see anything?" I asked.

We sat and watched for ten minutes or more. At the same time, we both pointed and said, "Animals are out there."

"Can you make out what they are?"

Fannie shook her head no. Then the mule dropped his head and went to eating. I shrugged, turned and rode back along the rim of the basin. We needed to find a campsite, so we looked down in some of the draws for a spring or water. I wanted a small flat where we could at least have a place to put the bedrolls. After an hour, and just before the sun went down, we found a spring, in a small meadow that was really nice. We didn't find much for firewood, but after walking out away from the spring, we found a couple of dead bushes that worked. We made a small fire, heated the sandwiches, and then shook out our bedrolls and crawled in

We had been lying, enjoying the fire, and visiting about the trail down, when the wild dogs howled. First they were close and then way off in the distance to the west, then to the north, and the south. It sounded like they were talking about those strange things on the ridge above the valley. I went to sleep listening to them.

When I awoke, Fannie was up and had the fire going. She was watching something off to her right.

I said, as I sat up, "You're up early."

She put her fingers to her lips and motioned for me to be still. I rolled over on my stomach and, at the same time, I picked up the rifle lying by my side.

I whispered, "What is it?"

She pointed slowly toward some timber at the bottom of the slope we went down yesterday. A bunch of the big deer was feeding along quietly, with the horses. As we watched, a big male walked out of the timber. He had a huge set of horns. They spread out wider and longer than his body. I couldn't believe it. He was twice as big as the does with him. I counted, and there were twenty-five head.

Fannie whispered. "They're beautiful. That male is magnificent, isn't he?"

We sat watching them. They turned and walked over to the side of the flat. They walked over the rim, down on the hillside, then out on the basin floor.

We fixed breakfast, saddled up, and went over where the animals had disappeared. I thought maybe we could follow them down, but it was too brushy, so we rode north along the lip of the valley for a couple of hours.

The ground was smooth enough here to bring the wagons along without any problem. The valley walls became more of a gentle slope. We found a nice open ridge that went completely to the valley floor. A fair sized stream was running down on this side of the valley. Willows grew along the side, marking where it ran.

I said to Fannie, "I don't think we need to go any further, do you? I think we can get the wagons down in the valley without too much work. Let's go get started. I'm eager to see what the valley has to offer, and take a hot bath."

The sun was setting way off in the west when we got back to the wagons.

"It looks like we found the valley just in time. I think winter is not too far off. The days are getting shorter. Hope it doesn't get much snow in this area. I've never lived where there was a lot of snow. On top of that, we're not very well prepared for snow and cold yet. Have you ever lived where they had both?" I asked.

"Yes. It did get very cold. We had a lot of snow at times in Pennsylvania. It can be very beautiful when the trees are all white. It can also be really uncomfortable when you're trying to work outside. Sometimes your hands get so cold your fingers feel like they are going to fall off." She giggled, "And your nose, too, like when you wake up here in the morning."

CHAPTER 17

When we awoke the next morning, frost covered everything. The air was clear and cold. I soon hunted up my coat and a pair of gloves we had found in the wagons. I got the axe and bucksaw out of a wagon while Fannie fixed some hot cereal for breakfast. We didn't have milk so we had learned to eat our cereal with brown sugar. That's not my favorite, but tasted good and gave us lots of strength.

After we finished breakfast, Fannie asked, "How are we going to do this today? What do you want me to do?"

"I'll chop down the small trees and you can come along behind and drag them off to the side. Anything we can't get that way we'll drag with a team of horses. I think we can move most of the stuff along the ridge by hand. Be sure to put on those heavy boots and some of the gloves from the wagon."

I began to cut the smaller trees and we soon had a system worked out. I fell the big, tall trees so the tops went out of the trail. Then I cut them into smaller pieces that were easier to turn around, so the wagon would straddle them. We thought we had worked a long time, but the sun had not reached the noon position.

Fannie asked, "How long did you say we would have to work to get the top of the ridge clear?"

"Well, at this rate, a lot longer than I thought. We may get through in a couple more days. Just think about that hot bath waiting down in the valley." I replied.

"If I do this for two more days, I won't be able to walk down the hill, let alone take a bath." She said with a smile.

It didn't take us two more days. It took five. By that time, we were completely worn out. However, the work seemed to be getting easier. The open area was getting closer, but some of the bigger trees, by the open area, had lots of limbs." How are we going to cut them down?" Fannie asked, as she pointed to the big ones.

"We'll saw them down. Those are going to be our drag trees."

"You've got to be teasing. The horses can't pull them plus the wagons."

"Remember, we have lots of horses. I would rather have them pulling all of the way down than trying to outrun the wagons."

When we got back to the wagons, late in the afternoon, I climbed into the short wagon of mine and got out a long crosscut saw, I found in the Clements' wagon. The saw would be useful now and probably later, also. I took the bucksaw and went down the hill a ways and found a dead, down log. I cut a short piece, about a foot long, out of the center and took it back to camp. I split the wood in half and split a couple of pieces about three inches thick. From these I cut tapered pieces and made two wedges. I would use these to fall the trees with, like Bart had shown me.

Early the next morning, I brought the stock into camp and harnessed the big gray teams of Fannie's. I saddled Charlie and the stallion. We ate breakfast and reloaded the wagons. Morning was half gone by the time we moved out with Fannie's wagons. I hooked only three teams to the wagons instead of the five.

Fannie wanted to know, "Just the three teams? Why? I don't think they can pull that much."

I answered, "Working three teams between the stumps and the brush along the ridge will be hard enough. The longer the span of teams, the harder it will be to make the turns. You drive and I'll walk in front and help turn the leaders the way they need to go."

I tied the saddle stock on the back of the trailer and we eased the wagons out and onto the trail. Those big horses walked along like nothing was behind them. They weren't bothered when the wagon wheels went over the small stumps and jerked the tongue back and forth. As we traveled down the ridge, we had to stop once in a while to remove a small tree or brush to make the trail wide enough for the wagon wheels to fit between the tree stumps. The teams moved slow and didn't get excited or worried about the many turns and stops. I thought to myself, we will use the same horses on the next trip. These horses are jewels.

When we got close enough to the big trees, we stopped and tied the leaders to a tree. I took the saw and axe over to the first tree that needed fell. Fannie jumped down and came over and said, "I want to watch this. No way you're going to cut that huge tree with a saw."

I smiled and said, "You're right. I'm not going to cut the tree by myself. But you and I are going to cut that tree down."

I explained what we had to do, and how to use the saw. We worked for a couple of hours, sawing and chopping, before the tree was ready to go. I told Fannie to go back and talk to the teams and hold the leaders reins so they didn't get frightened. When she said she was ready, I cut a little more with the saw and chopped some more. Then I took the other axe and drove the wedges in the back crack of the tree. A couple of hits and the tree went down with a crash. The horses snorted and stepped around a little, but calmed right down.

I went around the wagon teams and walked the extra two teams past the standing team. I hooked them up and fastened a chain around the top of the tree. I took the lines and asked the horses to pull the tree out. It was a hard pull, but they turned the top uphill and pulled the tree so it was lying on the flat top of the ridge. That put the butt of the tree pointed downhill. I decided not to cut the limbs off, but let them work as a brake.

I led the wagon team past the tree so we could back the wagons up, which took some doing. We finally got the tree and the wagons t in a straight line and headed down the hill. We chained the tree to the framework of the back wagon. I unhooked the lead team and that left four horses to pull the load.

I couldn't tie the saddle horses on the back or the sides of the wagon because, if the wagon got away from us, they would get hurt or killed. Finally, we talked the situation over and decided I would drive the team. Fannie would ride Charlie and lead the stallion and come down behind me. We would leave the extra teams tied at the top. If we needed them we would ride up and get them.

Now, with my heart in my throat, and a fear in my knees, I spoke to the teams. They started to pull the log over the hill. They had to really pull to move the log. But suddenly the tree slid over the brink and we started down. No stopping now. Here we go, for good or bad. I had guessed right. The four horses had to pull a small amount but they had no trouble pulling the load. The trouble was trying to keep the wagons going straight down. We had a scary time or two when the tree started to roll sideways, but I would turn the team a little to correct the problem.

The horses sunk almost to their knees on the soft hillside. The wagon wheels also sunk in leaving deep ruts. The tree dug into the soft ground and plowed a furrow about a foot deep. Without stopping for a rest, we covered the half mile or more to the bottom in a short time.

When we hit the bottom, the team buckled down and started out on the flat. They didn't go far until I had to stop them. The load was just too heavy. Fannie wasn't far behind. By the time I stopped the team and started to unhook the chains from the tree, she came to help. I decided to see if I could drive the wagon over to the next drop off.

I had gone just far enough to get the wagon out of the way for the next one to come down, when I realized the four horses could pull the load but I didn't want to hurt the team's shoulders so I stopped.

I would unhook the teams leave the wagon, and then with the four horses, pull the log over to the next place. The flat was almost a mile across. When I got the log in place, I stopped the team out on the flat, all lined up with the hill.

We still had time to take the teams back up the hill and to camp before dark. By the time we climbed the hill and gathered up the other teams we had scattered around, it was almost dark.

We both pitched in and prepared a big supper. We hadn't had anything to eat since before daylight. I felt a chill in the air and knew everything would be frosty in the morning. The full moon and the stars shone in the clear night sky. We sat by the fire and talked about the wagon trail and the old tracks running down the ridge.

"I wonder where the wagon had gone. I didn't find any sign down on the shelf this afternoon. Maybe the black mule was watching some cattle or horses. If so, someone beat us to the valley and we will have to share it," I thought out loud.

"Well, from what I saw from the flat, the land is big enough for a lot of families to live on. It looks awful big to me. What would one family do with that much land?" Fannie replied.

"I want lots of land for cattle and horse pasture. After spending the winter with Bart and hearing his stories about the big cattle ranches out here, I dreamed about coming west and having a cattle ranch. A lot of range is needed to support a large herd of cattle. I understand out here they don't feed hay or grain to the cows like we did back home in Virginia. I bet your granddad fed hay and grain to the cows he milked. I know my dad did. He fed most of the summer and all winter. He said you had to give the milk cow grain for her to give you milk. Bart told about herds of cattle in Texas that numbered in the thousands. That would be something to behold."

Fannie sat on a block of wood, leaning close to the fire. She straightened up, looked around and asked, "Have you been hearing anything moving, other than the horses?"

"No, what do you think you're hearing?"

"Something else is moving. I hear the horses over in the meadow, but this is moving around out in the brush. A twig snaps once in a while. It's walking, and then stopping, like an animal feeding." Fannie said.

"I don't hear anything, but I'm tired. We have a big day again tomorrow. Just in case, when I go to bed, I'm going to put the rifle next to me so I can get it out fast. You better do the same. However, the horses don't seem to be bothered. Some deer may be feeding in the timber."

I banked the fire with a big dead stump, hoping for a good bed of coals in the morning. The fire burned very bright for a couple of hours. I lay looking at the stars. I wondered who could be with the other wagon. I drifted off to sleep. I have no idea of the time, but some time close to daylight I sat up so fast I hit my head on the wagon seat. I woke up to the most awful sound I had ever heard. The hair on the back of my neck stood up and, I will assure you, I was awake. Every muscle and nerve in my body tingled.

I lay back down and listened. Had I been dreaming? A short time later, the noise came again. It started out with a huge horse bawl and whistle, then a couple of horse deep grunts, then a sound like something taking in a deep breath, and a whistle grunt combined. I had the rifle ready and looked out of the wagon trying to see what in the world type of demon made a noise like that. I saw a movement over by Fannie's wagon. The next thing I knew, she was in my wagon and under the seat by me.

She cried, "What can that be? Did you ever hear anything so scary before? Sounds like a bull, bawling, along with all the grunts, and other sounds".

She was shaking like she was cold. I covered her up, crawled out, and slipped my clothes on. I stirred up the fire and added some more wood.

Dawn started to break in the east. I went out into the meadow to find where the horses had gone because of all of the noise. They stood in little bunches, around the meadow. They didn't seem to be frightened at all. I gathered the ones I wanted to use and took them to camp. As I entered the camping area, Fannie stuck her head out of the wagon and asked if I was still alive.

She asked, "Have you figured out what caused the awful noise?"

"No, but the horses aren't scared. You better come out. Let's get going. It will be full day before we get the wagons ready to go now. With any luck we may be able to get both wagons on down into the valley today. Come on now!" I scolded.

We had the horses hooked to the wagons, and had eaten some cold jerky for breakfast. Then we loaded everything. By the time we finished, full daylight had come. We had the same teams hooked that we used the day before. They seemed to know what we wanted. They started right out, following the trail along the ridge. Things went a lot faster this time. We had cleared all of the small trees the day before. We made good time and reached the other big tree we needed to fall, a lot earlier. The saw and axe stood by the tree, so I went down and started to work.

Fannie came down in a bit. She had learned to use the saw the day before, so we made good time getting the tree on the ground. However, the tree did not fall quite where we wanted. I took the axe and cut the top back some, then drove the four-horse team over to the top. I hooked them up and started pulling. We only made a few feet and they stopped. They couldn't drag it uphill. The tree had fallen down on the side of the hill a little too far. I studied, trying to figure out how to turn the dumb tree uphill and pull it to the top of the ridge. I finally harnessed another four horses, brought them down and hooked them in front of my team.

There wasn't any way I could drive them when I was on the ground. I tied all of the reins up to the harness hames and just held the leaders' lines. I talked to them in a loud voice and asked them to pull. They all hit the traces at about the same time. That big tree seemed to fly up the hill. I had a hard time keeping out of the way.

We hooked up the same as the day before, but I had everything off to the side of yesterday's trail. I jumped on the wagon and started down the hill. In no time at all, I hit the flat. Now we had two deep trails down the hill.

Again we unhooked the drag. But this time, when I went to the other tree, we backed up to the one from yesterday. I let the team rest for a spell and rode the stallion down to check the trail I would have to go with the wagon. It was not as steep and there were no big rocks that I could see.

By late afternoon we had both wagons on the valley floor. We found a place to camp until we could ride and find the warm creek. By the time we had camp set up the loose horses had all come to the bottom and trotted out into the deep grass. We found no water close. We hobbled most of the workhorses so they wouldn't stray off in the night.

The next morning, we saddled and got ready to go explore the valley and try to find the canyon with the hot springs. Suddenly, we heard the whistle, grunting sounds of last night. These sounds came from up on the hillside. I turned and tried to find what on earth made the noise. One of the big buck deer walked out into an opening. He turned my way and pointed his nose in the air. The sound of his bugling floated down to us. He walked over and shredded a small tree with his horns. I mean he really beat that tree up. Now we knew no monster existed on the hill and we relaxed.

We rode north from the wagons, along the foot of the slope, searching for the warm stream. It would be flowing into the stream out in the middle of the valley. We rode way past noon and decided we had gone the wrong way. This is a large valley. A lot larger than it appeared from the top of the rim. There were deer and the small animals that ran so fast. A wild dog showed no fear of us. He just trotted along hunting mice. He was bigger than a fox and a gray color, with a sharp pointed nose.

When we returned to camp, about dark, a herd of the big deer grazed out on the floor of the valley. The male herded the does out away from the hillside. Fannie stayed in camp and I went looking for water for the horses. I rode west, out into the valley a couple miles and south as far, but found nothing. After returning to camp, I took the hobbles off of the horses and let them go, knowing they would find water. The stallion and Charlie would have to spend another dry night, but they had gone a couple of days without water before.

The next morning we rode south and noticed the horses were gone. We searched for their tracks. They had drifted south about three miles during the night. A cool stream came from the side, out of what looked like a small canyon. We followed it and when we got closer to the hillside, it was apparent that the stream came from around a point of land. We rounded the point and another small valley lay at an angle to the larger valley. The opening of this small valley was at least two miles wide. It seemed like it ran a long way back into the mountain.

I turned to Fannie and said, "I think we found our side-canyon. Let's ride over to the other side and see if we find another steam."

When we got close to the other side of the small valley, sure enough, we found the other stream. Fannie jumped off, walked over, reached down, and felt the water.

"I don't believe this. The water is warm to the touch. Not hot, but warm. Not hot enough to take a bath in, but will be really warm someplace up the canyon."

"So, we have found our warm water. Now what? Do we ride on up the canyon or go back and get the wagons and bring them down here and make a camp?" I asked.

"Well, I didn't see the horses. Did you say they went someplace else for water? I think, we better find them first and decide what we want to do." Fannie said.

We turned and followed the stream out into the valley floor for about an hour. The stream was swinging northwest, toward the center of the valley. We found the horses grazing close to the stream. When we rode around and started back we could tell we were almost straight out from the marks the wagons left on the hillside. It didn't look too far out, but we rode about three hours to get back to camp. Tracks of a lot of different animals showed along the stream. Some of them looked like cattle tracks. I couldn't tell if they were cows or the big deer tracks. I thought I had seen some horse tracks out away from the creek, but since our stock had been all over, it might have been some of theirs.

We decided to wait until morning. We would move down to the mouth of the canyon and up it a ways. I had no doubt this was the right place. If not, it would be a great place to make a permanent camp for the winter, with lots of water, and grass aplenty. I had seen a couple of dead trees, on the hill, for firewood.

We moved camp the next day. We swung up along the north wall of the valley. Early in the afternoon, the valley suddenly became narrow and the streams were about a half mile or less apart. I called for a stop and parked the wagons.

I asked Fannie, "Do you want to ride ahead and see what we have."

"Okay. I'll take a look. Don't unhook the teams for a while. I'll be back as soon as I find the end of the valley or the cave."

She was gone until after dark. I had taken care of the stock and had a fire going when she rode into camp. I helped her down.

"Well, what did you find?" I wanted to know.

"This valley goes through a narrow place, but it stays about the same width as it is here. About a mile further on it widens out again and makes another small valley. Suddenly it comes to an end against a very straight up and down circle of cliffs. The hillsides are too steep for anything to climb out or get down."

"What about the cave?" I asked.

"Yes, I found two of them, about a hundred feet or more apart. This stream comes out of the middle of the north cave. The other cave is where the hot water comes from. It doesn't come out through the cave like this stream, but comes from a hole in the rock, about as high as I can reach. The water falls out and makes a pool about the size of the big wagon and maybe twice as long., and is really hot. I put my hand in the pool. You couldn't take a bath in that stuff or you would be scalded. I think we better cross the stream down here some place. The streambed in the upper part is really soft with no rocky bottom. We better go check in the morning, before we hook up and try to move into the upper part of the canyon. We can turn the wagons at the end of the canyon between the streams." She informed me.

"Is the hot water coming out on the right side of the cave or on the left side?"

She answered, "The right."

"So is the cave between the two streams?" I asked.

"Yes," She said.

We took our time the next morning. Then we saddled up and rode to the caves and looked around. She was right about crossing before we took the wagons into the canyon.

CHAPTER 18

"Let's get down and investigate the cave."

The entryway was about eight feet wide and ten or more feet high. The cave opened up into a room about twenty by forty feet, more or less. The back of the cave was dark so we couldn't see very well. I didn't find any animal sign. I didn't think a bear or anything else claimed the place as home this fall.

"What do you think?" I asked.

"We will be warm, but dark a lot of the time. Where are we going to cook? If we build a fire in here the smoke will fill the cave. I don't see any holes in the top for smoke to get out," Fannie answered.

"We might have to build the fire pit outside of the door and use the cave for sleeping. I think that would work." I said. "Anyway, we better get the wagons up here and unloaded as soon as possible."

We went down the creek and took turns walking the horses across the streambed. We didn't find any firm bottom until a couple of miles below the wagons. We found a narrow gravel bar, about three or four times the width of the wagon.

"This may be the only place hard enough to hold the wagons. We'll have to drive straight on so we don't slide off into the soft dirt." I commented.

We had plenty of room to get the string of horses and the wagons in a straight line before entering the water.

The next day we decided to take one pair of wagons at a time all the way to the cave. I turned my wagon around. As I approached the crossing, I swung the team wide and hit the water straight on. The team went across okay, but as the narrow wheels of the wagon got about to the streambed, they started to sink. I stood up and let out a yell for the leaders to go. The main wagon went across, but the trailer wagon sank to the axels.

Now what should we do? Should I go get the other team, or unhook the trailer and take the big wagon to the cave and come back for the short wagon? I was afraid if I hooked all of the horses to the wagons I would break an axel or something. We had come all this way without a breakdown. We unhooked the wagon from the trailer. The day was nearly gone before we got the second wagon out of the mud.

Now, what about Fannie's wagon? We had hers loaded heavier than mine. With the bottom of the stream all torn up it will be impossible to get her wagon across.

The next day I rode along the creek, out about three miles into the valley, before I found a place with a firm bottom. I rode back and forth across the stream a couple of times to make sure the bottom would be solid enough to hold.

We took Fannie's wagon down to the crossing. When we had the wagons ready to go I asked, "Do you want me to drive across or do you think you can?"

Well, of course she would drive her team. They knew her voice and wouldn't quit half way. I also knew her voice and she wasn't going to back down. I waved her ahead and she put the leaders into the crossing very quietly. When the wheels got about to the water she stood up and, at the top of her lungs, yelled at the team.

They were so surprised; they had the wagon on the other bank with the first lunge. They got right down on their knees and literally drug the trailer wagon through the mud up onto dry ground. Of course, her horses were bigger than my team and had worked together most of their life. The big gray team was quiet, but just a bundle of power. The young team really liked to work, and she knew how to drive them. They loved her and would walk up to her out in the pasture to get petted.

Late in the afternoon we dug around in my wagon and found the lantern for light. We went inside to explore the cave. We stood in the room trying to find any sign of an opening in the roof.

Fannie walked to the back of the cave and said, "Well, look what I found. Here is another entrance. Bring your light."

I walked over and let the light shine down a walkway, at least four feet wide and seven feet long, going back into the mountain. The wall completely blocked the opening from the room until you stepped to the end. I got to the end of the walkway, turned the corner, and another large room appeared, about thirty feet wide and at least that long. The ceiling was about twenty feet high. The walls and ceiling were solid rock. This room showed no sign of ever having large animals or water leaks. We searched for cracks that might let smoke out, but the ceiling appeared to be solid.

No fire rings showed in this room. We walked back into the first room. I could not see any opening for the smoke to escape. The fire rings scattered about the floor showed signs of being really old rings, and some Bart may have made.

"I'm going to try something," I said. I went out and gathered some firewood.

Fannie said, "You're not going to start a fire, I hope. It will take all night for the air to clear.

"Maybe not, I have a feeling, with all of the signs of fire rings in here; the smoke must escape some place."

The fire started easy with the dry wood pieces on the floor. I put a couple of bigger pieces on. The smoke built up, went to the ceiling, and disappeared. I couldn't tell how the smoke got out. I went outside and looked all around, but no smoke. Evidently the smoke seeped through small cracks to keep the cave clear. In a few minutes the small fire heated the interior of the cave. We had to figure out a way to close the front entrance and we would have a warm house for the winter.

Fannie unloaded the camping utensils and cooked supper. I went outside and took care of the horses. I walked around and planned how to fence all of the upper part of the canyon to keep some of the horses in so they would be ready to use when we needed them. I wasn't afraid of Charlie leaving, but any of the rest of the saddle horses would stray off with the bunch. They might be hard to catch out in the big area of the valley. I picketed the stallion and turned the rest loose. I would also need to keep at least one of the teams close by to get firewood. I went to the wagons, got the bedrolls and took them into the cave.

Fannie asked me to get a bucket of hot water to wash in. I had not been over to the hot spring yet. I walked over and dipped the bucket full of hot water and returned to the cave. I thought this would be all right. We had a plentiful supply of hot water. Now we had to figure out how to fix a place to cool the water enough for us to bathe and still keep it private, so we could enjoy the bath.

We unloaded the wagons the next day. We put all of the food storage and the extra saddles, harnesses, guns, and shells in the back room. We used a lot of the boxes with the gold in them, to stack other things on. We finished unloading the wagons. I took a screwdriver out of the tool chest and went out to my wagon. I began to take the extra floor out. The job took a long time, but I wanted to find what was underneath before things got wet. We took the lantern out so we could work into the night. We got the floorboards loose, and Fannie pulled out bundles of money and carried them to the cave. She stacked them on her bedroll.

About an hour later, I had the floorboards out of the wagon. I stacked them up inside of the cave to keep them dry. After we ate, we sat down and counted the packages. We had eight hundred and sixteen packages, with ten one hundred dollar bills to the packet.

We wondered why the men carried so much money. They were not soldiers. When we went through the clothes nothing said US Army. No markings showed on the gold bars in the other boxes. We sat and talked and felt sure both the gold and the money had been stolen. But stolen from where? We knew the mule train came from Mexico, but where was it headed? The two wagons were headed out west some place. One of the wagons had all of the Yankee money plus the case of new guns and all of the cartons of shells. There also had been a lot of gunpowder. We had dumped it on the ground and mixed it with dirt so Indians wouldn't get to use it.

While going through the packages Fannie said, "Look! What's the package on the floor? I must have dropped it."

I walked over and picked up a large sealed envelope. I opened it and found some legal looking papers. I took them over to Fannie and we sat down on her bed. We removed the papers and started to read them.

The first letter, on the top of the pile, was from Brigadier General Rudolph Scott ordering Sergeant Wolf to take five men and go to the Mexican boarder town of Juillo to receive a shipment of gold for the Confederate Army. He must return to Richmond immediately upon receiving the shipment. The mystery of the gold is solved.

What about the bundles of money? They are Yankee dollars, and a large shipment to someone. We may never know where they came from.

First we had to find out about the valley. Did we have neighbors or not? We took about a week to get things put away and some firewood cut and stacked inside. We took the canvases off of the wagons and tried to use them to close the open entrance to the cave. I came to the conclusion we would, need to build a frame to fit in the entrance. Then we could fit the canvas to it. Meanwhile, the weather stayed warm during the day and cool in the evenings in the canyon. During the day, while we worked, we heard a lot of whistling from the big deer. They seemed to be all around.

Once we thought we had enough wood and things fixed, we decided to ride to the other end of the valley. Then we would come back and scout out the rest of the valley floor. One morning, I rode out and found the horses and mules. They hadn't drifted too far away. They had a lot of grass and water close by.

I wanted to catch Molly to use as a pack animal, but she would have nothing to do with me. But every time I turned around, the big black mule came tagging along. I finally stopped and dismounted. He flapped his ears, walked up and nuzzled me. I put the halter on him, mounted the stallion and started for home. He wanted to go wherever I went. About half of the way home I threw the halter rope over his back. He just trotted along.

The next morning we loaded the mule and started north along the base of the hill. About noon we reached the drag marks coming down the hill. We rode on and noticed a small draw coming to intersect our path. It looked like an old wagon trail was going up the draw.

"What do you think? Should we check into this?" I asked Fannie.

She nodded her head and answered, "Yes, that might be the place where the wagon tracks end."

We rode up the draw a ways. Suddenly, as we came around a bend in the trail, a cabin sat in a clearing. We stopped and looked the place over and rode up to the door. I hollered, "Is anyone home."

Fannie said, "There are no horses or even new tracks around. Go inside and see if it's abandoned or what."

I walked to the door, pulled my pistol, and opened the door. The owner was in there alright. But he wasn't going anywhere. He had been dead for a long time, maybe since last fall or longer. I walked outside and told Fannie. We had found where the wagon had gone.

She got down, and peeked in and said, "I think we need to give him a burial."

I walked around hunting for a shovel and found one in a lean-to on the end of the house. I also found a set of harness and an old saddle hung on the wall. A light wagon, parked in back of the house, was covered with a canvas top. I went to find a place to dig a grave. I found where someone else had dug a grave, so I dug a shallow grave there and went to get the remains. Fannie had already rolled him in a blanket. I picked him up. The body had completely dried out and consisted of bones inside of clothes.

I went inside and found that Fannie had brought the bedrolls in. She swept the floor while she heated water for soup. We spent the evening going through the personal things trying to find a name or any way to identify the dead man. We found nothing.

I pointed to the cabin wall and asked Fannie, "Do you see what I do about the cabin?"

She said, "No. What am I missing?"

"The cabin is made out of lumber. I wonder where he got the boards. He must have hauled them in from somewhere. The light wagon wouldn't have hauled this much unless he made three or more trips. We will have to find where the boards came from before we head back home tomorrow."

In the morning, before we left, I checked outside but found no horses. The only tracks in the small corral were old or either made by cows or those big deer, where they had come to the block of salt that was almost gone. I pointed to the salt block. "A store must not be too far away. Let's ride north again and see what we can find".

We had not gone far until we picked up a wagon trail going north. We followed the trail until almost dark. We hunted for a camping spot. The trail had been climbing slowly through scattered trees and grassland. We found a spring off of the road, and made camp for the night. The next day after we had been riding for three or four hours, we broke over the top of a ridge. Below us was a town, setting in a fair-sized draw. A big river flowed down the draw beside something like a road.

I pointed to the town and said, "This must be where he got the lumber."

We sat for a few minutes and I asked, "Do you want to go down?"

She shook her head no, turned Charlie, and started toward home. When we got close to the valley I drifted off to the side so we would come into the valley way out in the center, I hoped. It wasn't long until we picked up a small stream and followed it. We followed the stream for two days. The black mule stopped and gazed off towards home. He stood for a few minutes, and put his nose to the ground.

I hadn't been paying any attention to tracks, but now I looked carefully. Cow tracks covered the area along the stream. In a short distance we found a pile of cow manure. I paid more attention and finally I saw, out to our left, a small group of cattle. We turned and rode over to them. Some of them ran as soon as we came close, but about a dozen seemed different. They didn't have the huge horns the wild ones did. Most of them had no horns at all and were a solid red color. One had a big bag and was a light brown. She looked very fat but her hip bones stuck out.

Fannie said, "Oh look, a Jersey milk cow. She must belong to the dead man. I think she's going to have a calf soon. How far do you think we are from home?"

"If we start going towards the mountains it's probably a long day's ride, why?"

She smiled and said, "I sure would like some cream on my hot cereal in the morning, wouldn't you?"

"We will need to go slow. We can rope and lead her but she would probably walk a lot faster if we chased her."

I tried to cut her out from the other cows, but she didn't want to do that. I motioned for Fannie to get on one side of the red cows and I would take the other side and we would take them all home. That suited the little cow and she took off walking where we wanted her to go.

A couple of hours later we found more cows. Again the ones with long curved horns took off running. The other ones, some with short horns and some without horns, ran just a little ways. When I rode around, them they walked over to the first bunch and followed them. We were surprised. This bunch had about twenty cows. So all together we had thirty head of cows, and a milk cow that was heavy with a calf. We would have milk to drink. Boy, what a find.

We took two full days to get home, but we had no reason to hurry. We found out another thing. Charlie was not a cow horse. He hated to chase them. On the other hand, the stallion liked to work the cows. He would put his head down, lay his ears back and walk after a cow and make her trot to keep up. I learned also, if one of the red cows turned and went running away from the herd, he took after it without even being told. But when that cow turned back into the bunch, so did he, at a full gallop. He just about left me sitting on the ground the first couple of times.

When we rode into the canyon most of the horses had come in and scattered around the big meadow. We went through the neck of the canyon and saw the wagons and the cave. I stopped and looked real close to make sure no one had moved in. We had been gone for a week and everything looked good. We rode on in, leaving the cows closer in than the horses. This felt like home.

The next two days I spent riding after the cows. They wanted to go back out on the flat. I decided I needed to build a fence across the narrow neck in the canyon to hold them here. But what would I build it out of?

The next day I told Fannie I was going to ride south and try to find something to use to build fences. I rode out early and followed the toe of the hill while looking up at the timber. Suddenly I knew the answer the long, tall trees were about six to eight inches on the bottom and seventy or so feet tall. I would fall them down the hill and drag them back where I needed them.

The next day I worked getting things ready to start cutting in the morning. I caught up two of my teams and had them ready to go early. I had to get the saw, the axes, and the log chains to the trees. I caught the black mule and another brown one, put the packsaddles on them and tied everything on. It was funny when I left home that morning. The mules were not happy about having so much stuff just hanging on them. A little way out, the brown mule decided he had had enough and went to bucking. The harder he bucked the harder the log chains rattled and bounced and slapped him in the legs and on the shoulders. He soon realized the error of the bucking thing so he went along fine the rest of the way.

During the day I fell about twenty trees with the bucksaw. As I walked down the hill I cut the tops off of them. I tried to skid some down with the team, but that didn't work very well, so I tied one of the horses up and skidded the rest of the day with one horse. I worked until late and then took the horses and rode home. I was dog tired and half starved. I took care of the stock and went to the cave. When I went through the door, I was greeted with a funny sight.

There, on her stool, sat Fannie. At her feet laid this little brown calf. Both of them were sound asleep, so I started to eat the food she had fixed. Fannie woke up and began to chew on me about being gone all of those hours. She had been worried about me. The cow had calved without me being home. Why didn't I come earlier? Mostly, all in one breath, so fast I had no chance to explain. She acted so mad, I laughed, which upset her more, I guess. So she started on me again.

I finally got her to listen and told her what I tried to do. Later, at bed time, she let me know if I planned to work in the trees; I should go one or two days and fall them. Then take the team down the next day. She would go along to help me skid them home. We could take two teams and bring a bunch back.

It was a good plan, but what about the milk cow? She needs to be milked or her bag well get huge and hard and she won't be good as a milk cow.

No, I have to figure out something else. The next day I took two teams down with me. I used one of the grays to skid the trees down on the flat and into a pile. That took almost a half a day. I tied the pile all together and hooked up the horses and started home. They worked hard to move the big load. They were sweating really hard by the time I traveled for an hour.

I stopped and rested the team. This is going to take a couple of days to make a drag. That meant at least three days round trip for twenty of the small trees. I had a mile of fence to build. I figured, at that rate, I would work all winter to get the logs home.

I had to find a faster and easier way. This way I had to walk all of the way home. I put in another long day. Late in the night I finally got into bed. I had to come up with some other way. If I worked the teams that hard, they would all be tired out in about a month.

The next day I went into the cave and asked Fannie if she had seen a fence built out of poles. She said she had seen fences built two ways. One by laying the logs on top of each other and the other by making a cross out of the butts of the small trees and fastening the top parts of the trees to the crosses. Done that way it would only take about four or five trees to a long span.

"To do that, I need to go to town and get a lot of long nails. There must be some other way. I've seen wire fencing when I came across the east but never paid much attention." I told her.

She didn't like the idea of me going to town alone. We talked about the trip for the next few days. I didn't see any other way. One morning I saddled up Charlie and the black mule and started to town shortly after daylight. I rode hard all day and made it over halfway. Again I camped on the hillside, in the timber at the end of the valley. I had two things I wanted to do. I needed to check into the fencing thing and I felt I needed to file a claim on the land. At least I needed to find out how from someone in town.

Before I left, I took the papers the banker had given me in Tennessee. Also I took one of the hundred dollar bills, as an afterthought. I put my rifle on the saddle and strapped the pistol on my hip. Most of the way in, I practiced drawing the pistol, so if I needed to I would know how. I certainly wasn't going to look for trouble. I also had a box of bullets in the saddlebags.

I did something I had not done before. I drew the pistol and fired to try and hit a stump or a rock. I shot the whole box of shells that day. I was getting better at hitting what I aimed at.

CHAPTER 19

After a day and a half of travel, I arrived in town about noon. I rode down the street to see what stores were there. I hadn't been wearing the buckskins, Bart made for me, since the wagon attack. I put them on before I left for town. They are warmer and if I got caught in a storm, they would keep me dry.

As I rode through the town, people turned and stared at me. I needed a haircut. My hair hung almost to my shoulders again. I was riding a mule instead of a horse. My buckskins needed some cleaning. The town had lots of business: a blacksmith, bank, general store, hotel, café, two saloons, livery stable, and a barbershop. I took the mules over to the livery and paid for a night's board for them and made arrangement to sleep in the hayloft. My next stop would be the barbershop.

I learned that the barbershop can be a good place to find out about the town. Barbers liked to talk. When I entered all heads turned my way.

The barber said, "Twenty minutes." I nodded and took a chair against the far wall.

Five other men sat in the shop. Only one still needed his haircut. I sat and listened to the talk about the area. Nothing much of interest came up until one of them asked the barber if he had heard how long the railroad figured it would be before they completed the line all the way through. My ears picked up immediately. I didn't know what the railroad was. I had never seen one. The discussion went on about the railroad and what it would do for the country.

When the barber finished the man he was working on, he turned to me and said, "Next."

One of the men pulled money from his pocket and paid for all of their haircuts. They all left as a group. That left me alone with the barber. I climbed into the chair and he asked what I wanted.

I said, "A hair cut."

He asked, "You want a shave with that, young man?

I thought he was kidding me. I smiled and said, "Not much there. I think it's hardly worth the soap."

He smiled and said, "How long since you looked in a mirror?" And he held one up in front of me.

I had some hair on my face, down along the jawbone, and my mustache had grown out.

I answered him, "Yeah, I guess I do need one, don't I?"

He went ahead and cut my hair. Then laid me back in the chair and put a hot towel on my face. I though he had scalded me. I sat straight up with an, "Oh Boy!"

He laughed and said, "A little hot. I'm sorry. The kettle is hotter than I thought."

Next he took a cup and made some soap suds. He put the suds on my face and wrapped the towel back on. I heard him rubbing something on a piece of leather. When he took the towel from my face, he began to shave me. I sat very still because that razor looked sharp, but slid over my face very easy.

When he finished, I asked, "How much?"

He said, "Twenty five cents, please."

I went out on the street, and then remembered I had left my rifle on the saddle. I walked back to the livery and took it out of the scabbard. I started over to the bank.

When I crossed the street, someone hollered, "You with the buckskins, I want to talk to you."

I stopped and glanced around to see if he wanted to talk to me. A man, standing on the walk across the street, smiled at me.

I asked, "You talking to me, Mister?"

"Yeah, I am. Come over here kid. I want to ask you some questions."

I didn't like this. He didn't appear to be a sheriff. Two more men stood behind him.

I asked, "What do you need?"

"I need them buckskins you got on. Why don't you just take them off?"

I stood still. And yes, I was scared, but I also knew he was not going to make me give up my clothes. He walked out in the street and started to pull his gun. I jerked mine as fast as I could. It surprised me. I had my gun pointed at him before he got his even half way from the holster.

I said quietly, "I don't think so. Turn around and go on your way."

He looked so surprised. His buddies quit smiling. They looked very shocked. He put his gun back in the holster and said, "You're mighty handy with that thing, aren't you?"

Now, I wouldn't let him get the idea I was afraid of him. "Only when I need to be," I answered.

A man stepped up beside me and asked, "Any trouble, young man?"

"I hope not," I replied. He had a badge on his shirtfront.

Now, nothing good had come from my meetings with the law as I came across the country. I talked to him quietly and tried to answer truthfully any questions he asked. I visited with him for a few minutes and turned and went into the bank.

I asked to talk to the banker. The man behind the counter turned and pointed to a back room. When the door shut behind me, the fat man behind a desk asked what I needed.

"I want to file on some land. I thought you might know where I can do that. I also need to change this into smaller notes."

"I can take care of both of your problems right here. First, have you found where you want to file? Then we'll do the money part."

He walked to a door off of the office. We went into another room. He had a lot of maps on the wall and a long table in the center. I asked what map showed the ground south of town. He walked across the room and pointed to a large map.

He smiled and said, "I understand this ground is not very good for farming. Now if you want good farm ground, this over here is the best."

I stood looking at the map trying to figure out how to read all of the lines. I asked, "Has anyone filed on any of this land?" I drew a circle around what I thought must be the basin.

"No, that's too far from town for most people now. I'm sure some day someone will file on those sections"

I stared at the map thinking, how will I ever find out where the canyon is? Finally I asked him, "How much does a section of land cost?"

"You want to homestead or buy outright?"

"I would like to buy outright. I don't want to wait to prove up on the land."

"If you buy land outright, the sections must be further than twenty miles from town. The railroad owns a lot of the land close by."

"Do you have some way of showing me where the railroad land is?" I asked.

"Sure do, the railroad has surveyed their land. Here's a map showing where the railroad land lays." He said, as he pointed to many squares on the map. "The ones marked with the crosses are railroad land. The plain squares are open rangeland."

"Okay, now how much for each one of these section? How long and wide is a section?" I asked.

"The price from the government is eight hundred dollars for each section, including all timber, mineral, and water rights. Now for the size, each section is six hundred and forty acres. They are one mile square."

"Thanks. If you will change this into smaller bills, I'll be going. I want to go to the café and get something to eat. I ate breakfast a long time a go."

I walked out onto the street and tried to decide if I wanted to eat or go to the store first.

The sheriff stopped beside me and said, "Looks like you can't make up your mind. Can I help?"

I jumped a little because he startled me. I told him what I had been thinking.

Smiling, he said, "You must not be too hungry if you have to stand here debating what to do."

That made up my mind. I really was hungry.

"Well?" he asked.

I nodded my head and started for the café. He dropped into stride beside me. When we entered the café only two men sat eating. We took a table and the waitress came and took his order. I hesitated.

She, seeing this, smiled and asked, "Would you like the same as the sheriff?"

I nodded my head and said, "Please." I was not used to ordering in a café. I had only done it a couple of times in my life.

The sheriff asked me where I had came from and what I planned to do in the west. While we sat eating, I told him how I had been forced to come west because of the war and the loss of my family. I liked this man. He told me about his life and we made friends that afternoon. I told him I wanted to start a cattle ranch south of town if I could figure out the map and how to read it.

We visited about lots of things while we ate. When the waitress came with the pie, I told her I hadn't ordered any. She said, "Pie comes with the dinner."

Wow, I was so full I didn't want to move, but the café started filling up fast. I hurried and finished eating my pie.

We left and I went across to the store. The man working there finally finished with the ladies and came and asked if I needed help.

I asked. "Are you the owner of the store?"

He stepped back with a disgusted look on his face and said, "We don't give out handouts here, so why don't you move along, Sonny."

That shocked me. I certainly didn't want a handout from anyone, let alone a stupid grocery clerk like him. I looked him up and down and said; "I will see the owner now, if you don't mind."

I guess I sounded a little more disgusted than I wanted to, but he made me mad with his attitude.

"Well, all right, but it will do you no good, I'm telling you."

He turned and went into a backroom. I heard him talking to someone. In a little while a man walked out and came over to me acting like he was put out.

I introduced myself and asked if he had any barbwire.

He said, "No, I don't. No one has wanted any. I can order some for you to come in on the train the first of next week."

He wanted to know how much wire I would need. He told me the price. I asked him a bunch more questions about how you fastened it to the posts and all of those things. I thought about something the banker said earlier, about the railroad owning so much of the land. I told the storekeeper I would think on it and come back in the morning. Then I walked back over to the bank.

I went in and the same guy came out and said, "We're closing up now, you'll have to come back tomorrow morning."

I still didn't like him, so I walked back to the door of the banker's office and knocked.

He looked up and said, "Oh, it's you again. What can I do for you this time?"

"I would like to talk to you alone if you have time tonight. I need to talk in private about something important."

He said to the clerk, "You go ahead and close up and go home. I'll see you in the morning, Andrew."

I watched as he went out and locked the front door. I turned to the banker and said, "I think I can make it worth your time to listen and help me get done what I want to do."

We talked until about midnight. I left the bank and went to the hayloft to get some sleep. I crawled into the hay above the mules. I hadn't been lying in the hay very long when I heard Charlie start doing his puff, puff. I stood and tiptoed over to the top of the ladder and I saw two men messing around by the mules. They eased over to the ladder. One of them started up, being very quiet. I knelt down and let him come to the top. Just as he started to climb out into the hay I swung the rifle, really hard, into his face. He let out a yell, turned loose, and fell to the floor. He lay still for a while. Then his buddy helped him up and they went staggering out of the wide door in the front.

I went to sleep and got up early and over to the café. When the sheriff came in, I told him about the two men. For breakfast I ordered the special. The special, consisted of a huge steak, eggs, fried potatoes, and coffee or hot chocolate. I didn't like coffee, so I took the chocolate. I was so stuffed I didn't eat everything. I asked if they would wrap up what I had left to take for lunch on the way home.

I went over to the store and bought a mirror, some shaving soap, a brush, and a strop to sharpen the razor with. I also bought a winter cap for myself and one for Fannie. I got a pair of mittens for each of us. They didn't have any wire so, I had an empty mule. I bought a barrel of kerosene to use in the lanterns. To balance the pack load, I bought some grain for the cow. That would have to do until spring when the wire came in. I would let the cows go back out on the flat and round them up again in the spring. I figured if we kept the milk cow's calf penned up some way, she would stay around.

I rode out of town early in the morning. As I rode down the street I saw two men standing in front of one of the saloons. One had a black and blue bruise on the side of his face and his one eye swelled shut.

I smiled and nodded to them and rode on. I pushed the mules hard and made the deserted cabin shortly after nightfall. It took me a few minutes to get the stove started. Then I went out and took care of the stock. The next morning I checked to really find out what the man had left. The wagon seemed to be in good shape. A lot of the things will be useful in the cave. He also had a nice pile of lesson books. I filled the saddlebags with them and got less than half. I knew we needed to have more schooling so we could buy and sell cattle for a ranch.

Sitting with the banker made me aware of the fact. He took time to explain what he was figuring, but when the time came for me to do the figuring I had to know how. I only went to school three winters. I wrote fair, but hadn't learned much math. Fannie had schooling to the seventh grade, so maybe she would teach me what I needed to know. She didn't know how to do a lot of things, either. I would bring the team back and load up the furniture from the cabin, then come and get the boards. They would be great to fill in the entrance of the cave and make it almost like a house. That would keep the cave warm and the wind wouldn't blow in through the front.

When I got home, I filled Fannie in on all that had happened. I told her we would go to the cabin the next day and load everything we had room for on the wagon. The weather turned colder in the mornings down in the valley floor. By the feel of the air, winter would soon set in. We were about halfway to the cabin when the rain came down hard, with hail pellets mixed in. We were cold and wet when we got to the cabin.

Fannie started the fire while I looked around to see what we wanted to load first. I heard a noise and stepped out of the door. A nice looking sorrel team stood in the corral, licking the salt block. I walked slowly to the corral and put the poles up. I had them shut in. They didn't like it at first, but after I talked to them, they quieted down and I could get the halters on them. I put the harness on them and walked them around the corral a time or two. They wanted to go to work. I went in the cabin and told Fannie what had happened. Instead of one wagon we now had two.

The rain stopped. In the morning we loaded all of the furniture we could get on the smaller wagon. Then we loaded the big wagon with the lumber from the cabin. We got most everything on the wagon by piling it high and running ropes over the top. The hardest thing was the heavy kitchen stove. But, the oven would bake biscuits better than the Dutch oven Fannie had been using. We loaded that day, and with the help of a full moon, made it all of the way home about sun up. This was going to make living a lot easier. When I got the opening in the front of the cave filled in we would be warm and dry.

CHAPTER 20

The air felt cold enough now for me to kill some fresh meat for winter. I fixed a tripod in the other cave. That cave stayed cool all of the time because of the cold water running through. Fannie had made a small dam inside. She fixed a pool to keep the milk pail in. She made butter from the cream. We had hot cereal with cream in the mornings and cold milk to drink anytime we wanted. The cow was worth a small scoop of grain once a day to keep her coming to get milked. Now, I had to fix a winter shelter for her and a place to sit and milk out of the wind and snow.

The next month was a busy one. The cave was snug and warm. I had made many trips to the lodge pole pines, as the sheriff called them. I cut many logs about two feet longer than the wagon bed and made a barn for the cow and filled the cracks between the logs with mud and grass.

The sheriff also told me the big deer were the elk Bart had talked about. He called the wild dogs coyotes. On one of the trips to get more logs a herd of deer trotted out in front of me. I shot one and loaded her on top of the logs. I took the deer home, skinned and hung the meat in the cave. We now had fresh meat. We had the cave ready for winter, so I rode to the log patch every day to cut posts for the fences. If I worked really hard I got about a hundred cut into seven foot lengths in a day. The big, butt ends, I cut eight feet long. I didn't pile them up, but left the logs lay where the tree fell.

My body had filled out with all of the rich cooking and all of the milk and cream to eat. I now stood five foot ten and probably weighed around a hundred and fifty pounds of solid muscle.

We had a small amount of snow during the month, but not too much. The cold had frozen everything, including the ground. We had eaten most of the deer, so I saddled the stallion one morning and went to scout in the valley. Fannie said she wanted to go along. She took Charlie and we rode out. I watched for the cows and she just the enjoyed the ride.

We came to a bunch of cows out in the tall grass and rode their way. They were watching us, when all of a sudden one of them trotted towards us. He let out a bellow and came some more. I could tell it was a bull with massive horns. He planned to protect his cows. I rode a little closer, thinking he would turn and run, like all of the other cattle had. He made for us as fast as he could run. I jerked the rifle from the scabbard and, when I saw he was not going to stop, I shot him between the eyes. He went down on his knees and right back up. He shook his head and lowered his horns and here he came again. He would have speared the stallion if he had not jumped aside. When the bull turned back I took more time. This time when I pulled the trigger he dropped. I jumped off and cut his throat so he would bleed out good.

Fannie asked, "Now, what in the world are we going to do with that much meat?"

I shrugged my shoulders, "I wasn't going to let him kill a horse. He would have if I hadn't stopped him. I wonder how many bulls out here feel the same way. These cattle must have drifted in from a cattle drive, or a rancher drove cattle out into this basin and some got away. I wish I knew how many are here. We know there are about thirty of those red cows that are tamer. I think we better have a brand made when we go to town this spring and brand the calves. That will be the start of our herd."

I looked at the bull and said, "I'll skin him out and take the hide for rawhide to patch things."

I proceeded to skin the bull. I worked nearly two hours to finish the job. I tried to put the hide on the stud, but he would have nothing to do with my plan. I told Fannie to step down and we would put the hide on Charlie. I tried, but I couldn't lift the hide. Charlie laid his ears back when I got too close to him. I looked at Fannie.

She smiled and asked, "Now what, mighty hunter?"

I didn't think it was funny, but after a few minutes I said, "I'll have to bring the wagon out and get the hide in the morning. Let's ride on up the creek a ways and see what else is out here."

We went a mile and found another bunch of cows with a red spotted, hornless bull. In the next couple of miles we counted almost a hundred head of cattle. We still had not found the first herd of thirty head we had taken the milk cow from.

I said, "Hey, we may have a ready-made herd going here. If we get a fence around this land, next spring we can cull out these bulls with the long horns and keep the bulls with no horns or just short ones."

We turned and rode back where the dead bull was lying. I cut the back steaks from him and put them in my saddlebags. I took down my rope and tied on the hide and headed for home with the hide in tow. The stud jumped around a bit, but he finally settled down and pulled and everything went fine. When we got close to home I took the hide over and put it in the warm water and piled some rocks on top. I'll come back in a week or two and see if the hair has slipped.

I worked around the cave getting everything in order for winter. I did another inventory and decided I needed to split some more wood to store in the back of the cave in case we had a bad storm. The wood took the rest of the day before I decided we had enough.

I worked in the daytime and we studied the books, that I brought from the cabin, late into the night. Fannie helped me learn math and spelling. I learned a lot. I was getting more confident. This will make life easier. We spent most of the winter going through the pile of books.

CHAPTER 21

I started to the pole patch again to cut poles and fence posts. I noticed the farther up the hill I worked the taller and bigger the trees became. Some of the trees would measure almost a foot thick. I stopped for a break and sat down to rest. I looked at what I had been cutting and suddenly I pictured those long, straight logs laying on top of each other and building a house out of them. Why hadn't I noticed that before?

I began to plan. I saw a house setting at the end of the hill, out in the meadow a little ways so the sun would hit it. I would have a barn around the toe of the hill, and a set of corrals out on the flat. We would have room for a good sized bunkhouse with a wide porch in front. We will plant fruit trees and have a nice big garden, like my folks had back east. I worked and thought about all of these things and planned what I needed to do. When I got home, I told Fannie what I had been thinking about while I worked.

The next morning was cold. A west wind blew too hard to fall trees. I learned that from experience. I had tried one day when the wind blew and nearly killed myself. I was cutting a tree when the wind came up. I just went ahead and cut it almost off when the wind gave a big puff. The tree did a complete spin on the stump and came down, going sideways on the hill. The top hit another tree and sagged way down in the middle. When it straightened out, the butt end of the large tree went shooting by me like a bullet. Wow, if my leg had been in the way it would have been crushed. If the tree had spun a little more my way, and hit me in the middle I might have been killed.

Fannie and I walked out where I thought we wanted to build the buildings. All day we talked about where we needed to put the house and how big to make it. She thought just a small one. I knew how long the logs were, so I stepped off a bigger one, much larger. I thought laying long logs wouldn't take any more work than laying short ones.

I stepped off where the bunkhouse, barn, and other outbuilding should go. I measured off an area for the corrals. I had a picture of everything in my mind. I had to figure out how many logs I would need. I had all winter to cut them. I would use the tops of the trees for fence posts. Yeah, that would work. I might be able to get most of them cut before spring if I worked really hard.

I told the banker I would come in and buy some land and bring the money sometime in the winter. He had given me a price for a square plot of land, twenty sections each way. That would be four hundred sections. Since they were not classed as farmland, he said he would try to make a deal for the land at half-price. I told him if he could, I would pay him a thousand dollars for doing the paper work.

I wanted to get the house logs and as many posts cut as possible during the winter. For two months I worked from daylight until dark nearly every day. Once in awhile, when we had a storm, I rode out on the valley floor and killed a deer. I also killed a coyote and tanned his hide. When I got a couple of them I would make some mitten liners for my hands. I made Fannie a hood for her coat so her ears wouldn't get cold while she was milking the cow.

I figured spring would be here in about two months, so I asked Fannie if she wanted to go to town with me. "Are we short on any food?"

"No, not really, but I would like to have a meal and to talk to someone other than the cave walls."

I guess, with me working so much, I hadn't thought about what she had been doing. She had been shut in the cave most of the winter, other than when she went out to do chores or get water. The cave had no windows, so all she had was lantern light.

"Do you want to ride in, or would you like to take the light wagon?" I asked her. She thought it would be nice to take the wagon and use a couple of deer hides to keep our legs warm. I went out and caught one of the teams of horses the next day and we prepared to go. Fannie helped put the camping gear and some food in the wagon. She also made two beds, with plenty of blankets, in the back.

We traveled until we got to the Cabin Draw and made camp up on the flat, where the cabin had been. Even with a nice fire, we were still cold. We went to bed early and rolled up in the blankets to stay warm. Sometime in the night, I felt Fannie moving around next to me. The next thing I knew she curled up around my back,

She said, "I'm so cold."

I had never had a girl put their arms around me and curl up tight. I lay there the rest of the night, but I didn't sleep. For some reason I had these weird thoughts. I know this was not going to work more than one night. She went to sleep and slept until morning.

I got up with the sun and got a big fire going. There were a couple of old stumps and I put both of them on the fire. Fannie heated up some jerky in a pot of water. We sat next to the fire and drank the broth like coffee.

When we had traveled down the road a while, Fannie turned to me, with a twinkle in her eye, and said, "I slept pretty good last night after I got warm. How did you do?"

I felt my face getting red, I nodded my head "Not too bad, but you took all of the covers, and I got cold."

She laughed and said, "Well if you had not spent all night crowding the side of the wagon bed, and cuddled up a little more, we both would have been warm."

When we got to town I drove up to the front of the hotel and helped her down and we went in the hotel. I asked for two rooms. The man looked at me and then at Fannie and raised his eyebrows. "You sure you want two rooms?"

I nodded my head and said, "Yes, sir. My sister and I want two rooms. How much are they for the night?"

"They are fifty cents each," he answered.

He gave a key to Fannie and I went out to put the team away. When I got back to the hotel and got my room key I went upstairs.

Fannie stepped out in the hall and motioned for me to come to her. She was standing there with this smirk on her face. "Your sister?"

I caught on quick and said, "Yes, my sister. Did you want me to say my wife?"

We washed and walked over to the café. The sheriff sat at his table against the back wall. When he saw me, he motioned for us to come over. He stood and held a chair out for Fannie saying, "And who might this be?"

I said, "Oh, this is my sister." Then I introduced them.

I noticed, while we ate, the sheriff looked at Fannie every few seconds. After awhile other men came into the café. All of the young ones would stop and do a double take. I wondered if there was something wrong with Fannie, if she was not dressed right or what.

We finished eating and, when we walked across the street, one of the young men walked up to us and asked if Fannie would like to go down the street to the dance hall and dance with him?

Fannie answered him, her face turning beet red, "No, thank you. I don't dance."

Now, I got this funny feeling, wondering what was going on. Why did I feel so upset about the attention Fannie was getting?

We went back to the hotel and up to our rooms. As we parted, she looked at me and said in her sweet voice, that I had learned not to trust, and with an impish smile, "Thank you for bringing me to town. I've never been to a town this size before, except with my folks once, and we just drove through."

I answered, in a troubled tone of voice, "I am tired and I'm going to bed."

I couldn't go to sleep. I lay there and went through the whole trip. What was going on? What were these feeling I had? I suddenly wanted to protect Fannie and distrusted all of the men who were looking her way, and watching as she walked by. I wanted to pop them in the nose and tell them to get. What was wrong with them? Didn't they know she was just a freckled face, red haired kid, and not some bar floozy? Oh well, we'll be going home in the morning and I can relax and go back to work.

The next morning, after we ate, we went to the bank. The banker took us into his office. I introduced him to Fannie. I asked, "Have you got the land spoken for so I can start doing what I will need to do to make a home and buildings?"

He smiled and said all of the paper work was done except for one small piece of property. It seemed there was a quarter-section a man started to prove up on about ten miles from town. He had sent a man out to the property. There were signs of an old cabin, but it had been torn down, and no one was around. He would have to wait for a year to file an abandonment of property claim before he could get the legal deed for me.

"When do you want to give me the money for the land purchase?"

I stood and looking at Fannie said, "I promise you I'll be in sometime next week and pay you."

When we went out and were walking towards the store, I told Fannie to go get anything she wanted while I talked to the owner. I wanted to ask him to find a man he would trust to hire some men to work. We'll need a crew to survey the property and a crew to build a fence all of the way around our land. Later we'll need a crew to help build the buildings we want.

I went to the back of the store and visited with the owner for a long time. I told him what I needed and asked him to make the arraignments for all of those things, if possible.

"I'll be back sometime next week, so would you make a list of all the things I'll need to start a crew working? I'll go over it with you. I'll need enough provisions for two crews, of ten men each, building fences. We can begin work as soon as the surveyors run some lines."

He said, "There are a lot of trained surveyors looking for work since the railroad is completed."

I asked if he would have some of them come in so I could talk to them next week. He thought he would be able to.

We left town about noon. I pushed the horses along at a brisk trot. We went on past the cabin spot where we always stopped. Fannie chuckled.

I glanced over at her and she asked, "What's the hurry? Why didn't we stop and camp? Are you afraid to camp since I made you sleep next to me?"

I thought a little and said, "Yeah, I guess I am. But really I want to get home. We will load the gold in the small wagon and get a fresh team and go back to town."

She asked, "Why? What's the hurry?" She got a funny expression on her face and said, "You don't trust the banker do you?"

"I don't trust anyone with that much money. You know, all it would take is one slipped word about a huge amount of gold coming into the bank and a dozen armed men would be waiting on the trail for us."

I drove on through to home. We got to the cave late in the morning. Fannie went in to fix some food and I saddled the stud and went out to find another team. I found a group of them fairly close to the canyon. I caught the sorrel team and took them to the cave.

CHAPTER 22

We ate and lay down and slept for a few hours. Then we started to load the wagon with the boxes of gold. They were heavy. We worked for three hours to get all of the boxes into the wagon and ready to travel. I had taken one of the canvases from the wagon tops and covered the wagon bottom and then folded it over the load. We took our bedrolls and tossed them on top with some camping gear. That pretty well covered everything up. I put extra ammunition for the rifles and pistols under the seat. Fannie filled all of the loops on the belts. We put on our traveling clothes, me in the buckskins and her in men's pants and our hats and heavy winter coats.

I watched when she laid an extra pistol on the seat beside each of us. "Now, who isn't trusting?" I asked.

She smiled and said, "Me."

Early in the afternoon we left the cave and headed towards town. The sky darkened. Maybe, if we're lucky, we will make town before the storm gets this far.

I set the team on a fast pace. The miles went by and about daylight we got to the cabin draw. We drove in and stayed until late afternoon. We cooked some food and slept part of the day. We left shortly after dark and again the sorrels set a good pace. At this rate, we would be at the bank early in the morning. That is what I had planned. We should arrive before a lot of people are moving on the street. When we broke out on top of the ridge, we could make out a few lights in town. I stopped the team to give them a rest. As we sat resting, we heard a horse walking from the left side of the wagon trail. Suddenly a horse and rider came up on my side of the wagon.

"Well, well, Andy, look what we have here, two people going to town in the middle of the night. I wonder why they're out so late, or early. I wonder what they have under the tarp. Something we could use maybe. Our grub is getting a little low lately." The first man leaned over to pull the canvas back.

I said, "Don't touch anything in the wagon. Just move on and let us be."

The man on my side sat still for a minute. I couldn't see his face so thought he couldn't see mine but he chuckled, then I heard a gun cock.

"You know who this is Andy? He's the dumb kid who moved so fast with the gun in the street last summer. Okay, smart guy. We're living out in a hut freezing our rears off because of you. Now I'm going to lift up the tarp and if you as much as move, I'll blow you apart."

I looked over at Fannie, but she wasn't on the seat. Where had she gone? I had my hand on the extra revolver. I had cocked the pistol when the two horses rode up to us.

"Now be a smart kid and you won't get hurt."

Again he leaned over to raise the canvas. His horse went straight in the air with a snort the man came off of the horse. He hit the ground with a thud and groaned. I was watching Andy. He cursed and raised his gun as if to shoot. That's when I shot him. He also fell off of his horse and tried to stand. He was cussing and holding his right arm. Then both horses disappeared from my sight.

I shouted, "Fannie, where are you?"

Her answer came from out in the timber, "I'm out here and I have both of their horses. Who fired the shot, anyway?"

"I did. Are you okay?"

"Yes. I rolled off when the guy on my side went behind the big tree. I hoped he couldn't see me move."

I stepped down and walked around to the back of the wagon. I had in mind to get the lantern from the back where we put it. The moon came out from behind the clouds, bright enough to see clearly. The one I shot sat against a tree holding his arm.

He looked really sick and asked me, "Are you going to get me to a doctor?"

I looked down at his buddy on the ground by the wagon. I couldn't believe what I saw. When his horse dumped him he hit his head on the wheel hub and that killed him. His eyes were open and staring at the dark sky. I walked over, took him by the feet and dragged him out of the way. I asked Fannie to bring the horses over. I helped Andy up into the saddle, turned him toward town and told him to go find a doctor. We tied the other horse on behind the wagon.

I told Fannie, "We'll tell the Sheriff where this guy is and he can come get him."

We pulled up to the back door of the bank about an hour before full daylight. I walked over to the sheriff's office and banged on the door a couple of times. Finally he opened the door. In a very grouchy voice he wanted to know what I wanted. I told him who I was and he jerked the door open

"What's wrong, Ken? Is there trouble out at your place or what?"

I laughed and said, "No, I came to visit you. You've been asleep a long time for a sheriff. It's time to get up and go up to the top of the hill and get a dead man."

"Okay, okay. Slow down and tell me about it."

I shook my head no and told him I didn't have time right now. "I want to know where the banker lives. I have a delivery for him and I need to make the delivery before daylight."

He told me how to get to his house. I untied the horse from the back of the wagon and, following his directions, found what had to be the banker's house. I knocked really hard a couple of times to raise him. He came stomping to the door.

I told him, very quietly, that I had come to deliver what I owed him and I would meet him at the back door of the bank as soon as he could get dressed. I rode back to the wagon. The sheriff stood talking to Fannie. She had already told him about the two men and about sending one to the doctor. I told him what had happened when I shot Andy in the arm.

He turned to me and said, "Okay, it's time to tell me about this delivery you've got here that is so secret."

I chuckled quietly. "If you want to know about it, you are going to have to help unload the boxes into the bank. Then we'll buy you breakfast and go to your office and discuss this in private."

The banker walked up and asked why we had to do this now instead of after the bank opened.

"I said, "Just open the door and we'll unload some boxes into your vault."

He unlocked the front door, locked it again then came out the back door. I stripped the canvas back and the sheriff helped Fannie and me unload the boxes and take them into the bank. When we were through I went to the wagon and got a hammer. I ripped the top off of one box. I handed one bar to the sheriff and one to the banker.

"Here is what you just unloaded."

The sheriff stood with his mouth open and finally asked, "My God, what have you got here?"

The banker couldn't believe what he had.

I turned to the banker, "Do you want us to help unpack the boxes before your help comes, so you can get the bars locked in the safe? I would also like the sheriff to be here when we count the bars so we both have a witness."

He never said a word, but nodded his head. I started removing the bars from the boxes. The banker and sheriff began putting them in the vault. His vault was a large one because he had handled a lot of railroad money while they built the railroad. As I took the bars from the boxes Fannie took the empty boxes out and put them in the wagon. We worked an hour and a half to unload the wagon. We closed the back door of the bank. The banker counted the bars and the sheriff counted them, and they looked at each other.

The sheriff said, "I got seven hundred and twenty bars. Is that right?"

The banker nodded, "Same as I did."

The banker sat down at his desk and wrote a receipt for that many bars.

I asked, "Do you want me to come back tonight and help weight them so we know what the value is?"

The banker shook his head and said, "No, we have had over a million dollars at times. I have a trusted employee to help. We can take it from here."

"I'm hungry. Fannie, why don't you and the sheriff go over and order while I put the team up? What do you want me to do with the saddle horse?" His owner won't need him anymore?"

"Put him in the livery and tell Billy I'll be over after I eat."

I took the stock over and put them in the livery barn and paid the owner the dollar he wanted.

He turned to me and asked, "Where did you get the team of sorrels?"

I told him a neighbor of mine had them, and one day my sister and I stopped at his place and found him dead, sitting at the dinner table.

"That's too bad. He was a nice man. I sold him that team and wagon three years ago. He and his wife made a real nice couple. Did the wife sell you the team?"

I told him we found a grave and figured he had buried his wife, so we buried him beside her. I turned and said, "The sheriff and my partner have ordered breakfast for me over at the café so I better go."

While we were eating, I thought over what the liveryman had told me about the team of sorrels and the couple who bought them. After I finished eating, I went over to the bank and asked if the banker had come back.

The man, who had been so rude to me before, smiled and said, "Yes, sir, just go on back."

I went into the banker's office and told him what the liveryman had told me about the team of horse. He said he would check on the land to see if the couple had filed the required papers on the quarter section. If not, he would file and include the piece in the land purchase.

I walked over to him." You know my name, but I don't believe I have heard yours. If we're going to be doing a lot of business, and I guess we will, we need to get better acquainted."

"Yes, I guess that's right. They call me Mr. Job, but I would like you to call me Quinton when we're alone."

"My name is Ken and the redhead with me is Fannie. I think we'll go book rooms at the hotel for tonight. How long will it take you to come up with a figure on the money? I want to start hiring men to build a house, barns, bunkhouse, and corrals. I will also need to buy some cattle before long. There are some wild cattle but I don't know how many. Not enough, I know for sure. We'll need a bunch of those to feed the work crews while I'm doing all of the building."

I found Fannie walking through the store aisles. She looked bored and wanted to know where I had been. So I told her about the man and the sorrel team and what the banker and I talked about. I asked her if she wanted to go home today or stay in town another night.

She said, "I'd like to stay in for the night and have a long night's sleep before we start back."

"I'm going over to the sheriff's office. Do you want to come? I promised to tell him all about the gold and where it came from before we leave town. You can add to the story from your side. I might leave something out."

"That would be better than sitting in a hotel room, I think." Fannie's replied.

We went to the sheriff's office and told him about the gold and how we had gotten it. We also told him about the rest of the trip and why we lived in the cave.

He was interested in the hot springs and the big bowl of land we had filed claim on.

"How many section have you filed on?" He asked.

I said, "Twenty square sections or I think about two hundred and fifty thousand acres. That should carry a thousand cows, I hope. That's all I can do for now, but if someone else doesn't file on some of the other ground, I will file on more later, as soon as we get some cows and the building done. We have to get cattle going for income."

"I guess you had the bank working on this before you came in with the money."

"Yes. I talked with him last fall. When we came in the other day he said the papers could be signed, so we went out and got the money and brought it back after dark. Oh, that reminds me. What are you going to do with the man up on the ridge top? You have to bring him in for burial don't you?"

"Yes. I'll go get him now, I guess."

"Do you want some help? I can pick up a horse at the livery and go with you. Better yet, we can rent a packhorse and I'll ride his horse."

Fannie and I had spent over three hours at the office, telling our story. I glanced at her and she looked beat.

"Why don't you go get rooms for us? I'll come over as soon as we get back. We'll eat a good supper, get a good night's sleep, and go for home in the morning. Hopefully the weather will hold and we can get home without any problems."

CHAPTER 23

We got up early and left town by daylight. The weather didn't look too good but we decided to go any way. We had our bedrolls in the back of the wagon and our work clothes on. We had the tarp to make a shelter with if we needed to, so we didn't worry too much about a storm. Before we left, the storekeeper came out and motioned for me to come into the store,

"A storm is brewing. You better take a couple of these buffalo robes. You might need them. You can bring them back the next time you're in."

"Do you really think it's going to be that bad?" I asked.

He nodded.

"Why don't I open an account with you now? You can give the bill to the banker so if it's months before we get back you'll have your money."

I took the heavy robes out to the wagon and Fannie, laughing, asked, "Are those for the team to keep them from freezing?"

I assured her they were to keep her precious little pinkies warm.

Laughing, we headed out of town for a long, cold ride. Oh, if only we had known how cold and how long the ride would be, we would have stayed in town for another night.

The clouds and the wind came from the west as we climbed the ridge. The team traveled at a brisk trot. They seemed in a hurry to get home. We broke over the ridge top and glanced to the west. A curtain of clouds lay across the valley, about halfway down the western rim. The wind that had been coming from the side, now turned so we had to drive straight into it. The horses started to throw their heads and act nervous.

"I think you better get those robes out of the back. We can wrap up in them in case this gets worse. The wind is getting awful cold. What do you think"? I asked.

Fannie turned, reached down and lifted one robe and handed it to me. I wrapped up in it. She struggled to get the other robe pulled to the seat of the wagon when a big gust of wind tore the robe from her hands. She grabbed the side of the wagon to keep from flying out with the robe. I heard her scream as she struggled to stay in the wagon. I stopped the horses in time to see her go over the side. I jumped from the wagon, picked her up and lifted her into the wagon bed.

"Are you hurt any place?"

She shook her head no. I turned and ran out from the wagon and picked up the robe. By now the wind was screaming so hard I couldn't carry the robe. I put it on the ground with the hair side up and drug it back. I was completely caked with snow. We managed to get into the wagon bed and wrap up in the robes. I spoke to the team and they started along the trail, but all of the coaxing in the world would not get them into the trot again. They would go for a while, and then start to drift to the side, trying to turn from the wind. Finally, I stopped them and went to their heads. Their eyes were completely covered with packed snow, frozen in place. I cleaned their faces and loved them so they knew we trusted them.

I climbed into the wagon covered with caked snow. Fannie had given up trying to sit on the seat and was sitting on the floor of the wagon wrapped in the robe. I wrapped up again and climbed down into the bed of the wagon and drove. The wind slacked off and the team began to trot again. But the snow came down so fast I couldn't see more than a hundred feet or so ahead. I was cold, even with the robe wrapped around me. My coat was soaked through, but I wouldn't take it off. We slowed to a fast walk again. The team walked in snow, knee deep by now. Finally they stopped by themselves. I stood up to help them and they were standing in front of the cave.

I touched Fannie's shoulder. "You're home. I'll take care of the horses and you can go in and start the fire. I'll only be a few minutes."

I heard no reply so I unwrapped the heavy robe.

She groaned, "I hurt everywhere. I don't think I can walk. My legs feel like I've been beaten."

"Okay, I'll turn the horses loose then help you into the house."

I unhooked the team, took their harnesses off and let them go. They turned sideways to the wagon and put their rumps toward the snow and wind. They were completely worn out.

I went to the back of the wagon and scooted Fannie back so I could pick her up. When I picked her up, she put her arms around my neck and hung on hard. When we got inside I laid her on her bed and covered her up with some blankets. Then I started the fire and took off my soaked jacket and lighted the lanterns.

That's when Fannie sat up and said, "Come here."

I walked over to her. She reached up and gave me a big hug and said, "Thank you for saving our lives tonight."

I looked at her, "You said you were hurting. Where do you hurt?"

She got a big smile and the twinkle in her eyes. "Oh, that hug fixed everything up great. Do you want me to fix something to eat? It must be close to breakfast time.

"No, I just want to sleep. I haven't slept for a long time.

The fire warmed the cave and the warmth soaked in. I relaxed and the warmer it got the sleeper I became. I went over to my bed, took off the wet clothes, and crawled under the covers. That's all I remember for I don't know how long.

When I woke up, the fire had gone out and the cave was cold. I pulled on dry clothes and started the fire. I looked behind Fannie's curtain. She slept soundly. I opened the door and looked out. The world had changed completely, no grays and browns only total white. Everything was covered with snow, even the two horses standing backed up to the wagon. I had never seen so much snow in my life. The cold air hurt my face and when I breathed my lungs hurt. The sun must be up in the sky somewhere. Light filtering through the clouds created a dull gray appearance. The stream of hot water was completely covered with a cloud of steam as the warm water mixed with the cold air. I shut the door and fixed something to eat.

I put on my heavy coat and shoes and walked over to the cave where we hung the meat. I wanted to cut some steaks for breakfast. I walked in and the meat had disappeared. Something had come in and taken it from the rack I hung it on. What could have come in and taken half of a deer? I found no tracks, even in the caves dry dust. I went back to the house and finished getting breakfast. By now Fannie was up. I told her about the deer being gone.

After breakfast I put on heavy clothes and went out to change the stud's picket line. He stood in knee deep snow and shivered from the cold. He nickered as he watched me come for him. The snow was quite light and easy to walk through.

"I think I'll saddle the stud and ride out and see if the other stock is okay. Maybe I can find another deer while I'm out. If we had Charlie close by you could go along. That would be fun."

I took the stud to the cave and went in to get my saddle and rifle. When I came out of the cave, out on the flat was the group of horses. The sorrel team walked to meet them. I called and Charlie came up to me, hung his head and wanted his ears scratched.

"Fannie, come see who came to go for a ride with us."

She opened the door and looked out. "I'll be right out with the saddle, Charlie. Ken, do you want me to fix a lunch while you saddle both of the horses?"

"Why not? I think the air is warming up some, so let's go check on the cows. Maybe the snow will help us find them. At least we can track them." I said.

We rode out into the valley, following the warm stream. I thought the cows might come to the warm water to drink. We had not gone far until we saw some cows gathered along the banks of the stream. We rode far enough away from them so they wouldn't spook and run.

In the afternoon, we rode to where the warm water stream joined with the bigger creek that worked its way down the length of the valley. We counted over two hundred animals along this stream. We rode north until we found the other stream and rode toward home. We had cold feet, so we hurried along. A movement off to the right caught the stud's eye. He threw his head in the air. With ears up, he stopped and snorted. I let him walk that way, when all of sudden, from a clump of tall grass, a large cat jumped up and started to trot away from us. The stud laid his ears back and wanted to give chase. I swung off, taking the rifle with me. The cat stopped when we did and I took a bead on him. When I fired he jumped in the air and went running away. He ran for a hundred yards or so, and then fell down. I mounted and rode toward him with the rifle ready. When we got close he tried to get up. I could see I had not missed completely. He had a broken leg. I turned the stud sideways and shot the cat again.

Fannie rode over to where he had been laying when he jumped up the first time. She laughed and motioned for me to come. I looked down and there was our half of deer with almost all of the meat striped off. We went to pick the cat up so I could keep the hide. When I picked him up to tie him on behind the saddle, I saw that he had an injured foot. He had been hurt and not able to hunt and make his own kills so he robbed ours.

We rode home, following the stream. We found twenty-five cows along the creek. Five big, old bulls with these small bunches. That made quite a few in just a small amount of the range. We hadn't ridden more than a five-mile circle.

We still didn't have any meat. So the next day we both took rifles and swung south along the foot of the hill, toward where I had cut the trees. We rode for about an hour and came to fresh tracks in the snow. A big bunch of animals had passed this way some time yesterday afternoon, going toward the creek out on the flat. We followed them and they were feeding. Due to the depth of the snow, the small herd of elk had come off of the steep hillside and out on the flat where they could paw for grass.

I got off the horse and walked toward them. They paid no attention to me and I got less than a hundred yards from them before one of the cows turned and stamped her front foot. They all started to act nervous, so I aimed on the first one's head and fired. Thanks for the practice I had on squirrels, she dropped. The rest of them trotted off some distance, stopped and went to eating again. I dressed her out, put my rope around her head and headed for home. The carcass slid along easily in the snow. The stud didn't even notice the extra load.

That night we had fresh liver, fried potatoes, and hot biscuits. Fannie had become a really good cook by now and I told her so.

The cold and snow lasted for two week or more, before the sky cleared, then turned really cold for a few more days before I could feel the air warming.

CHAPTER 24

During this time I talked seriously to Fannie about going east to check on her grandparents. Finally she got mad at me.

With tears in her eyes and a temper in her voice, she said, "Alright, I'll go, but if it's a wasted trip I will come home and never speak to you again. Do you understand me?"

We waited more than three weeks before we were able to travel to town. When we set the date for her to go, she became less talkative and more sullen. I realized that she was scared. Neither of us had ever traveled on the train, or had traveled that far alone. The morning we left for town she was crying. She wouldn't talk to me most of the day.

We had stopped at the cabin draw for the first night. She turned to me and, with tears in her eyes, asked, "What am I going to do if they are both dead, what then?"

"Come home the way you went. You know you have plenty of money, so you can buy a ticket home."

Remembering the advice the woman had given to me, I said, "Listen, while you're traveling, don't keep more money than you will be spending that day where anyone can see what you have."

We arrived in town and went to the hotel and booked rooms. We went to the bank and told Mr. Job what was going to happen. I wanted some small bills for Fannie to take with her. I didn't tell him about the five one hundred dollar bills she already had.

Next we went over to the store and I told her to buy what clothes she would need and at least two dresses. She started to object and said one was going to be enough.

"No, it's not. You get some really nice dresses. Remember you are a very rich girl, so dress like it."

While she was doing that I was browsing the gun counter. They had a small pistol in a thirty-eight caliber. They called the gun a Derringer. It held two shells, like a double-barreled shotgun. I got a box of shells to go along with the gun.

When she had all of the things she said she would need, the clerk started to wrap them in paper.

I asked, "What are you going to carry everything in?" I turned to the clerk and asked, "Do you have any, what do you call them?"

He smiled and answered, "Satchels, sir. Yes, we have a few."

We followed him to the back of the store where he showed her three or four. Fannie picked out one large enough to hold all of her clothes and appeared to be strong. He showed Fannie how the lock worked and gave her the keys. We took all of the things to the hotel room and went to the café to eat supper. The sheriff was at his usual table so we ate with him.

I asked, "What time does the east-bound train come through?"

"Well, today or tomorrow?" He asked. "Today's will be in about three hours from now. The next one will be the same time tomorrow afternoon. Why, is one of you going east?"

I nodded and looked at Fannie. She was as white as the snow we just had, and her hands were trembling. The sheriff saw how afraid she was so he didn't make a joke. We went on talking for a while. He turned to Fannie and asked, "How far are you going?"

She told him she was going to Wickerville, Pennsylvania.

"He whistled and said, "That is a long trip. When you're ready, come by the office and I'll walk down with you."

We went to the room and she packed all of her clothes in the bag. The ones she brought from home and the new ones she bought today. She turned to me as she held up two dresses.

I said, "I think the one in the left hand will be the best to travel in."

I left the room so she could get dressed. A few minutes later she knocked on the door, went back to her room and motioned me to follow. When I entered, she turned and threw herself into my arms and sobbing said, "I don't want to leave you. What if I never get to see you again?"

I held her tight and said, "We will write and if you can't come to me I will come and get you, if you want me to."

She turned to pick up her bag.

I said, "Fannie." When she turned I handed her the small pistol and the box of shells. "Put the shells in your case and the loaded pistol in you dress pocket. You know how to use it so don't be afraid to. Remember; if the time comes, make sure you shoot straight."

She put the pistol in her dress pocket and opened the bag for the shells. I reached out and handed her a chain with the locket. "This is your mom's. I saved it the day I buried her. Now you will have this to remember her by. We must go if you're going to catch the train."

The train left the station March 20, 1871, at six p.m.

CHAPTER 25

The sheriff and I walked back to his office. I missed Fannie already. We talked about the things I planned for the ranch. I confessed I really needed someone with a lot more experience to guide me. "I guess I need to hire a man to help with the hiring, firing, and as a ramrod."

The next morning I went to the bank and talked with the banker. I asked about the gold and how much was left after the land and his commission was paid.

"The gold weighed 3600 pounds. You're lucky the wagon didn't break on the way in with the huge load. As for the accounting, you asked me to purchase a square block of land, twenty sections by twenty sections. I was able to get a good price, because of the large size, both from the government and the railroad. The railroad land cost more, but the average was six hundred dollars a section. I prepared a draft to each of these for you to sign."

I looked a little confused, I guess. So he explained. A draft is a piece of paper that requires the bank to pay the amount requested to the holder of the paper. He put two legal documents in front of me. I signed where he pointed. He picked those up and put them aside, each in an envelope.

He put another paper in front of me and said, "This is for my fee. It's a draft to me for five thousand dollars, if you approve that much."

I nodded and answered, "That will be fine."

"Now, the current price of gold is eighteen dollars and ninety-three cents per troy ounce. You deposited eight hundred seventeen thousand, seven hundred seventy-six dollars. I subtracted the amount paid from the original deposit and that leaves you with a total of five hundred seventy two thousand, seven hundred seventy-six dollars."

Next he opened two large envelopes and removed two bundles of paper from each.

"These papers are the deeds from the government land office to you. There are two copies of each. I will put one in our bank files and you can take the other home with you or you can rent a locked box here in the bank to keep all of your legal papers and other valuable things safe. It's only fifty cents a year for the box."

I took out some change and paid for five years rent on one of their biggest boxes. I talked to him about setting up an account with the store so I didn't need to come in for all my supplies. He showed me how to write, what he called a check, to pay bills with and told me how to keep track of the money I spent. I asked him if he had found a surveyor to run the lines on the property.

He shook his head no. "I think Frank, over at the store, can do that a lot better than I can. He has a lot of contacts from the railroad crews."

I stood, thanked him for his help and started to walk out of his office. When I opened the door to the outer room, I heard a loud voice. I looked up and Andy held a gun on one of the men behind the teller's cage. He demanded money now. I came out of the office door in back of him. He had no idea I was there.

I drew my pistol and, on tiptoes, walked up behind him and pushed the barrel of the pistol into his back and said, "Andy, you never seem to learn do you? Just hand me the gun slowly and go sit in the chair over by the front door."

I walked him over and he sat down in the chair. I stood, holding the pistol pointed his way, while a customer went running for the sheriff. The sheriff came hurrying in and started asking a bunch of questions. Then he took Andy and headed to the jail. I followed along. After he put his prisoner into a cell, he came out and shook his head.

"What am I going to do with this guy? He really isn't that bad of a guy. He can't find any work here and has no money to get a ticket on the train. He worked for the railroad, as crew boss, cutting ties for a long time. Then he got caught up with the no-good who tried to hold you up. Since then he has just existed from one handout to the next."

I sat and thought about the situation and then turned to the sheriff. "Do you think he can be trusted to run another crew and cut logs for my buildings and hundreds of fence posts?"

He shrugged. "I don't know. Do you want to talk to him?

"I'm asking for your opinion. So, what do you think?"

"Let's go talk to him. I'd like for the poor guy to get going again. He used to come to town and drink a beer once in a while, but never was a drunkard or caused trouble until lately."

We went into the cellblock and Andy was sitting on the bed with his head hung down. He was sobbing. The sheriff walked up to the bars to talk to him. I stepped up and motioned for him to let me do the talking.

Andy looked up with tears in his eyes and said, "I really blew it this time, didn't I? How many years will I get in the state pen for this dumb stunt, Sheriff?"

I asked, "Andy, how old are you?"

He hung his head again. "I'm twenty-five, why?"

"What were you doing before you got stuck in here?" I asked.

With some pride in his voice he answered, "I was a crew foreman on a tie cutting crew. My crew cut logs and hauled them to the sawmill where they were made into ties for laying the track. Why?"

"If I can get the charges dropped for this little stunt, do you think you could be trusted to cut timber for me and run a crew? The crew will be about ten men. I need someone for the job. But if you screw up, the sheriff will come take you back and hold you for bank robbery. What do you think?"

"Hey, if you can do that, I will do anything. I don't want to go to jail. It would kill me and also my mom."

I turned to the sheriff, "What about it Sheriff?"

He smiled and said, "I'll go talk to Mr. Job. Be back soon."

We walked out of the cell area and he said, "I think you made a wise move. If Quinton will not press charges, I think Andy will be your man forever, and may become a real friend."

"I'll go to the store and make arraignment for some supplies. I'm going to need lots of things for the work crews. I'll have to order a lot of stuff, so I better get started."

I found Frank in the back of his store and asked if he had a few minutes to order some supplies. Three hours later the arrangements were made. I went over to the livery, talked to the livery stable owner and gave him an order for three chuck wagons. He thought he would get them in a couple of weeks. He had one on hand now. I also ordered five heavy duty wagons to haul supplies and fence equipment.

Frank knew of two surveyors to hire. If he would hire them and have them hire ten men each, we would build fence as they ran lines. I told him about the wagons at the livery and said I would bring teams in for the wagons. He would equip them and send them out with supplies. I needed tents for sleeping and tarps for cooking under and all food supplies for a month.

I went back to the jail to ask what the sheriff had found out. I entered his office and he smiled. "You hired your first man. He's waiting in back for you."

He went and got Andy and they came out together.

"Where is your horse?" I asked.

"I sold it to live, but the money ran out the other day. I was hungry," he answered.

I reached into my pocket and handed him a five-dollar bill and said, "Go eat and get what you need for clothes at the store. If that isn't enough, come and get me, and I'll pick up the tab. You'll need work clothes. Don't be cheap. Get good stuff and enough to last for the summer. It will be several months before you get back to town. I have hot water so you can wash clothes at the ranch."

I went to the hotel and booked a room for him. Then went to the store and picked up a supply of work socks, gloves and the things I thought I would need. I also bought a spool of heavy rope and asked about wire. He asked how much I needed. We talked about the amount and decided I would need a boxcar full, at least to start with. The wire will be here in five days.

Andy came in. I introduced them and told Frank Andy would be running a crew for me and if he came in to fill his orders.

I turned to Andy asking, "Do you know of any good men from your other crew who need work?"

He turned it over in his mind while he gathered up the things he needed. When we went to the counter to pay, he said, "I can get you at least twenty men the railroad has laid off, if they are still around. I can send some wires and see what shows up."

I nodded and said, "I want nothing but good men, not trouble makers or slackers. I don't have time to be messing with them. Let's go to the train station and you can send your wires."

While we were walking to the station he said, "I lost my gun to the sheriff. What about getting another one?"

I waited to answer. We went to the station and he told the telegraph agent what wires he wanted sent and to where, then we walked back towards the store.

"I have extra rifles out at the ranch and I hope no one will need a side arm. If that happens, we will take care of it." I told him he had a room at the hotel for the night.

"We have some time now before supper. Let's load the wagon with what's ready to go. We can eat and leave shortly after sunup."

The next morning we were an hour out of town when the sun came up over the trees. We topped out on the ridge. I stopped to let the horses rest. The air was cold. It made my eyes water, but the sun was going to shine and the snow would melt in a few days. Spring would be here soon and everything would turn green.

After we had traveled for a long ways, Andy turned to me, "Thank you for the chance. I was at the end of my rope. I hadn't eaten for three days. I slept in the alley behind the bar and didn't know what to do. I didn't want to start begging for meals. All I wanted was enough money to get on the train and go find some work. I thought if I found work I would come back and pay for what I had stolen."

After dark the second day, we drove into the valley by the cave. The stud let me know he was not happy about being left by himself. We took care of the horses and I went in the cave and started the fire. Andy came in and could not believe how we had fixed the place. He made the comment that it was nicer than a lot of houses. We cooked supper and, after visiting for a while, I banked the fire for the night and we turned in.

After breakfast the next morning, I went out and brought the stud up and saddled him. I was going to look for the horses. All of a sudden he whirled around and trumpeted with his head raised. He tried to get away. I held on to him and got him under control when a bunch of the horses came running into the lower end of the valley. They came all of the way up to where we were standing. They stopped and looked out towards the flat. They were snorting and milling around. I noticed that all the horses were geldings. I quickly grabbed my rifle and mounted. The stud tore out like he had been shot. He went out onto the valley floor on a dead run. The rest of the horses milled in a circle. I couldn't figure what was going on. Then I saw a big, bay horse that I didn't recognize. It was another stallion. He had chased all of the geldings away from the mares. No mules were with them. He had also sorted them away. I swung out so I would come up on the outside of the herd.

The mares started to go into the valley where the other horses were. I got behind them and pushed them right on in. The stallion was through the narrows before he was aware of what was going on. He tried to turn back but I had him trapped. I took down my rope and crowded all of the horses up next to the cave between the two streams. He tried to stay away from me, but with Andy on the ground and me on the horse, he finally milled around so I could get a throw at him. To my surprise, the rope settled over his head. He squealed and tried to pull free. Also to my surprise, he fought the rope just a few minutes and then led right out of the herd. He was halter broke and had escaped from somewhere.

I had Andy get a halter from one of the wagons and we worked around him quietly. He soon let us put the halter on. He stood trembling, and accepted us handling him. Now, what was I going to do with two stallions? One was pain enough, but two. They had to be kept apart or they would injure each other or worse yet, one might be killed.

However, he had brought the teams all into the valley, so we started to catch and put the harness on them. I was going to take most of them into the livery barn so when a crew was hired and the wagons came in, the teams would be in town ready to come back out with the wagons.

We caught all of them, but I decide I wanted to keep the big gray teams and the sorrel team at home. When everything was harnessed I had Andy pick out one of the horses from the saddle stock. I went into the cave and got a saddle and bridle for him. He was gentle with the horses and I liked that.

I said, "He may be a little spooky. He hasn't been ridden for almost a year. So watch out when you get on. He may buck."

Andy took a stirrup and up he went and down went the horse's head. It was a toss-up for a few of minutes, and then the horse quit and trotted around.

We divided the horses into two lines. With one line each we headed for town. I tied the bay stud on the end of the string I was leading. We got to town late in the night. The horses traveled a lot faster than a wagon and team.

I went to the livery owner and made arrangements for the teams. I also had him put the bay stud in one of his box stalls. With that done we went to eat. I hoped the sheriff was at the café. Sure enough, he was at his table, so we sat down with him and had a big meal.

I asked him if anyone had lost a bay stallion. He shook his head no, but said he would ask around. He got up to leave and I followed him outside. I told Andy to go ahead and get us a couple of rooms. I followed Chad over to his office. I said, "I need to talk to you about something really important."

We went in and he turned to me with a questioning look. "Yes," Like what now?

"I need a good man to help me. I don't have the experience to run thirty men and to do everything. I know what I want out there, but I can't be everyplace at one time. It's going to be a two or three man job. Do you know anyone I can hire, I guess to be a foreman. I'm going to be busy just going from one crew to the next, let alone being a boss. I now understand this is over my head and I need help."

He smiled and nodded his head. "I'm glad you realized that this soon, before it got away from you. I was wondering how far you would go before you made the discovery. You've undertaken a big job."

I sat and thought for a while. "There is only one person I know who has the experience to do the job and I could trust."

He asked, "Who would that be? Anyone I know?"

"Yeah. I get the feeling you're not happy here on this job. I think you've been a range man and are used to being outside. You know horses and I bet you know cattle, too. You know how to handle men and can back it up if you need to or you wouldn't have been an officer during the time the railroad was going through. I bet this was a tough town and that's why you're here. I don't know what they pay you to sit around and get bored, but I can do better."

He sat there with no expression on his face. Then, with a smile, said, "Thank you for the confidence. That's an interesting offer. I've been a foreman on a big ranch down Texas way. There came a time to ride on, so I ended up here throwing drunks into cells and selling my gun. I don't like to be a fast gun. It's not a pleasant life. Let me give it some thought. I have my own saddle and equipment. But I would have to buy a horse. There aren't many really good ones around here."

"If no one claims him, there is a really good one over in the livery stable that you can have. I would bet he's completely broke. He came charging into the horse herd and, when I got a rope on him, he made a play at fighting me. But a few pulls and he stopped and we walked right up to him. He was nervous but not frightened. Look at him tomorrow and think about the job offer. I'll be going out in the morning. I'm going to bed. See you in the morning. Oh, by the way, what do you make as sheriff?"

He smiled and said, "Not nearly enough for the crap I have to put up with. I think I might take you up on the job, but let me think on it tonight.

CHAPTER 26

I went to the hotel. Andy waited in the lobby for me. He stood up when I walked in. He said, "They wouldn't give me a room unless you told them to."

I walked over to the desk and asked, "How do I get to talk to the owner?"

He frowned at me like I was a punk kid. "You don't, Kid. If you want a room just pay the fee and drop it."

Again I asked, "Does the owner live in this building?"

"Yes he does, but I'm not going to disturbed him over one room for one night."

"Go get him. I want to talk business with him."

A door opened down the hall and an older man walked up to the desk and asked if I had a problem.

I said, "Not any more. I wanted to talk to you but your hired clerk didn't think I was old enough to be of any importance. We were having a little discussion about the fact."

He told the clerk they would talk about this later. He asked what I wanted.

I said, "How much will it cost me to rent two rooms on a yearly basis? I would want one of them reserved just for me and the other one for my help when they come to town."

He seemed surprised. "Well, I don't know for sure. I can give you a rate. I rent them for a dollar a night, so that would be thirty dollars a month."

I said, "Twenty a month a piece. With the railroad gone you're not going to rent them most of the time. We'll check in every time we come to town and the rooms can be cleaned after we leave. You're not going to rent any other room that much."

He took a moment and said, "Okay. When do you want to pay?"

I answered, "I'll pay two hundred now and the rest the next time I come to town.

I took two one hundred dollar bills from my pocket and gave them to him. I want a receipt, please. What rooms do you want us to use?"

He took two keys from the board and handed Andy one and the other one to me.

He said, "You keep the key. If you forget yours, we keep a spare in the office. No one will go in unless you give them permission. You may leave something in the rooms if you want to."

"Thanks. Oh, by the way, I'm Ken Clausen. I'm going to be building a ranch south of here. I bought the land and will be starting to build the ranch buildings as soon as I can get a crew together. I'll need help, so if you know of anyone who needs a job, tell them to come out to the ranch. I don't want drunks and hard cases, but I want good men."

"Let's go to bed, Andy. Daylight comes fast."

As we climbed the stairs I asked, "Did you check the telegraph office to see if you had any answers while I was talking to the sheriff?"

He answered, "No. I'll check in the morning."

We went to our rooms and right to bed. Sometime in the night I woke up with a start. I heard gunfire some place down the street. I turned over and went back to sleep. In the morning Andy and I walked over to the café for breakfast. We were about through eating when Chad walked in. He sat down and looked like he had aged ten years. I said, "Short night?"

He said, "Long night. Did you hear the shooting?"

Andy and I both nodded our heads. He shifted in his chair. "Some young kid, about twenty, decided to draw on me when I asked him to come down to the jail and sleep. Is the job offer still open?"

Andy looked surprised but said nothing. I nodded my head and went on eating. Chad ordered his breakfast and sat staring at the room until his food came. Andy stood up and went out the door. He went to check his telegrams. When Chad finished, I stood up and paid for all of the breakfasts, then we walked out.

I asked, "Want to look at the horse?"

We turned and walked towards the livery barn. We exchanged good mornings with the livery man and I walked into the stall and petted the stallion. He acted happy to see me. I put the halter rope on him and walked him out. When I saw him this morning, he was a beautiful animal. The stable attendant had brushed and cleaned him up.

The liveryman walked over and commented, "That is one fine animal. Someone has made a pet out of him. Did you know he has a bullet graze on his side?"

We both walked around him. Sure enough, a straight line ran across his lower hip. The wound healed, but left a white scar. I put him back in the stall and turned to walk away.

Chad said, "We need to talk."

I walked toward his office. We went in and he sat down. He spoke quietly. "I tried to talk to the kid but all he thought of was killing someone. Damn, I hate this job."

He stood up, unpinned and threw the badge on the desk, then walked out the door.

He turned and said, "I'll be ready in one hour. Are you waiting or are you going on first?"

"I'll wait," I answered.

Andy said, "I found my ten-man crew, so what else do you want me to do?"

"Let's go to the store and tell Frank that we will need a wagon full of supplies and a chuck wagon,"

When we finished in the store, we decided that Andy would wait and come to the ranch when the crew got in town. He would bring the wagons and the supplies along with the men.

I heard the train whistle blow and, for some reason, started toward the railroad tracks. When I got about to the station, a man, a young woman and another younger boy walked out of the station and stood, looking around like they were lost. I thought I had seen him someplace. I walked on toward them.

The man stepped forward and asked, "Do you know where I can find work?"

I looked at him more closely, and then it registered. "John! What are you doing here?" I knew he did not recognize me. "I'm Ken. You helped me a couple of years ago. Molly is still with me."

The light came on and he smiled all over.

I asked, "You're looking for work you said?"

"Yes, we're broke and need work and a place to live." He turned and pointed, "This is Elisabeth. Do you remember her? And this is the kid with the double-barrel shotgun." And we all chuckled.

"Yes. I need you. I will have all the work you can do and then some. Let's go get you in the hotel for a day or two."

When we had them settled in some rooms, I took John down the street to the blacksmith shop. I asked if the smithy had any idea where I could buy all the things I needed for a shop.

He was surprised. "Yes, right here."

The railroad had moved on. He had twice as much as he needed of almost everything.

I asked, "What about iron?"

He motioned for me to follow him. We walked out back. He had piles of iron of all sizes.

I said to John, "Get everything you'll need. You're going to have about twenty teams to shoe and hinges to make for corral gates and houses. You'll need repair parts for wagon beds and to sharpen tools. We have enough work to keep you and the young one busy forever. We'll talk about wages later, but now, how long has it been since you had a good meal?"

"At least two days I guess," he answered.

We walked over to the café. I went into the kitchen, talked to the owner and asked if she would keep track of the meals for my crews that were coming in. I asked her if she knew Andy.

She said, "Yes, I know him well."

I told her Andy would sign the meal tickets, so go ahead and feed the men.

"This family will be coming for a few days, so do the same for them, please. I hope to be back in a week or so."

She agreed to feed them. I went out and down to the smithy again.

"We need to talk about prices on your extra equipment."

"We'll wait and see what all he wants and then when you can come in we'll talk."

"I want John to get out to the ranch with everything he needs as fast as he can. Will you let it be loaded and hauled before I pay?"

"Sure, I don't need most of the things now, so there's no hurry."

I went back to the store to talk to Frank again. I need tents for the crews to live in.

He said, "How many do you need?"

We walked out to a shed full of tents and canvas. He had furnished tents for the railroad crews so he had about any size tent we would need. I told him to check with the crew bosses when they came in and let them figure out what supplies they wanted. I told him what I had done with the smithy and asked him to send up a complete kitchen with a tent for the family to cook in and four smaller ones for sleeping tents. They'll also need blankets and beds.

"There are ten teams over at the livery, so make use of them. I've ordered a bunch of wagons. We'll need the chuck wagon as soon as the post crew gets here. Oh, I've hired Chad. He'll be ramrodding the crews and most of the other things on the ranch. Give him whatever he wants or needs, no questions. He is the boss now as far as I'm concerned."

Within the next two months we had two survey crews working, one on the south line and one on the north. We had increased the logging crew to twenty to keep up with the cutting and hauling of posts. Some of that crew also was building two bridges over the streams close to the home place. They made plans to build a bridge across the creek that ran down the center of the main valley. I made a rope corral by the cave for the studs. We kept them in the corral so they were out of the way. However, they were ridden almost every day. The pack mules had been separated into teams and were in harness.

Elisabeth and Molly had come together again and Molly was happy and gentle as could be. I rode Charlie every time I had any long distance to go, like to town. I could go from the ranch to town about two hours faster with him than with the stud. All of the wagons and teams worked every day.

I had some men building a small house in the cabin draw. The old shack had been about half way between town and the ranch. The new cabin had two bedrooms and a kitchen-dining area. The cabin was not big but it made a good place for the teamsters to spend the night and rest the teams.

The logging crew hauled a few logs for the house and other buildings. I needed to find a builder to start on the house soon if we wanted to be finished by winter. We had a very busy three months. I missed Fannie a lot, but as I got busier I was too tired to think about anything but eating and sleeping.

One night I felt lonesome, so I sat down and wrote a note telling her about the ranch.

~~~

Fannie

I miss you since you left. I've worried because I have not had any word from you. I hope you are alright and made the trip with no problems. I started the building of the ranch. I wish you were here to help with ideas and just to watch what is going to happen this summer.

Write when you get time.

Ken

~~~

I took the letter to town to mail. When I entered the post office the man gave me a letter from Fannie. I mailed my letter and went to the hotel room to read the one from Fannie.

~~~

Dear Ken,   *May 20, 1871*

I meant to write and tell you what has happened to me. I had no trouble on the train getting here. The trip was long and tiresome. When I arrived I went to a hotel and rented a room for a night. Then I rented a buggy to go out to the farm. The man in the livery was afraid I couldn't handle the team and wanted to send a man out with me. I assured him there would be no trouble with the team.

As I approached the farm, I noticed everything was in bad shape. The fences leaned in all directions. No sign of life appeared around the barns. Only weeds grew in the yard. It made me so sad, because Grandpa's farm had always been so pretty with the fences painted and the fencerows all trimmed. The countryside is green and lush. We had some rain last night so the air is clean and fresh. When I drove into the farm yard I went up to the house and got out.

I went to the front door and knocked, but got no answer. I walked around to the back door, but still no answer. I pushed on the back door and it opened, so I walked in. Dirty dishes covered the counters. I called and thought I heard someone answer. I walked into the front room and Grandma was sitting in a chair looking out the window.

I ran to her and she asked, "Who is there?" I said, Grandma, its Fannie. She started to cry and said, "I knew you would come. I have been sitting here praying that you would. I am so alone. Everyone has left." I hugged her. She was crying and said, "No one has come for a week." I looked around the room and there was no sign of food.

I asked about Grandpa and she said "He has been gone almost a year. The neighbor has been coming in once a week and cooking for me. I can't figure out why I couldn't go too, but I just sit here and worry."

It is so sad, Ken. She is so thin. I can lift her easily. She has been so neglected and she has large sores all over her body. I just sit and cry for her.

I have been here almost two months and I have been so busy caring for Grandma and getting the farm cleaned up. I miss the west and the open spaces. Mostly I miss our dumb cave in the rocks, with the hot springs to bathe in and you to talk to. In these two months I have learned how close we had become.

The neighbor, next to the farm, is going to do the farming on shares. That will give Grandma and me some income to live on. I'm getting the flowerbeds and the yard cleaned up this week. I bought a horse to pull the surrey so I can go back and forth to town and get food. I've had the man next door work the garden up for me and I will plant some things so we have fresh garden vegetables.

Oh, thank you for saving Mother's locket. Mom and Dad's pictures are in it. I was so broken up that day I had no idea what was going on. That was so thoughtful of you. I hope your ranch is coming along the way you want. I so wish I could help with the planning of the house and everything. It looks like I will be here longer than I planned. Grandma seems to be getting stronger by the day. It is wonderful what a little food and loving will do.

I do so miss you and your wonderful spirit. I'm looking forward to hearing from you and getting the news of your life and the progress of the ranch.

Please write soon.

Fannie

~~~

I read the letter through twice and put it in one of the drawers of the chest in the hotel room. I lay on the bed for a long time and thought about the year we had together and things we had done. Yes, I missed her. I missed her bright blue eyes that snapped when I teased her and the bright red hair as it fell to the ground when I cut it off. She went from a cute little girl to a spunky slim young man with the few strokes of the scissors. She sat on the wagon seat and handled the team of large horses better than most men could. I missed seeing how she could ride and how much Charlie had taken to her instead of me. He would follow her and beg for her to scratch his ears. I went to sleep wishing she was with me. She was a trooper and had gone through so much, and it had changed her life as well as mine.

CHAPTER 27

The days all ran together. The work was progressing. I spent many days riding the range, searching for cows. Chad and I were going ahead of the fence crews and moving wild cows we found, into the area behind the fence. Sometimes we would ride for miles and not find a thing. Then we would hit a jackpot and find fifty or more in a bunch, hidden in a small draw with water. One day, we rode onto a flat that showed signs of plowing years before. We explored and found the remains of a small, caved in cabin. A water trough was set in the ground. Fresh tracks covered the ground, so we spread out searching for the cattle. I found a small group, under some big trees, bedded down in the shade. I moved them out, and four big, gray bulls with huge bodies stood up. They all had rings in their noses. Chad rode up with twenty or more. They all looked the same. They were nearly all bulls. I pointed to the four with rings.

Chad said, "They were wagon oxen. They've been here a long time. Those bulls are so old they won't be any good for food."

"Let's ride around and try to find cows. I'd like some cows for brood stock from them. Look at the size of the bones on those big boys."

After we worked through all of the draws we found thirty cows about the same size and type. A few were crossed with longhorn, but were good looking brood stock.

As fall drew near a lot of the fence work was coming to an end. The men moved in close and we started to build the corrals and barns. The bunkhouse, large kitchen, and dining room for the help were nearly complete. The main house was up and the roof was shingled, but it had no windows or doors yet. The foundation was in for a long barn made to hold twenty teams on one side; the other side would hold fifteen saddle horses and a storage room for the saddles and harnesses.

I ordered planking for the floor of the house. We were waiting for that to come in on the railroad. I had gone through Frank's catalogs and ordered all of the most modern household fixtures and bathtubs for the house. I found I could order the new and modern toilet paper by the case. I ordered a hundred cases. A lot of men and families would be using it. They had new cast iron sinks for the kitchens. Planking had been ordered to make the horses stalls out of. We had a tent city with all of the workers. Wagons were hauling supplies from town every day. We fixed up a wagon as a butcher wagon. Three men went out at least twice a week and killed some of the wild bulls to feed the crew.

Chad suggested that we take a crew and start at the far end of the property and make a drive and round up all of the cattle into a herd, so we would know what we had. We took a chuck wagon and twenty of the men who were experienced cowboys. In two weeks we had all of the cows in a herd. I was surprised to find close to a thousand head. The large majority of them had long horns, but we found about three hundred hornless cows.

A week after we made the drive, Chad came home from town and said, "I sold the herd of bulls, and those longhorn cows that you don't want to keep, to a cattle buyer. You need to go cut out the ones you want to keep for breeding bulls along with the red cows you want. He'll be here in four days with a crew of men to drive them to the railroad. He'll pay thirty five dollars a head for them."

After we cut out the cows I wanted, and some of last year's young stock to feed the crew, we still had four hundred head. The crew came and moved the cattle to town. The buyer came asking for me. He gave me a check for fourteen thousand dollars. We visited, and I asked him if he would be able to supply me with brood stock to put out this fall.

Chad said, "We want them to calf here so this is home for the calves."

He asked how many cows we wanted. I looked at Chad and he raised his eyebrows.

I asked, "A thousand?"

He nodded his head and said, "At least."

"If you can, get twice that many good stock."

"Oh, I can get twice that many out of Texas next week." The buyer assured me.

I shook my head. "That's the drawback. We don't want longhorns. I want no horns and a gentle type of animals. I don't care what color, but I don't want those big horns. I hear about shorthorn cattle. They're what they call muleys. Can you find hornless whiteface bulls? I have a few big gray cattle out here with no horns. I think they're from oxen bulls. Chad, do you think we can handle two thousand head? If so, that's what we'll take, if you can find them. I would like them to be three or four year old stock."

I hadn't taken time to go to town for four months to check the mail. I'd been out working with one crew or the other. I wasn't even eating in the cave. I ate with the crew and fell into bed and got up again before daylight.

One of the teamsters came with a load of supplies from town. He said a man wanted to meet me tomorrow afternoon at the hotel, if possibly.

"What does he want? Did he say?"

"Something about cows is all he said." The teamster replied.

I found Chad and told him we needed to be in town before noon tomorrow. We better leave right away.

When we got to town and met the cattle buyer, he said he had two thousand bred cows for us to look at.

"Where?" I asked.

He smiled and said they were in Texas at his ranch. He had shipped them in from many places.

"Chad, you go look at them and if they're good enough, buy them."

After Chad and the buyer boarded the train, I went to the café to get something to eat. When I was through, the owner motioned me into the kitchen and handed me a bill for a lot of meals. I put the bill in my pocket and told her I had to go to the bank and would be right back with the money. When I came back and paid, I put in an extra ten for a tip.

I walked down to the post office and picked up a letter waiting for me from Fannie. I went to the hotel where I would have some private time.

~~~

Dear Ken   *Aug. 30, 1871*

I hope this finds you well and of good cheer. It seemed like a lifetime since I was able to take a few minutes for myself. Things are going about the same here. Grandma is still strong and now is helping me can food for the winter. The farm is again looking like someone cares. The man, who is farming, is doing a good job and the crops are good this year. Plentiful rain keeps the pastures deep in grass. He made hay on a couple of them. Oh, I'm going to school part of the time and the school board have approached me about teaching this fall. The time will go a little faster and give us more money to live on.

I think about you a lot and long to see you again. The ranch must be getting pretty close to finished. I wish I could stand on the top of the divide and listen to the elk do their bugling and see forever across the mountains again. But I think I will have to wait a while longer.

One of the members of the church approached me last month with a proposition of marriage. He said something like this: "Fannie, could we go someplace private? I would like to talk to you, please." We went outside and sat on the front steps. He reached over and took my hand and leaning close said, "I think you are beautiful and I would like to marry you. Do you suppose that would be possible? I have a nice little farm and if we both work right hard we could raise a nice family. Please think about this and let me know next week."

I will be looking forward to hearing what you think I should do. You know, I will be sixteen soon and that is marrying age here. I would hate to become an old maid. His offer might not be too bad. He is at least thirty and a nice man. I suppose he has his farm paid for. I have waited a long time for some word from you. I know you are busy but I really need to hear from you. I get so lonely I can hardly stand it. You just wait. When I get to see you I'm going to give you a big kiss or maybe a slug on the nose. Oh, one more thing. Will you give Charlie a love for me and take some time to tell him how much I miss the ugly beast.

A man here wants to buy the farm but he isn't coming up with enough money. He is offering about half as much as the place is worth. He thinks I'm some dumb kid. Oh, if he knew where I have been and what I have seen in my short life he would not try to push me. I will write again soon.

Thinking of you,
Fannie

~~~
</div>

Again I was in the hotel room, on the bed, reading the letter from Fannie. I read the letter twice before I went to eat. After supper I came back to the hotel room. I started to think about her and got really lonesome, so lonesome I couldn't go to sleep. I tossed and turned most of the night. The thought of her even holding someone else's hand was driving me crazy. I remember the feeling of her hugging me and telling me goodbye the morning she left on the train. I know she was just a kid, but the feeling of her arms about my neck and the strength in her arms as she clung to me for strength was burned in my memory.

I jumped up, dressed, went to the livery and took the stud from his stall. I rode home in the middle of the night. It took about two days before I had control of myself. After supper I went to the cave and lighted the two lanterns. I got out the writing stuff and wrote.

# CHAPTER 28

*Dear Fannie*                                               *Sept. 10, 1871*

*I received your letter and I'm sorry I haven't written for so long. I've been so busy that I lost all sense of time. I buried myself in the working of the ranch so I could put the thoughts of you from my mind. It has not always worked. I find myself seeing something new or a picture of something and the thought comes into my mind, "I wish Fannie could see this." Like last week, I was fifteen miles from home and suddenly, in front of me a doe deer stood up. She had a small baby by her side. The fawn was not more than a few hours old with wobbly legs. She was so cute, I wanted to swing down and pet her but that would not have been good either. I don't know why she was born so late in the season. She won't have much chance to live through the winter.*

*The house is all finished, with a big fireplace in the living room. I put the elk horns, from the big bull elk I killed the first winter, over it. Remember the bull that charged us? I saved those horns and they are hanging on the wall to one side. I put the thief's hide on the other side. You remember the old mountain lion that stole the deer when we were in town?*

*I'll be moving into the house sometime this month. The barns are about completed. The bunkhouse is all done except, one of the men is fixing it so the hot water from the spring will be running to the bathroom. He has built a bunch of tubs in a separate room. It will be nice. The men can come in and take a hot bath after a hard day. There is a chicken house with a large wire pen to keep the coyotes out. Some of the crew is building a home for the blacksmith and his wife. It is above the main house. There will be a place for a garden. Well, I say his wife. I think they will be getting married this fall.*

*Elisabeth is the same age as I am. We met when I was traveling the first summer away from home. She has had a hard life. She is quite good looking and a very serious girl. She has been working in the cook*

*tent with the cooks all summer. She will make someone a good wife.
She has been cleaning the house since the construction is through. She
needed work, so I gave her a job the day they got off the train. She is a
good worker and pleasant to be around.*

*I gave Charlie a love and told him you loved him. He just acted
sadder and shook his ears and walked away. I think Chad will be
buying two thousand head of cows this week. He is gone with a cattle
buyer to inspect them. He should be home in a day or two and then I
will know. He might be in town when I take this in to mail. It is late so
I must get some sleep.*

*As for you even thinking about marrying some eastern farmer, stop
and think about how rich you are in the west. I will enclose money for
you so you don't have to teach school or do anything that will keep
you longer than you need to be.*

Forever yours,
Ken

~~~

I enclosed four of the hundred dollar bills in the envelope and
sealed it. I went to town the next day and mailed the letter and the
money to Fannie.

The days are getting shorter, I noticed, and the weather is crisp in
the mornings. However, when the sun comes out it is getting really
nice in the daytime. Most of the crew is gone. Ten men are staying all
winter. Chad thinks that is enough to manage the cattle and ride herd
on them. We are making plans to build a line shack close to the other
end of the property. We will build a cabin where we found the gray
cows. There's a really nice spring and a meadow that can be fenced
and raise enough hay to feed the saddle stock and a team of horses
through the winter. We'll put in a nice set of corrals to help with the
working of cattle on the far end of the ranch. I think the cabin needs to
be able to sleep at least six, so that is what's planned for next spring.

Chad was in town when I took the letter to mail to Fannie. We met
at the café and had supper together. "Well, what did you find out about
the herd he has?" I asked.

He took some time and finally answered, "How rich are you? He's
got what you want and they are mostly good stock. Might be a hundred
with a little too much age, and fifty on the small side, but they'll give
birth to a calf next year and those calves will make good cows. You

can cull the cows next fall. All in all, they are quite good. I was surprised."

"So what's the drawback? You seem to be worried about something, so what's wrong?" I wanted to know.

"The price is a bit high, I think. However, he shipped them from about twenty ranches, all over the country, to make up the herd."

"Alright, what's his price?"

"Well, bred cows are worth thirty dollars on the market. But, with his expenses tacked in, he wants forty dollars a head delivered here." Chad said, "That amounts to a bunch of money."

"When does he need an answer?" I asked.

"He would like to know tomorrow so he can make shipping plans. He needs a lot of boxcars and help to do the job. The railroad will make up a special train to ship them all at one time. It will take about fifty-five cattle cars."

"Let's go sleep and think about what to do. I'll check with the banker to see how rich I am after this summer's spending spree."

We walked over to the hotel and went up to our rooms. I lay in bed for a long time, thinking about Fannie and our lives. Why couldn't we bring Grandma out here so she would be with Fannie? We had plenty of room in the new, big house. And I plan on hiring some help to take care of the housework for Fannie so she can get outside, where she wants to be.

The thought crossed my mind; you're planning on marrying her and planning everything that way. What if she doesn't want to marry you? What then? Half of the ranch is hers. What if she marries someone else? Have you ever thought about that? She is entitled to half. Good lord, she worked as hard as I had, except for this last summer. But she worked back east just as hard as I did here.

By now I was so worked up I couldn't go to sleep. I had nothing to read, so got up and paced the floor for a couple of hours and then I thought, "Oh, forget it." And I lay down and went to sleep.

I was late getting up in the morning. When I got to the café, Chad was through eating and sitting with his second cup of coffee. He smiled and asked, "Tough night?"

I just nodded and gave my order to the waitress. She gave me a flirty look and smiling said, "Coming right up."

Chad laughed. "I guess the word is out."

"What word?" I wondered.

Chad changed the subject." What time are you going to the bank?"

"As soon as I eat. Get the smirk off your face. She's almost old enough to be my mother."

I ate, got up and walked to the bank to see Mr. Job. I was led right into his office.

He stood, held out his hand and said, "Well, this is a surprise. Do you need something or is this a social call?"

"Oh, I just dropped in to see if I'd run out of money yet. I've been trying."

"Yes. I've been watching. What the devil have you done out there anyway, other than hire half of the men this side of the state line and fed them steaks?" He jokingly said.

"I dropped in to see how much money is left in the account, after I built a ranch from nothing but grass. You need to drive out some day. What I really want to know is where my account stands."

He nodded and called to the teller in the next room. "Bring in the KC Ranch account, will you please."

He read the numbers to himself and smiling asked, "How big of a loan do you want?"

My mouth flew open. I was shocked.

He laughed and said, "Got you on that one, didn't I? You have, as of today, about three hundred thousand in your account."

"It's time to stock the ranch, so I've had a stock buyer buying some cattle. I don't want longhorns because they're too hard to handle. The range is all fenced. I can buy two thousand head of bred cows. They're a mixed herd, but no horns. They will mostly range in age from three year olds to five or six. Most of them are three and four. The price is a little high, about ten dollars over longhorns. I think, in the long run, they will pay off. I'll try to find some good bulls to go with them next spring. The cost will be eighty thousand, give or take a few dollars. That was why I wanted to know if I had enough to buy that many right now. I think I can, if I tighten the belt for a while."

I went from the bank to the hotel to find Chad. He was not in his room. I went to the café and found him drinking another cup of coffee and eating a piece of pie. "You're going to get fat if you keep eating pie every time you sit down."

He nodded and answered, "What a great way to die, don't you think?"

"Okay, let's go telegraph the buyer. I want to know what they are bred to. I hope not longhorn bulls."

I had Chad send the telegram saying we would take the herd if they were not bred to longhorn bulls. An answer came back in an hour. The deal was solid and they were bred to mostly whiteface and shorthorn bulls. He would make a delivery in one week. We wired back saying we will be ready in one week.

I asked Chad, while we were walking toward the livery barn, "What do we need to do other than bring the crew in to get the herd? Is everything out at the ranch taken care of?"

"We'll take them home, push them on across the creek, and spread them out on the pasture. We'll need to take a week or so to spread them out to the water holes or springs." Chad answered.

"Let's go to the hotel. I've been thinking about something this past week and we need to talk. The horse barn and all of the things are ready at the ranch, but there is no hay for the horses when we put them in the barn or corrals."

I stopped walking and asked him. "Have you given any thought to the problem? What are we going to do for feed? I guess we let the crew go too soon. What do you think we should do?"

Chad shook his head and said, "I guess this winter we'll put them out on pasture every night and keep a roundup horse in the barn."

"Let's go talk to Frank over at the store and see what he has to say," I suggested.

We found Frank standing outside of his store looking at the front. The front had been pretty well filled with holes and the lanterns were all busted.

"What in the devil happened to you?" I asked.

He shook this head and said, "This town should sue you or refuse to let you do business here. Do you know that? Ever since you went and bribed our town law to go to work with you, we've had nothing but trouble from one young man, who likes to destroy anything that will break with a bullet. He shot this up a couple of nights ago. Whenever someone approaches him to pay up he laughs and says for what?"

"Who is this guy?" Chad asked. "Where do I find him?"

"He calls himself Willie. He hangs out with a couple other guys down at the end of the street in the saloon. He claims he is the fastest man alive with a gun."

Chad turned and went down the street with a determined look on his face. I had seen that look a couple of times out at the ranch. I knew someone was in trouble. I walked really fast to catch up with him.

I said, "You know, this is not any of your responsibility. You're no longer wearing the badge."

He looked over his shoulder and said, "That's right, but Frank is a special friend of ours and we need to help him."

I thought, "Wait a minute. What was this "we" bit? I don't want to get into a fight, much less shoot someone."

By the time I came to a decision I was needed some place else, Chad turned and walked into the bar. He stopped inside of the door and looked around for a second or two. In a loud voice he asked, "Is someone named Willie in here? I understand he's the toughest, fastest, man with a gun around."

One young man jumped to his feet and walked right up to Chad and said, "I'm Willie, so what?"

I was watching the other two sitting at the table. Chad never said another word. He hit the kid as hard as he could right on the point of the jaw, reached out and caught him when he dropped. He threw him over his shoulder and walked to the door. The two other guys jumped to their feet and started to draw their guns.

I drew my gun and said, "Put them away fellows and get your stuff. You're going along."

Chad didn't walk towards the jail like I thought he would. He walked to the store and turned to the other two and said, "Take off your guns and boots." He called to Frank.

When Frank walked outside Chad said, "What's the cost to fix up the damages to your store?"

Frank asked, "Which time? They've hit me twice and they shot up the café three weeks ago or more. They still hassle her every day."

By now the tough guy was awake. He jumped up and started to cuss and swear and threaten Chad. Chad reached down and picked up a holstered gun from the street and asked, "Is this yours?"

When Willie said, "Yes, give it to me and I'll show you how tough I am."

Chad pulled the gun from the holster and tossed it to Willie. As he was about to catch it, Chad drew and shot the gun in the air and sent it spinning out of reach. Then he shot the hat off of the kid's head. The next one nicked an ear. Willie was standing, trembling with fright.

"Now, I have your attention I want to know how you plan to pay for the damage you have caused here in town. Do you have horses and saddles? What can you sell to pay for it?"

One of the other young men said, "Justin and I are sorry. We were carried away with his big talk. We're from the farmer's area across the tracks and this was our first time away from home. I can sell my saddle and horse to pay my share."

The other young man said, "I can too."

Chad turned to the troublemaker.

Willie looked at him and said, "Go to hell."

Chad nodded and picking up the kids boots and gun, he turned to Frank and handed them to him saying, "Let's go to the livery and see what kind of crow bait this kid has."

When we got there, Chad told the attendant he wanted him to bring out the kid's mount. When the man came out he was leading an old, white mule, at least twenty years old, with a broken down saddle on it. We looked at each other and started to laugh. The other two young men stood with a shocked expression on their faces.

One of them said, "That's your mount?" They also laughed.

Chad turned, took Willie by the shirt collar and walked him down the street to the railroad depot. He went into the station and said, over his shoulder, "Go get the mule and bring it here." He motioned to a man outside of the station.

When he came in Chad asked him, "What time does the freight pull out?"

"About ten minutes," he said, "Going east."

Chad said, "Dustin, I'm going into the ticket office. You take this guy and his mule and load them into a boxcar. I'll give the ticket man a ten. You put a lock on the door and don't take the padlock off until he has ridden out his ten, okay?

As we left the station, Chad turned to the two boys and asked, "Have either of you put up hay out on your farm?"

They both nodded their head. He asked how they did it. One answered, "With a hay scythe and a wagon. We cut it, let the grass cure for a few days, load it on a wagon, and haul it into a barn or to a stack."

"We need hay," he said, "And you need a job. Find your way out to the ranch the first of the week and you have a job until snow flies, and then we'll go from there."

He went to Frank and asked about the damages and told him to hold their guns until they came in and paid him. They both said they would. I gave one of them five dollars to eat with until they could get to the ranch. I explained how to get to the ranch and told them to come to the hotel and I would show them their room.

Chad shook his head and said, "Wait until we come back in and you can help move a couple thousand head of cows out to the ranch."

They both stood with their mouths open. Finally they both said at once, "A couple thousand head! Good lord, I hope you don't want us to cut enough hay for that many?"

Chad and I broke out laughing. I told them, "Not really. See you the first of the week."

CHAPTER 29

We went in to talk to Frank before leaving for home. I asked what he had to help us put up hay. He went over to a catalog and showed us a new machine called a mower, pulled buy two horses, and cut a swath five feet wide. A machine, called a dump rake, gathered the hay into bunches. I ordered four of the mowers and everything to keep them operating. I figured one dump rake would be enough for this winter.

We left for home before daylight. As we dropped into the valley, we were watching and trying to decide where we would cut hay. We thought about cutting the big flat out toward the creek. The grass had been pretty well eaten off by all of the teams last summer. Chad suggested we go to the other side of the creek and cut the area we had not pastured during the summer.

The next night, after we got home, I sat down and wrote another letter, to Fannie

~~~

Dearest Fannie,   *November 20, 1871*
  It has been three months since I heard from you. Hoping you are well. I hope you received the money I sent. I'm worried, since you haven't written for a long time.   It's almost winter here in the mountains. We are getting frost every night.
  We moved the herd of cows in and they are scattered over the western part of the range. They are all colors, but very few of them have even short horns. They are a lot tamer and do not want them to chase the horses when we ride into bunches of them.
  We also bought some new machines to cut hay. John made four of the wagons into hay wagons. The wagons have a flat bed with a standard at each end to hold the hay from sliding off. I hired a couple of young men, who were raised on a farm. They are a big help. Chad and I think we will keep them on to help for the winter. They are good workers.
  Did you take the job of teaching school? How is your grandma doing? I moved into the new home and the house is so different from the cave. There are two big windows that look out on the flat meadow. You can see the west rim though them. Water is coming from the

springs into the houses through pipes buried underground. The pipes are also running into all of the buildings. We equipped the houses and all the living quarters with the newest features. We put in hot and cold running water fixtures. What a nice thing that is. All you do is open the faucets and out comes hot or cold water. Indoor toilets are great, no going out in the cold.

I think about you a lot. This house is awful lonely at night with no one to talk to. Elisabeth cooks dinner for me and goes home. She and John went to town a month ago and got married. They didn't tell anyone until they had been married for two weeks. Elisabeth's brother moved into the bunkhouse one day and we all wondered why. Then John said they had gotten married. That made me all the lonelier. I wonder what your plans are. Is anyone asking for your hand?

Forever,
Kenneth

~~~

I went to town today and picked up a letter from Fannie. I didn't take time to read it. I was in town to order some things for the help for Christmas. A storm was brewing and I wanted to get home before I got caught out like Fannie and I did. I was riding Charlie and he felt the weather changing, so he was glad to hit a fast pace most of the way home. He was sweating hard when we rode into the barn, so I took time to rub him down. When I walked out of the barn, the wind and snow hit me in the face. I ran for the house. When I got home Elisabeth had started a fire in the fireplace. Supper was cooked and left on the back of the stove for me. I looked out, but she was gone. She left before the snow hit. I ate, then opened and read the letter.

~~~

Dear Kenneth,   *Nov 15, 1871*
Yes, I received your letter in the fall. I'm sorry I didn't answer sooner. A lot is going on here. Shortly after your letter arrived I had an offer on the farm that the banker thought we should consider. It was for a nice sum and would keep us for a long time. After a lot of talking, I have Grandma convinced to accept the offer. The family wants to move in shortly after Christmas, so we are packing and disposing of forty some years of Grandma's things. That's been hard on her and on me as I go through boxes of my mother and father's things they left here when they went west. I told Gram about the trip and she can't understand why I would like to go back west. To her the west is a

world of awful cruel men and murder. I arraigned to rent a part of a boarding house for Gram and me for the rest of the winter. Then we will see what comes up.

No, I didn't accept any proposals from men. Yes, a couple of men would like me to go to dances with them and on dates. One is quite nice but I don't have any feelings for him. His father is quite wealthy and I think he is a little spoiled. He has never worked for a living. He has definitely never missed a meal. He has no idea what it is to wonder where he is going to sleep the next night, or if there will be wood for a fire to keep warm. No, he has never rolled up in a bedroll in the back of a wagon and had to jump into bed with the opposite sex to keep warm. I think maybe he would like that

As to your question about Grandma's health, she is strong and going good again. She keeps telling me I need to get out more and socialize. In other words, go to parties and giggle like the other girls my age do when a handsome young man walks by. I lost the giggle after driving a ten-horse team for days on end in the heat and cold.

Oh, Ken, I miss you so much. I will try to write more often, I promise. Thank you for the money. It came just as we really needed it.

Love,
Fannie

~~~

CHAPTER 30

The following weeks were a blur. The snow piled up and the men and I rode every day keeping the cattle from piling up in the draws, out of the wind. January turned into February and the weather started to warm during the day. Chad had us slowly move the cows toward the home ranch. The cows would start calving soon. He wanted them close so we could ride through the herd night and morning. We moved them all within five miles of the house and barns.

One morning Chad and one of the men rode up to the barn. Chad said, "Get your horse and follow us."

I mounted and we rode out toward the herd.

Chad stopped, raised his arm and said, "Here is the future of the KC Ranch."

At least two dozen baby calves bucked and played in the warm sun. They all had white faces, but their bodies were all different colors. What a beautiful sight. I sat with tears in my eyes. Oh, how I wish Fannie could see this. She would want to pet each one.

The next month went by so fast we hardly had time to sleep. The cows calved and we were out night and day in case one was in trouble. February turned to March and I told Chad to get a hold of one of the fencing crews. I wanted some cross fences put in and told him where I wanted them. He thought that was a good idea.

I went to town and looked through Frank's catalogs. I looked for some more farm machinery. I wanted more haying equipment. Over the winter I had decided to plow up some of the bottom land and plant oats and corn for winter feed. I ordered what I thought we would need and included two of the new stationary hay balers, also a hand turned machine to put the corncobs in and remove corn from the cob.

I checked the mail and had nothing from Fannie. By the time I got home I had made up my mind. I was going to go get her. I had waited long enough. It had been a year.

The next morning I told Chad that I had another ranch in Tennessee. I needed to go check on it, and see what had happened to my folks place in Virginia. I told him about ordering the farm equipment and asked him what he thought about putting the redheaded young man, who had been in trouble in town last fall, in charge of haying, plowing, and seeding oats and corn for feed.

He thought about it and asked, "How much do you mean in charge?"

"Whatever you think he can handle", I said.

He nodded his head and said, "It's his."

We talked about where I wanted to cut hay and plow fields for planting crops.

He asked, "When are you was leaving?"

"In the morning I'll take the sorrel team and light wagon with my stuff and you or one of the men can bring it home. The place is now yours to run until I get back. Good luck. I hope I won't be gone more than a month."

As a parting shot I said, "You better get with the cattle buyer and get some bulls ordered pretty quick. We'll need them in a month or so won't we? When they come, go to the bank and get a draft to pay for them. I'll talk to Quinton and tell him to give you a draft for whatever you need for the bulls. You better find out what the guys think they will need for the spring plowing and this summer's haying. I would like enough hay in stacks so the cows can be brought in closer to home during the worse part of the winter.

I went to John and told him we would need some way to handle the hay bales and for him to get with Chad and the redheaded young man to see what they wanted him to make. There were going to be more wagon beds, for sure. He needed to make sure there were plenty of shoes ready for teams. I told him I was leaving for a while and I would lock the house.

The next morning I left the ranch, with no idea what was ahead of me. I got to town the next day, with plenty to time to buy a ticket on the train to Pennsylvania. I went to the store and got two complete new sets of clothes, including new boots and a western hat. I had taken five thousand dollars from the safe, so I bought a money belt and put it on under my shirt. A loose jacket covered everything. I bought a short nosed gun and underarm type holster; also, what they called a satchel, like Fannie had. I was ready and waiting at the station early.

CHAPTER 31

Six o'clock in the evening, April 14, 1872, I boarded the train and headed east. To what, I had no idea. But I was going under a lot different conditions than I had coming west.

I'm now a grown man with a grown man's stature. Hard work filled out my body. I'm five feet ten inches tall, and weigh about one hundred sixty pounds, with not one ounce of fat. I walk like I own the world and I about do. My confidence grew because of all the things I accomplished. I really had been there and done things. I know what I want and I am going after her. The woman, who is to be my wife, is waiting. I am ready to take on the world if need be.

The train went day and night. When we got into the big cities I never left the station. I was not as brave as I thought. I marveled at Fannie going through this alone. I ate sandwiches and drank water and nothing else. One night I went to what they called the dining car to eat. They wanted two dollars for a small plate of something not fit to eat, to my way of thinking. They called the fish, cat fish. After the first bite I didn't want more. The car filled with stinking smoke. I almost gagged before I got to fresh air.

I went down the narrow aisle back to my seat. A man stood up and started my way, dressed in a fancy looking suit, wearing eyeglasses. His shoes had been polished until they sparkled. He wore a bright colored tie, tied in some type of fancy knot. When we met, I turned sideways for him to pass. He lost his balance and fell into me. I felt his hand go into my pants pocket where I had some money. I turned toward him and trapped his hand in my pocket. I looked him in the eye and said, "Your mistake, mister."

I opened my jacket and he saw the gun. He went as white as a sheet and tried to get away. A black man came walking toward us and stopped to wait for us to move.

I asked him," Who is in charge on the train?" and showed him why. He turned and called someone's name. A big man stood up and walked to us.

"What's going on here?" he asked.

I reached down, took the fancy dresser by the wrist and pulled his hand out of my pocket. He tried to pull away and I held him. He was not very strong.

That's when the big man said, "You, mister, are going to get off of the train."

He took him to the door at the end of the car. I didn't see him again.

The train took almost eight days to get to the town where I got off. Now I had to find Fannie. I walked into the office at the train station and asked how I could get to Wickerville.

The agent, in the cage said, "A stage will go in the morning if you want to wait."

"How far is it, anyway?" I asked.

He answered, "Way up north, at least ten miles, I believe."

"Well, tell me, where can I rent a horse or a buggy?"

"You must be in a powerful hurry. That will cost a good bit of change."

I got tired of his jabber. I tried again. "A livery?" I asked.

He shook his head and said, "Down the street and two blocks to the left."

I picked up my satchel and walked to find the livery stable. As I approached the front door, a man walked out to meet me.

"Can I help you, mister?" He asked.

"Yes, can you tell me how far to Wickerville?"

He studied me for a moment. "Well, a little over ten miles down the road. Kind of a long walk in those cowboy boots you got on,"

I said, "You've been west, I gather."

"That's right. I spent three years in California digging for gold and darn near starved to death. When I came home over the divide I almost froze. I ended holed up in a little town all winter and spent what money I had left surviving. I worked my way home working for the railroad. That is one trip I'll never forget and never try again. We Easterners are not made for that country."

"I need a horse or a buggy. I want to get to Wickerville today if I can."

"Well, let me think. It's nine o'clock, so your making the trip by early afternoon shouldn't be problem. Do you want a horse or a buggy? But, did you ever ride on one of the little flat saddles like they do here?"

"Yes. I lived in Virginia and when I went west I had part of one on a mule. When I got to the big river I was able to get a good saddle. If you have a good stepper and a buggy I'll take them."

"How long do you want her for? The cost will be a dollar a day. When you are in Wickerville you can keep her in the stable."

"Ok, I'll take the buggy. How soon will it be ready?"

"Right away, but if you just got off the train you might want to eat. They don't feed much that is fit to eat. The little café around the corner has good food."

That sounded good to me. I walked around the corner and went into the café. I ordered steak, fried potatoes with onions, and a big glass of cold milk.

About an hour later I got back to the livery. The mare was tied up out in front and ready to go.

The owner came out and said, "She'll take a nice long trot most of the way. The buggy whip is just for looks. She's sweet. I don't usually rent her out, but I think you know how to handle animals. She just needs to be talked to."

I put my things in the buggy and tried to give him a deposit. He waved me off and said, "When you get back."

I turned north on the road and jiggled the reins a little. The mare broke into a long trot. She seemed to be enjoying the trip. I sat back and watched the farms and fields go by. This area seemed a lot like home to me. The land was flatter than Dad's farm in Virginia, but the houses were the same and the grass had the same green color. However, dairy cows replaced cotton fields. The day went by fast. I enjoyed myself and before I realized it, lunchtime had passed. The sun was past the center and headed well into the afternoon when I entered the small town of Wickerville. The little mare had not broken a sweat and she held to the mile eating-pace. I loved her. She was truly a treasure.

Now, how would I find where Fannie and her grandma lived? As I drove down the street, I found a mercantile store on the right. I tied the mare in front and went in. A middle-aged woman stood behind the counter.

I walked up to her and asked if she had any idea where Fannie Magee and her grandmother lived. "I'm new to the area and want to find them."

She leaned back a little and looked me over right well. "Now, what would you be wantin' of Fannie, pray tell?"

I asked, "You do know them?"

She got a twinkle in her eye. Then she answered, "A wee bit, I think. But now, how do you know her, is the question. You don't dress like a suitor. I don't see any flowers or a bow tie, now do I?"

I shook my head and knew I was going to get hassled from this lady if I didn't get the best of her. I stared her in the eye and said, "What would you expect from a bum who has to beg for direction to his own wife's house."

"So, what do you think I'm supposed to do? Give every man, who comes along with a sad tale, the way to Fannie's home?"

I said, "I'm wasting time here. I haven't come all the way across the country to be put off by some Irish woman, who has taken it upon herself to protect a fair lady, so her own son can have a wife."

She laughed and said; "Now I do believe you are the one she's been moping around about. Their house is up the next street on the left. 'Tis a blue house with white trim. There are two doors. The one on the left is Fair Fannie's home."

I thanked her and started out the door.

She asked, "Where are the flowers, young man? You can't go calling without some flowers. She loves flowers, you know. Fannie always has some around. Here, take these. I can cut more for the next suitor."

I thanked her and went running out to the buggy and drove up the street. What did she mean; I can cut more for the next one? Was I not going to be welcome? Was there someone else? I hadn't written to let her know I was coming. I turned the corner and the blue house was the second one on the street. I drove up to the front walk and sat thinking. For some reason, I was afraid to knock on the door. Would I be welcome, I wondered. Nuts, here goes. I jumped down and walked to the door and knocked.

The door opened and a little, round-faced lady looked out, asking if she could help me. Right then I didn't think anyone could help me. I asked if Fannie was home.

She smiled and asked, "Who shall I say is calling?"

I said, "Just tell her Ken is here to see her."

I heard a scream from in the house some place. The next thing I knew, a sobbing something wrapped around me, almost knocking me down. I hung on for a while and enjoyed the hugs. She turned loose, took my face in her hands and planted the biggest warm kiss on my lips. I know my face got beet red before she stopped.

Her grandma stood and watched and then said, with a twinkle in her eyes, "Fannie, there's a young man at the door. He says his name is Ken. I do believe, young man, you better give me the flowers before they're completely crushed."

Fannie grabbed my arm and pulled me into the room, then turned and kissed me again. Now, I started liking this, so I took her in my arms and kissed her back. That turned her face red. She looked at her grandma as she came in from the other room.

Fannie said, "Grandma, this is Kenneth Clausen. I've told you all about him. He's the most wonderful young man you could ask for. We traveled for months over miles of country, just thirty horses and us. He never ever once treated me with disrespect or anything less than like I was a lady."

Her eyes started to twinkle as she looked at me and said, "Even one cold night when I crawled into his bed to keep from freezing. Now, Grandma, I want you to know he never ever tried to kiss me until now. Many times I wanted him to in the worst way, but he is always a gentleman."

I took my hat off and said, "I think we were about to meet before we were so rudely interrupted. I'm Ken, as you have guessed, and I can tell you're Fannie's Grandma. I can see you looked just like her a few years ago. It's nice to meet you and I hope we can get to be friends."

She looked at me really somber and answered, "The friend thing will depend on what your plans for my granddaughter are. But we'll wait and cross that bridge when it's time to make some decisions about our lives."

Fannie cried, "Oh, Grandma, he just got here. Don't go picking on him yet."

She took me by the arm and started for the door saying, "Ken, why don't we take the horse out behind and put her in the stable? She needs feed and water. That's a long trip and she needs to rest."

I smiled and walked out in front of her and went to the mare. I followed Fannie around the house to the stable. I unharnessed the mare and put her in the stall by Fannie's horse. When I stepped out of the stall, she met me with a long, clinging hug and a kiss.

"Oh Ken, what are we going to do? I can't leave Grandma here alone and I can't take her to live in a small house in the west. She has spent all of her life right here. She and Grandpa moved onto the farm the day after they were married."

"Why don't you leave that up to her? Let's not make a hurried decision yet. Let's talk about a few things first. Come on, before she comes hunting for us. I don't want to get on the wrong side of her to begin with. Come on."

We walked, hand in hand, back to the house. We found Grandma in the kitchen making a pie. Fannie walked over to her and gave her a kiss on the cheek and winked at me at the same time. We had a wonderful supper with hot pie and whipped cream on the top.

I commented, "The whipped cream and pie are delicious I've not made any for a long time."

Fannie asked, "What about the Jersey?"

"I'm sorry to say, I got so busy this year I didn't take time to milk her. I let John and Elisabeth milk and take care of her. I think Elisabeth probably did the milking. John is so busy with the blacksmith work; I don't think he had much time for anything but sleeping and eating. He was busy all winter, but nothing pressing like last summer."

Fannie asked, "And who is this Elisabeth that has been doing your housework and a lot of the house cleaning? You said she was pretty and you had known her before. Grandma was sitting, with a smile on her face and a twinkle in her eye.

I winked at her and with a straight face said, "She's a young woman I met not long after I left my home in Virginia. I rode into their place one evening asking for a place to sleep and hoping to get some hot food. She was outside working in the garden. While I talked to her, her younger brother came out and pointed a shotgun at me and told me to leave. Now, you know, I respect someone with a shotgun. Anyway, she is about five feet eight, slender, but not too slender. She has beautiful brown shoulder length hair, and always a bright smile. Her eyes are jet black and can cut you to ribbons if she doesn't approve of something. She's a really hard worker. I like her a lot. She's becoming a woman men are going to stop and notice. Is there anything else you want to know about her?"

Fannie frowned at me and said, with a touch of temper, in her voice, "No. I think maybe you have been noticing a little too much yourself."

I shrugged and answered, "Well, it's been a long winter and I didn't ride every day you know."

Grandma started to laugh. "You asked for it, Honey Child, and he got you, that's for sure. This is a young man not even you can get the best of. I think you've met your match, Fannie girl."

Fannie said, "Oh, it's bad enough without you taking his side. I had forgotten how he likes to tease. She probably is four foot three and built like a barrel."

I turned to Grandma and asked, "Do you have any idea how far it is to Richmond, Virginia? My folks had a farm near Wagoner's Corner before they were all killed. I would like to go find out if someone has taken over the place or if it's empty. If no one has claimed the land I'd like to do so."

"No, but a railroad might go through where you want to go. Richmond is a large town by now, I suppose. You could go to the train station and find out, I would think."

We visited for a couple more hours and I asked if I needed to go find a room to rent.

Fannie jumped up and said, "You'll do no such thing. I'll make a bed here in the front room for you. You will stay here. I will not turn you loose on the town. No telling what kind of trouble you would get into."

She went and got some blankets from a closet and made a bed on the floor for me. I knelt down and helped her. Grandma had gone into one of the other rooms and shut the door. Fannie stood up, turned to me, then walked over and gave me a light kiss and said good night.

"By the way, you better put the pistol in your satchel. You'll not need the gun here." She went into her room and shut her door.

I got up at my usual time. The sun began to light the eastern sky. It's going to be a hot day, I thought. I walked around through the town for about an hour, wondering how to approach Fannie's Grandma about marrying Fannie and taking her west. I wasn't going to leave without, her, I knew that for sure. I turned and walked toward the house. I heard this very Irish voice behind me.

"Well, Laddie, did the flowers get you in the door? Must have, ye be out early this mornin', with a smile as big as a spring morning."

I stopped, turned and smiled, "Yeah, they did. But someplace in the scuffle, as to who was going to kiss who, the flowers came out a little beat up. I want to thank you for the kind thought. I would like to pay you for them. If you have any more, I'll take another bunch this morning."

"Well now, if you stay long I'll not have any flowers left in my garden, will I? But I think we may be able to find a few more. Come with me." She ordered.

We walked around to the back of her house. She had a large flower garden, full of flowers in all colors. "Now, what would you like?"

I said, "You pick them out. I'm sure she'll like any of them."

She picked a good-sized handful and handed them to me. This time I handed her a dollar. She shook her head no.

I asked, "Do you buy the seed to plant?"

"Sometimes, when I want to get something new, I send an order to a seed company."

"Then order two or three next time. I like flowers, too. We both will enjoy them if I come again."

I walked towards the house. When I turned the corner and started down the street Fannie came running out to meet me.

"Where have you been this morning? Out charming our neighbor out of more flowers, I see."

"Do you like them?"

"Oh, they are beautiful, but you better quit spending all of your money on flowers or we might not have enough to get back west."

I looked at her and couldn't resist saying, "What is this 'we' bit"?

She got a real serious expression on her face and said, "That is not something I will even consider. You going home without me, is not going to happen, you know."

"I'm sorry for teasing. I would not even consider something like that."

Fannie wanted to go out to the farm and show me where she had been raised. We loaded Grandma in the buggy with us and drove around looking at all of the farms. We listened to Grandma tell about her old neighbors and how their farms were prospering. The home place was fixed up and had flowers blooming in the beds. The dairy cows appeared all fat and healthy. The fences had been fixed. Some of them appeared to be freshly painted earlier this spring. We could tell the farmer took care of his farm. We returned to town. Fannie and I got out of the buggy. Grandma leaned against me as I lifted her to the ground.

"Thank you. I enjoyed the ride. I feel better, after seeing the farm. It's going to be a family home again, and that makes me feel good."

After supper, she sat down in the front room and motioned for me to come and sit by her. "You've seen my farm, now tell me about yours. Fannie has told me some, but you've been working for better than a year, since she left."

We sat for hours while I told her about the thousands of acres and the buildings we had built. About the wonderful home made of peeled logs. I talked about all of the newest things. I told her you could sit in front of the two big windows and see for miles and watch deer and elk feed with the cows; and how we had lived in the cave all winter, and about Charlie. How he loved Fannie and would follow her and want his ears scratched. I told her a little about her granddaughter sitting on the big freight wagon and driving five big teams of horses in a line at one time. How proud I felt of Fannie for doing the things she had done. We laughed when I told about me cutting Fannie's hair, then her cutting mine. I couldn't see mine, but hers was a mess. I had never had nerve enough to tell her how bad.

After we went to bed, I lay planning what I needed to do to go see about my father's place.

CHAPTER 32

I told Fannie and Grandma I wanted to go find out about the farm. We stayed around home all day. The next morning I left way before daylight. I drove to the railroad station and inquired about traveling to Richmond. The train would leave in an hour. I returned the mare to the livery and paid the owner and told him if he ever wanted to sell her to give me a chance.

"He smiled and said, "I think shipping her to Nevada might be a little expensive."

I returned to the station and boarded the train going south. It would be a five-hour ride to Richmond. I left the train late in the afternoon. I went through the station and stopped at the ticket counter and asked if there was a hotel close by where I might get a room.

He said, not one he would recommend. I would be better off to take a ride up town. They have a lot of nice hotels, if you can afford one.

I picked up my satchel and went outside. Teams and buggies lined up in front of the station. I stopped and studied them.

One of the men, standing in a group, walked over to me and asked, "Do you need a ride, young fellow?"

He appeared to be a nice man. I said, "I'd like to go up town and find a room to spend the night."

"Jump in. I'll take you. The price is a dollar in advance."

I got out a dollar for him. He drove through the streets and pulled up in front of a big building. A man standing in front, wearing some type of uniform walked to the wagon and asked if I wanted a room.

"Yes." I told him. He reached for my satchel. I quickly picked it up and got out of the buggy.

He said, "Please follow me" And started to the door.

That's when two men ran out of a side street and tried to jerk the satchel from my hands. They had misjudged their victim. I didn't fight back. I just drew the pistol fast and jammed it into the closest one's face. He let out a squeak and they both took off like I had shot them. I turned to see where everyone went. I still held the pistol in my hand. The buggy and doorman had disappeared. I put the gun in its holster and walked into a very fancy hotel lobby with a man behind the counter.

When I asked for a room, he smiled and said, "Five dollars please."

I glanced around and asked, "Where's the man who was outside of the door? He asked if he could carry my bags."

"You must be mistaken. We don't have a doorman." He answered.

I smiled and said, "Someone made a mistake, but not me."

I took a key and went upstairs to my room, a lot wiser about traveling in the east. I made sure the key locked the door before I went to sleep. I awoke to the smell of food. That sure did smell good. I got more money from my belt and went down the stairs. A small eating place filled an area beside the lobby. I went in and a man asked if I wanted coffee.

I told him, "No thanks, but I am really past ready for breakfast. What do you have?"

He handed me a heavy piece of folded paper with the list of food to order for breakfast. I had never seen anything like that.

I turned to him asking, "What would you have if you had gone all day yesterday without eating?"

He smiled and asked, "The first time off of the range?"

I nodded.

He said, "I'll fix you up." And he headed for the kitchen door.

I thought he had forgotten me but he came back with pancakes, bacon and eggs, lots of hot syrup, fried potatoes, and a huge glass of ice cold-milk.

"Will this do to start?" he asked.

"Looks just right I think this will be plenty. Thank you."

I didn't waste time talking, but just dived right in. When I was through I looked for the man. He came over to the table and told me the meal was two dollars. He asked where I was from. I told him from Nevada, way out west.

"I've been there. I worked as a cook for the railroad starting in California."

"How did you end up here?" I asked.

He said, "I got drunk and robbed and I haven't saved up enough money to get a ticket back west."

I asked him where to find a livery stable close by. I needed to rent a team and buggy for a few days.

He said, "Most of the town horses are retired farm work horses. You would be wiser if you took a cab to the outskirts of town to rent something."

I followed his advice and got a nice team and buggy and driving direction to get to where I wanted to go. The stable man said the drive would take a couple of days.

 The drive really turned into three days, but I finally found the town of Wagoner's Corner. I had no trouble finding the farm. Not much had changed from the way I left it. The house and barn were burned down. The pigpen and chicken house were standing. The farmyard was completely grown up to weeds. The fields were also just weeds. It made me so sad. I sat and looked at the once good farm. I drove out of the farmyard and met a team and wagon coming down the road. I waited for them to come abreast and I asked, "Can you tell me about this farm?"

He said, "The story is a sad one."

He told me what he knew about the farm. He was partly right but a lot he didn't know. I asked how I could find out more, and he directed me to the courthouse in town. Now, that was the information I wanted.

I went to the courthouse and finally found a man who told me most of those abandoned farms were for sale because of back taxes.

I asked him, "How do I find out about the taxes and what needs to be done?"

He smiled and said, "I do most of the paperwork on them. Do you have any farm in mind?"

"Yes I do. I am interested in the Clausen farm."

He seemed startled and asked, "You wouldn't be the son would you?"

I nodded my head.

He turned and picked up a big book, opened to a page and turned the book for me to read. "A hundred dollars are due on taxes as of now." He held his finger on a column of numbers for me to read.

"If I paid the taxes on the farm would I own the place free and clear?" I wanted to know.

He answered, "Yes, you would. And you would have a fine piece of land. It was a very good farm until everybody left. A farmer has been showing some interest and wanted to buy the land this spring. He went home to talk to his wife about buying, but he hasn't come back."

"I noticed two other farms, beside my place, that look deserted. Are they for sale?"

He looked in the book and did some figuring and said, "If you want those two, the price would be five hundred dollars. You would have six hundred and forty acres of prime cotton ground. The price of cotton is beginning to come back, you know. The land may make you a rich man."

"Okay. Is there some place private I can go for a couple of minutes?"

He showed me a small room and walked out and closed the door. I loosened the money belt and removed eight one-hundred dollar bills. I went back into the other room and laid five of the bills on the counter. He wrote me out a receipt and handed me some papers. He said they were the deeds to the farms.

I asked him if he would write down the name of the farmer, who wanted to buy the land, and tell me how to get to his place. I left the courthouse and, following his directions, drove to the farmer's home. Three hours later, I headed back the way I had come. The farmer was overjoyed to have the farms to work on shares. He would deposit the money for one-third of the crop in the same bank Bart's farm income was being deposited in.

CHAPTER 33

Five days later I drove up to Fannie's house late at night. I put the mare in the barn and went to the house and knocked on the door. Grandma opened the door and let me in.

She asked, "Have you eaten today?"

I shook my head no and put my stuff in the corner of the room. She went to the kitchen, and in a few minutes she called. She set a sandwich and a glass of milk on the table.

I looked around and asked, "Where's Fannie tonight?"

She answered, "Oh, she's out, but will be back before long, I hope. She went someplace this morning and hasn't returned. I thought that was Fannie when you knocked. Did you have a successful trip?"

"I did. I went to find my folks' home in Virginia, as you know. Very little has changed. I was able to pay the taxes and the place is mine again. I also purchased a couple of other farms for taxes. I found a farmer close by who's going to farm the place on shares. Has Fannie said anything to you about money?" I asked.

She shook her head no. "Only that you sent some to help. I'll pay you back. The money really helped. We were running pretty low for a while."

I shook my head and said, "Your granddaughter is a very rich young woman, you know. Half of everything in the west is hers. She seems to think everything is mine, but that isn't true. It's as much hers as mine. If she wants to marry someone else she will still be worth almost a million dollars. I hope she'll marry me. But I haven't asked her. I wanted to ask you first for your permission to ask her to marry me."

She sat like she was in shock. "I did not know about the money, but I am happy for her. Now, as far as the marriage thing, that will have to be her decision. I'll be happy if she decides to marry you."

I hung my head and with tears in my eyes and said, "Thank you. She has a very kind, thoughtful Grandma."

Fannie came home sometime later. I heard her quietly open and shut the door. She tiptoed into her room and eased the door closed. I wanted to speak to her, but changed my mind.

Late the next morning, I came back to the house from walking around town. I stopped and visited with the Irish woman who owned the Mercantile Store. We had a long visit about Grandma Magee. They had been friends for many years. She told about the struggle Grandma and Grandpa had after the family left because of Fannie's father's health problems. The farm had slowly gone downhill because they couldn't keep up with the work. He died one morning while doing chores. Grandma found him and walked over to the neighbor's farm for help.

When I returned to Fannies home, a fancy, high-stepping team with a driver, stopped in front of the house. The door opened and a young man, about two years older than me, stepped out of the carriage.

He looked up at the driver and said, "I will hurry William, so don't go to sleep."

He walked past me as if I didn't exist. He went to the door and knocked very loudly. When Grandma opened the door, he didn't even say good morning. He said, "I want to see Fannie right away." He spoke to her as if she was paid help.

Grandma's face registered displeasure and said, "She's not awake yet. She came home late last night, I do believe."

I had walked up behind him by then. He said, "Well, wake her up. I must see her now."

The tone of his voice made it an order, not a request. I got upset with the way he was treating this sweet old lady. After all, she is Fannie's grandma, not some slave.

I said, "Excuse me. I believe you're blocking me from going into the house. Would you step aside so I can get to the door?"

He turned and demanded, "Who are you, anyway?" But he didn't step aside.

I had had it with this guy. I said, "That really is not any of your business, who I am. Another thing, you start treating this lady like the lady she is, or go get in the fancy wagon and leave."

He seemed shocked, as if no one had ever stood up to him. Then his face got red. He demanded, in a loud voice, "Do you, young man, realize who you are talking to?"

I smiled a sly smile and said, "No. Are you supposed to be a king or something special? All I see is a rude, disrespectful person trying to make himself look important."

He whirled and at the same time launched a roundhouse swing my way. I stepped back and hit him with everything I had in my right hand. His feet flew out from under him and he went backwards, almost to the gate. I stepped out after him, spun him around, put my foot on the seat of his pants and shoved hard. He hit the side of the carriage, hung there for a second or two, and slid to the ground. I looked up at the driver. He was sitting in the box, trying not to smile. He just shrugged his shoulders.

I turned and walked to the house, went in and shut the door. Grandma was standing just inside of the door smiling. She said, "I have wanted to do that for a year. Thank you."

I made a pert bow and said, "My pleasure, Madam." We both laughed.

Fannie called from her bedroom door, "What's so funny this morning?"

I looked at her and answered, "You are, standing in your nightgown with that red hair standing on end."

Fannie flipped around and went back into her bedroom. Grandma gave a snort and went in the kitchen with a big smile.

Later in the day, Fannie came to me, where I was sitting on the front step. "Ken, we need to talk. I was gone all day yesterday, as you know, and I've made a decision."

"Yes, I know you didn't come in until way late last night. I heard you come in after midnight."

Her face got red." I had a problem that I needed to make right."

Grandma said, from the doorway above us, "Don't worry about it child, Ken solved your problem this morning. He didn't take near as long, and was a whole lot more convincing than you could ever be." She had a big happy smile on her face as she turned and walked into the house.

Fannie gave me a questioning look.

I said, "Never mind. Yes, we do have to talk. Would you wait here for a minute? I want to go in the house and get something for you."

I went into the house and got a tissue wrapped package from my satchel. When I went back out, I motioned to Grandma to follow me. I sat down beside Fannie, on the step, and took her hand. I knew Grandma was standing behind us in the doorway. I looked into Fannie's eyes and took out the small ring and handed it to her.

"This is your mother's ring, I saved for this occasion. Fannie, will you marry me?"

She broke down crying and held the ring to her lips. "Oh, Ken! Yes."

"You know, I can get you a very expensive ring if you want. But I thought this was something more like you."

I got up, took the ring, and put it on her finger. It fit perfectly. She stepped close to me and kissed me with more passion than I thought any one person could express. I looked up at Grandma. She was standing there, with tears running down her cheeks. She turned back into the house. We stood in the front yard holding each other, not ashamed to show our feelings to the world.

On Sunday, we all went to church. The women all made much ado over Fannie wearing a ring. All the ladies wanted to meet me. I must have answered a thousand questions that afternoon. We went home and the ladies fixed a celebration supper.

After we washed the dishes and retired to the living room, Grandma motioned for me to sit with her on the sofa. She told Fannie to bring a chair and sit beside me.

"I want to know what your plans are. Are you going to be married here before you leave or are you going west to get married?"

I touched Fannie's hand and said, "Whatever Fannie wants is alright by me."

Fannie sat for a long time. She said, "I would like to be married here, in the church, where I grew up."

Grandma asked, "How soon?"

Fannie asked her if next Friday night would be too quick. "Can we be ready by that time?"

"I think so. Why don't you and Ken go talk to the minister, and we'll start getting the preparations ready."

When we got back from talking to the preacher, Fannie, Grandma, and I sat in the living room. I said to Grandma, "I want you to go west with us when we go. You have no one here, and in Nevada you can help raise your great-grandchildren. Our home is a big, new house with plenty of room for you. I might even teach you to ride a horse."

She sat with tears in her eyes and never said a thing.

I got up and said; "Think about this for the next while. We'll talk again later."

The rest of the week turned into a hubbub of confusion. Women were coming and going. Almost everyone smiled. Some, with long faces, worried that things weren't going to get done right. Women brought flowers from their gardens, the ones blooming early this time of the year.

Grandma asked me if I had a suit and tie. Now why would I need something like that? Aren't these clothes, I bought before I came, good enough? They are brand new, almost. She instructed me to go to town and buy a new suit, white shirt and tie.

"You might be able to polish those boots so maybe they will do."

Wow! If I had known how much work it would be to get married, I think I would have forgotten about marriage and lived a life of sin, as the preacher called it.

By the time Friday came around I had gone hungry, been told to leave the house for a dress fitting, whatever that was, and seen my wife-to-be maybe three times. Then she had a bunch of rags tied in her hair and hanging down in long strips. I had taken the buggy and driven three hours, each way, to buy suitable clothes, as Grandma called them. I had spent a couple hundred dollars for stuff I would never use again,

While in town getting the clothes, I walked over to a jewelry store. I saw what I needed, the most beautiful ring I had ever seen. I asked how much the ring cost.

The man smiled and said, "Only two hundred dollars, cash."

Whew, that was more than a good horse, saddle and all. I went back to get the clothes and thought about the ring. Then I walked back across the street and gave the man his two hundred. I probably would regret that someday but, for some reason, it seemed like the right thing to do.

Friday came as a beautiful, sunny, spring day. The lady from the mercantile store came about noon and told me I needed to go to her house to get dressed. I couldn't dress at Grandma's. Fannie would dress there.

Then she asked, "Have you made arraignments for a room at the hotel for Fannie and you to stay the night?"

I looked dumb and asked, "Why? There's room at Grandma's place."

She threw her hands in the air and said, "I do not believe this Kid. Where in the world have you been all of your life?"

Then she started to tell me why. She no more than got the first sentence out before my face turned red.

I said, "I get it," and fled into the house.

I got some money to pay for the room and also grabbed my suit and clothes and went to her place. I had been told to be at the church by six in the evening. I hooked the mare to the buggy and drove myself to the church. Lots of Buggies had parked all along the street in front of the church. Where had all of the people come from? Now this is not funny. I didn't bargain on all of those people being here. I drove up and a teen-age boy took the mare's bridle and started to pet her. He told me he would watch the horse. I stepped down, put my hand in my coat pocket, and fingered the ring box. With my head held high I walked through the door.

There was not an empty seat in the building. Now, this was not really happening. I couldn't make my feet move. I looked down the aisle. The preacher motioned for me to come. I started to tremble, but I knew I had to go. Somehow I found myself standing beside him. He smiled and took my hand as if to shake it.

He said, quietly, "You will be fine, just relax."

Oh, crud! That was easy for him to say. I thought I would pass out. About the time I thought I was going down, the music started to play and everyone stood up. Here came Fannie, walking slowly down the aisle, all dressed in white. Her red hair all done in long curls. She had a small bouquet of flowers in her hand. She was the most beautiful woman I had ever seen in my life. She looked at me, and smiled like I had never seen her smile before. My heart melted. All I wanted to do was hold her.

As she stepped up beside me, she slipped a little. I put out my hand to steady her. Her hand was all wet and cold. She was as scared as I was. That gave me courage.

When the preacher had his say, he asked me if I had the ring. I took the box from my pocket and she put her hand out for me to put her mother's ring on it. I opened the box and slipped the beautiful ring on her finger. She gasped and looked shocked, then started to cry.

When the service ended, Fannie and I changed clothes. We returned to the basement of the church and mingled with all of the family friends. Later, we got away and went to the hotel. We could finally be by ourselves. We were married May 18, 1872 at her church in Wickerville, Pennsylvania.

The next morning we got up early and went to the church to help clean up after the party. Some of the women had a big breakfast ready for us. They insisted that we sit and eat.

A little way through breakfast Fannie turned to me and asked, "Now, what do we do? When do you want to go home?"

"Do you think Grandma will want to go with us? If she does, we'll have to wait for her to pack her things and get them ready to be shipped. That will take at least a week. What about you? When do you want to go?" I asked.

She gave me a warm smile. "As soon as we can get the tickets is okay with me. I'm ready to get home where you are mine."

I laughed and said, "You know the man is supposed to be the aggressor in the marriage."

"We'll talk to Grandma this morning and ask her if she has decided what she wants to do. Let's go find out what we're going to do." Fannie said.

When we got to the house, Grandma was sitting in the front room, looking out the window. Fannie walked up and gave her a hug. "Thank you, Gram, for the wonderful party and the beautiful wedding It was fabulous. I can't express my thanks enough."

Grandma whispered to her as she returned her hug. "Thank you for letting me and all of my friends be a part of your wedding. Now let's get on with life. When do you and Ken wish to go home?"

Fannie put her arm around her. "As soon as we can get you packed and ready for the trip."

Grandma teared up and asked, "Are you sure you want an old woman tagging along? You have so much to do. I have all of my friends here. What can I do in Nevada?"

Fannie said, "You're not such an old woman. I don't want you to get the way you were when I came. It was awful for you and me both. I won't insist that you come but I think I will need you to teach me how to be a wife instead of a tomboy."

CHAPTER 34

One week later we boarded the train and headed west to our new home on the KC Ranch. While the train traveled across the country, Grandma sat at the window and marveled at the long expanse of open land. As we entered into the mountains she would exclaim, "How beautiful," when looking at the deep timbered canyons. The trees and swift running rivers were a joy to her. As the train pushed on, new scenery came into view every few minutes.

The trip was long. I decided the diner car served really good meals. One afternoon, two men walked into the car, dressed in suits, ties and were clean-shaven. They took the seats in front of Grandma and Fannie. They had not been there long until they turned and introduced themselves. I sat three rows up from them so I couldn't hear what was being discussed. They visited for a long time. When I walked back to get Fannie and her Grandma, the men stood and introduced themselves as Elder Patten and Elder Simpson.

I shook hands with them and asked, "Are you two women ready to eat some supper?"

We went to the dinning car. While we ate, the two men came in and ordered two slices of bread and two glasses of water. Grandma was the first to draw attention to the fact they didn't eat anything but the bread and water.

After we returned to the car, a porter came though with sandwiches and apples for sale. Grandma reached into her purse as she motioned to the porter and took out some money. She whispered something to the black man. He smiled and walked over to the two men and talked low. They turned and smiled at us. Each took two sandwiches, bowed their heads and asked a blessing on the food. When they had eaten they moved again, sat in front of Fannie and Grandma, and began to visit with them. I felt concerned about the two men. I moved to an empty seat behind Fannie. I could hear them talking about a book and about Jesus Christ.

One of them said, "We're Mormon missionaries returning from a mission in Europe. We served in England for two years. We are nearly where we will leave the train and go on south to Salt Lake City. Thank you for the food. It's the first we've had for three days. May I give you a book in payment for the kindness and the food? This book will give your family food of another kind."

Two days later we arrived at six o'clock in Grantsville, Nevada. We took our satchels, walked to the hotel and checked in at the desk. The new clerk didn't know me. He asked my name when I asked for the keys to the KC Ranch rooms. "Unless someone is in the one, we will be okay." I said

He glanced at me funny like and again asked my name. I told him, "I'm Ken Clausen., "You're new aren't you?"

He answered, "Yes, sir, about two weeks, as he opened the register. With a very surprised expression, he raised his head. "Oh! That Ken Clausen. I'm sorry sir. You will find your rooms are clean and ready."

I took Fannie and Grandma upstairs. I led Fannie to our room, and then walked with Grandma down the hall to her room. When I turned to leave, she looked at me and said, "You didn't tell me that you are someone of importance. What else haven't you told me?"

I laughed and answered, "Just wait and see, Grandma. I told you your granddaughter is a very rich person. Here some people will look on her as a queen. Get freshened up and we'll walk across the street for supper. The café is a nice little place and you'll enjoy the food."

I went down the hall and stuck my head into our room. I said, "Fannie, when you're ready, take Grandma over to the café for supper. I'm going down to the livery stable and see what's available for a ride home."

Fannie laughed and said, "Get Grams a good gentle saddle horse."

I chuckled and went down the street to the livery. I walked up to the attendant on duty and he said, "Welcome home, Ken. How was your trip? Did you get what you went after?"

I asked, "Who's been spreading rumors about me going east for something special?"

He smiled and said, "It's no secret. You went to get the red-headed girl who came with you when you first got here."

"Yes, Mike. I brought her home with a ring on her finger. But that isn't the problem. We also brought her grandma along, so do you have a nice big buggy to seat four? We don't have anything like that at the ranch, unless Chad bought one while I was away."

"Not to my knowledge, he hasn't. But he did bring the nice team of sorrels in and said you might need them."

"Okay, do you have a good buggy now?"

"Yeah. The boss had two of them delivered last week. Do you want to look at them tonight?"

I shook my head. "Bring in the sorrels and have the buggy ready in the morning. Go over to the store and get a couple of lap robes and make sure everything is already to go when we come down early. Put the buggy on the bill. I think we will need one from now on."

I went to the café. Fannie and Grams went toward a table as I walked in the door. The men in the café all stopped eating and stared at Fannie. I must admit she was beautiful. I walked toward their table.

The waitress glanced up and said, "Take a seat, Ken. I'll be right there."

Fannie got this twinkle in her eyes and said very quietly, "Yes, Ken, take a seat." Trying to mock the sweet tone the waitress used. "It seems like I got home just in time. I didn't know you had a thing for older women. What do you think, Grandma?"

She replied, "I'm finding out more and more about this shy young man you married. It appears he may not be as shy as he wanted you to think."

I blushed. "Okay. Cut it out or I will get the two saddle horses for you, and they won't be so gentle."

The waitress came over. When she saw us sitting together, she looked sheepish and asked, "You have a friend?"

I smiled, "No, I have a wife. She was with me the first time we came in. She went back east for a while. This is Fannie Magee Clausen and her grandmother. And this is Carol, a big flirt but a good waitress."

We ordered. When she brought the food, Grandma's eyes bugged out. Turning to me she said, "You didn't say they brought a week's worth of food at a time."

We all laughed and Fannie said, "You can take some of it with you tomorrow. It will be a long ride on the horse all day, if I remember right."

Grandma looked worried, "You are not serious about the horse. I have never ridden a horse in my life and I'm not going to start now."

We got up early. I went to the livery to get the team. Mike had them harnessed and ready to hook up. I drove over to the railroad station and told them to contact Mike at the livery when our freight came in. He would bring a wagon and pick up the boxes and send them out to the ranch. I went back to the livery and told him the same thing. I added, "Our freight should be along in a few days. Are any ranch teams and wagons in now?"

"Yes, two of each," Mike said.

"Has Chad been in lately?"

"No. Not for a couple of weeks. The crew came in and unloaded a bunch of bulls from the railroad and took them out to the ranch. They had some funny looking bulls in that bunch," He commented. "Some grey and brown ones had big, long ears and a large hump on their necks. I think a couple of them must be older bulls. They stood as high as a horse. They are as big as those gray teams of workhorses, but were not wild or showed any signs of being mean."

I went to the hotel and loaded our bags in the buggy. We went to breakfast and, an hour after sunup, headed out of town.

Fannie turned to me and asked, "When did you buy the buggy?"

"This morning. Mike had two of them. They came in last week so they're new. I thought one would make a good buggy for the sorrels."

When we got to the top of the ridge the sun was beginning to come up through the trees to the east. Grandma exclaimed, "There is nothing out there but grass and rolling hills. It's barren, but beautiful in a lonely way."

"See the fence ahead. That's where the ranch starts and goes as far as you can see, to the south and west. When we get down the road ten miles, you'll see a deep valley that drops off to the west. The valley is twenty or more miles across, and that far to the south, maybe more. That's where the ranch house is located. The ranch is twenty square miles. We own over two hundred fifty thousand acres."

I turned to Fannie and told her Chad had shipped in a herd of bulls last week. Mike, at the livery, told me they had some of the funniest looking bulls. All are as tall and as big as the grays. Gray and brown in color and had long floppy ears. Most of them had a big floppy hump on their shoulders. He claims they are huge, but seem to be gentle.

"I wonder what he bought. When I left I suggested for him to find at least a hundred good bulls. I added that they should have no horns and not be wild. I didn't care about the color. We need something to produce big calves. I didn't think it was going to be possible, but Mike swears none of the bull had horns. He said a lot of the young, red animals had white faces."

We stopped to eat lunch and let Grandma rest in the shade of a tree along the wagon trail. The trail had almost become a road because of all of the wagon traffic traveling over it this past year. We had no sooner started eating when one of the sorrels threw up his head and looked to his right, out towards the far rim. I soon saw what was bothering him. A herd of antelope came out of a small draw. They were trotting so they would cross our trail further along. I pointed them out to Grandma.

I said, "Just keep your eyes on them. When they spot us they will run like nothing you've ever seen."

They took about ten minutes before they stopped and raised their heads. They watched us for a little bit, and then started to run. Oh, how they could go. Grandma watched until they disappeared over a low ridge.

Then she said, "They are beautiful. They ran in a straight line, like you said they would."

I told her. "They are said to be able to go about sixty miles an hour. I know if you try to shoot one, the secret to hitting any is to shoot at the first one in line. With luck you might hit one of the last of the line.

We stopped and spent the night in the cabin. Grandma had never seen a house built of logs. She was surprised that we had traveled most of the day and hadn't seen anyone else. She couldn't believe no one lived in all of that space. I had to keep reminding her it was all part of the ranch.

After a good nights rested, we left to go on to the ranch. We traveled until the sun got low in the sky. A fiery red sunset crossed the western sky. Gray and white storm clouds were building up. The reflection of the sun was beautiful. Fannie talked to Grandma about the sunset. We broke around the corner of the valley. There, setting in our sight, were the ranch buildings.

Grandma opened her mouth in awe. Fannie turned to see what Gram was looking at.

I stopped the horses and said, "Welcome to the KC Ranch."

CHAPTER 35

They both just sat and stared. Finally Fannie said, "Oh, Ken everything is beautiful! I could never imagine this, so big with all of the barns and corrals. What's the long building away from the house?"

"That's the horse barn. The other one is the worker's bunkhouse. The kitchen and bath areas are in the building to the left. On the right end is the foreman's living quarters."

"The house," Fannie said," "is so big. And those logs shine. What did you do to them?"

"I don't have any Idea. They weren't like that when I left. Chad had something done to them. Come on. Let's get you to the house before dark."

We drove up to the front door. Elisabeth came running from their house. She ran up to the buggy and asked why I didn't let her know when we were coming. She could have had the fire going and some supper ready. Then she stopped, stared at Fannie and got a shocked expression on her face.

"Oh, Ken, she is beautiful. You said she was, but not like this."

Fannie smiled and said, "He told me how beautiful you are. I see he really does have a good eye. I guess we will need to watch him."

I got the women unloaded and took the team to the barn where Chad waited by the door of the stable. He looked at the buggy and said, "Boy, you came home in style. That must have been a great trip."

I turned towards him, "Yes, it was. In the morning come to the house and say hello to Fannie. I want to warn you, she's not the tomboy Fannie you knew when she left here. We also brought her grandma home with us. You'll like her. She can be a blast. Say, Mike, at the livery, told me you found some bulls. What in the world kind of freaks did you buy, anyway? He tried to describe them. They have long ears and are as big as the workhorses. He said something about a big hump on their neck."

"When you get settled in and ready for a ride, we'll go check on them. They are still bunched up, out on the flat. They're not out with the cows. I want to hold them away for another month and then turn them out so most of the calves come about the same time. Cows are still dropping calves every few days. Calving started two months ago. Did you see what that redheaded kid is doing out west of the barn? He tried to plow up the ranch. A field of oats is coming up. Next, he put all of the teams to work on what he calls the cornfield. They're still working on that, but he has worked up at least eighty acres. If the stuff grows, there will be more than enough corn to feed all of the horses in Nevada."

I answered, "Maybe the corn will fatten some steers for us to eat, also. I'd better go see if the women are getting settled. Oh, by the way, there'll be someone coming in a few days with a load of furniture from town. When it comes we will need help unloading the wagon."

I went to the house to find Fannie and Elisabeth going through the rooms. Elisabeth was explaining all of the new things. Fannie and Grandma followed, just oohing and aahing about many things they had never seen before. When I came in the door Fannie ran to me like a little kid. She threw her arms around me and hugged.

"Oh, Ken, where in the world did you find all of the lovely things? An indoor bathroom!"

Grandma asked, "Do you have any more surprises? Imagine running hot water in the kitchen and bathroom."

I said, "I told you we had many surprises at home. Now, I'll cook us some supper. Elisabeth, you go take care of your husband. Grandma, you and Fannie go take a bath and freshen up."

I turned and asked Elisabeth if she had any meat hanging in the cooler and she nodded. I went out to the building beside the main house where cold water was running. A hindquarter of beef hung from the ceiling. I cut some steaks to fry. By the time supper was ready, the two women came out. They had taken a bath and changed their clothes. They were so excited about the tubs and a bathroom attached to each bedroom.

Grandma, shyly, asked about the rolls of paper. I explained what they were for. Fannie looked shocked and blushed.

Grandma got a shy smile, "You mean no more stinking chamber pots? Good lord, you guys don't realize what you'll be missing."

The next day, Chad came to the house. He knocked on the door and Fannie went to let him in. When she opened the door he stood, looking stunned.

"He said, "Good lord girl, you grew up in that time away. You're now a woman. Give me a hug, girl. I wouldn't have known you if I'd met you on the street."

After he got his hug he asked me, "Do you want to go for a ride and see the ranch and the bulls?"

Fannie said, "I don't know about Ken, but I do. Is Charlie around some place? I'll go get into my pants if you guys will saddle up."

She went into our room and found where her man pants had been stored. She came out ready to ride.

Grandma saw what she was wearing and said, "Fannie! You are not going outside with those pants on. That is disgraceful."

Fannie smiled, "That's the way I traveled for months when we came across the plains. Besides, they're warm and comfortable. I can ride western style, sitting on a horse like a man."

We walked to the barn and Charlie was saddled and tied to the hitching rail. His ears flopped down and he didn't even look up. Fannie walked to him and spoke. His ears came up and he made his snuffing sound. He put his face over next to hers and started to nibble. I guess he was kissing her arm and rubbing his head on her. She scratched his ears and hugged him. She untied the halter rope and climbed up into the saddle. He stepped out with his ears up and took the lead toward the pasture. He was one happy mule. The old scoundrel never even glanced my way. We rode all day. I couldn't believe all of the calves. What was happening with the ranch was everything I had ever dreamed about or hoped for.

EPILOGE

The years slipped by and the mighty KC Ranch expanded and grew with the times. Charlie and I saw great changes in our lives as we grew older. There were more and younger Clausens for Charlie to love and be loved by, with hugs and sugar cubes. He seemed to know when we needed his protection from sorrow and delighted with us in our victories.

When the time for his departure from this life came close, he spent the last few weeks standing on an outcropping above the house and buildings of the ranch. Charlie stood with his ears up, looking west, and waiting for the next new experience that time would bring into our lives. He was always eager to start every day with his ears forward and his nose pointed to the trail ahead. He seemed to know new times were coming and he wanted us to be a part of it. When we found him, he was facing west where he had been lying, looking out over the vast open range of the ranch.

We had traveled from almost the eastern ocean to nearly the western ocean. We had crossed small creeks and great rivers. We had crossed deep canyons and great divides.

We had gone from great sorrows to great victories in our lives.

There is a headstone over Charlie's grave that reads:

ALWAYS LOOKING WEST
HAVE A GREAT TRIP CHARLIE
With love
The Clausen Family

HISTORICAL INFORMATION

Gold Bars: The price of gold in 1865 was $18.93 per troy ounce. A bar could weigh from two and one-half pounds to twenty-five pounds. Only the gold bars in fort Knox weigh twenty-five pounds. (Information from: www.answerbag.com)

One-Hundred Dollar Bills: The 1863 issue of the bills had an eagle with spread wings, United States and an identification number on the front. It was a gold certificate. They were literally "as good as gold," and were not printed until 1865. Their use at the time was exclusively for transactions between banks; general-circulation gold Certificate came along in 1882.

Indoor Toilets: The first American patent for a toilet was given in 1857. By 1870 the flush toilet was being imported from England. It was called a water closet.
(We did not have indoor toilets in our homes until the 1940s.)

Toilet Paper: Joseph Gayetty, of New York, produced the first packaged toilet paper in 1857. It was pre-moistened, flat sheets medicated with aloe. It replaced corncobs, newspaper, and the Sears & Roebuck catalog. (Wikipedia, Free Encyclopedia)

Galvanized Pipe has been used in the United States since 1870. It is made by dipping steel pipes into hot molten zinc to prevent the steel from rusting. (ehow.com)

Hay Balers: Stationary hay balers, introduced around the mid 1800s, were horse-powered units that required workers to pitch hay into the baler and tie the compressed hay into bales. The balers were later put on wheels so they could be taken to the hay, but the process still required a man to drive the tractor; a baler operator to push hay into the bale chamber, and a couple of workers to tie the bales. (History of Balers: ehow.com)

Freight Wagons: Hansen said, The freighter is a true icon of America's rich western heritage. While there were thousands of freight wagons supplying the western frontier in the 1800s, very few survived and even fewer are operational. We never cease to be amazed at the engineering feats of the early pioneers and consider it a privilege to assist in the preservation of the valuable part of the U. S. frontier history. The large wagons are said to be able to carry 30,000 pounds of borax from Death Valley. There was often a smaller wagon pulled behind the large one. (www.hansenwheel.com/wagon)

Railroad in Nevada: The 1861 Legislature passed an act allowing construction of a railroad across Nevada from west to east to encourage the building of the transcontinental railroad.

Central Pacific Company: Incorporated formally June 28, 1861. The route was surveyed in August.....joined with tracks of the Union Pacific Railroad at Promontory Point, Utah, May 10, 1869, completing the first transcontinental railroad system in the western hemisphere. (Information from: (Nevadahistory.org/railroadhtml)

Confederate Generals: There were many generals and brigadier generals for the Confederacy during the War Between the States. Rudolph Scott was not one of them. His name is simply a figment of my imagination.

Grantsville, Nevada: This location was used for my novel. Grantsville is now a ghost town. Gold was discovered in Grantsville Canyon in 1863. By 1879 the population was 800. There were two general merchandise stores, one hardware store, livery stable, two barber shops; a jewelry store, assay office, bank, two drug stores, a restaurant, and about twelve saloons. The town faded away in 1885.

Wickerville, Pennsylvania: This town is another figment of my imagination. I could not find such a place listed, however I did find Wickerville Cemetery in Pennsylvania.

Pictures

<u>Kicking Mule</u>: Mr. Garrett, of the Wahkiahum School District, 500 South 3rd Street, Cathlamet, Washington, granted permission for the use of the picture, Nov. 28, 2011.
Information from: www.welcometowahkiakum.com/mules

Duane Clatworthy is shoeing a horse and Leona (Bunny) is watching and talking to keep the horse calm. The picture was taken in 1959 near Darby, Montana. This is from the family photos.

ABOUT THE AUTHOR

Duane Kent Clatworthy was born in 1931 on a farm outside of the small town of Milledgeville, Illinois. He grew from childhood on a farm southeast of the smaller town of Stevensville, Montana. He lived in the Bitterroot Valley for fifty years.

He shot his first elk when he was twelve years old. His father had a hunting camp on Fish Creek in the Lolo Forest of Montana. Every year for many years, he filled his big game tags with elk, deer, and bear. He fished the streams for brook trout and Flathead Lake for sockeye salmon.

Duane began working away from home when he was nine years old. He drove a team of horses pulling the slide of the overshot hay stacker for neighbors. Soon he was driving a buckrake and stacking hay. By the time he was fifteen years old, he was shoeing horses and mules. At sixteen he worked for the Forest Service in the Libby, Montana Ranger District. He had charge of a string of mules and horses carrying cargo for lookouts and trail building crews. Some of that cargo was dynamite and its caps. He also worked on forest fire crews.

In 1950, when he was eighteen, he married his high school sweetheart, who was sixteen. He bought mustang horses, broke them to ride and resold them. In 1952 they, with his parents, bought a Lodge and Dude Ranch on the east fork of the Bitterroot River in Montana. They named it the D Bar 2 Lodge. He became a licensed outfitter and guide while also teaching hunter's training classes to young people. He guided many hunters and fishermen into the Pintlar Primative area, as well as to the many lakes in the East Fork drainage of the Bitterroot River. When he went out to get meat for his family, wife and four daughters, he would take his 30-30 or 308 rifle, put four shells in his pocket and come back with three shells and his meat.

He worked in sawmills and learned to operate all of the machines. In 1963 his wife and youngest daughter were badly burned in a house fire. He decided he needed to work where he made more money, so he learned to fall timber. He did that for many years, still hunting in the fall and fishing with his buddy, Rollie Clevidence, when the temperature dropped to twenty below zero and was too cold to run his big saw.

For more than twenty years he went to Alaska fishing for halibut. He worked hard to get the first one-hundred pound fish.

Duane is truly a jack-of-all-trades and can fix nearly everything. He loves to garden and watch things grow. He has built a new house and remodeled several others. He has made furniture, from doll beds to beautiful china hutches. He loves animals and continues to raise steers for the family freezer.

The Clatworthy's four daughters are: Susan Stahl, Dawn Olsen, Diane Good and Melanie Ploharz. There are nineteen grandchildren, forty-plus great-grandchildren and four great-great grandchildren with more on the way.

At eighty-six years old he still loves to fish. Two artificial hips hinder him some from climbing up and down the riverbanks in Oregon where they now live.

Duane says this book has been running around in his head for months. He finally had to get it out of this head and on paper.

Duane, at time of reprint of this book, is still active with gardening and raising steers.

[By his wife and staunchest supporter, Leona Wood (Bunny) Clatworthy]

www.ingramcontent.com/pod-product-compliance
Lightning Source LLC
Chambersburg PA
CBHW031330170626
46807CB00002B/633